W9-BVN-575

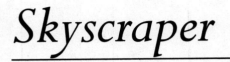

Skyscraper

Also by Zane

Skyscraper

A Novel

Zane

ATRIA BOOKS

New York   London   Toronto   Sydney   Singapore

ATRIA BOOKS

1230 Avenue of the Americas
New York, NY 10020

This book is a work of fiction. Names, characters, places and incidents are products of the author's imagination or are used fictitiously. Any resemblance to actual events or locales or persons, living or dead, is entirely coincidental.

Copyright © 2003 by Zane

All rights reserved, including the right to reproduce this book or portions thereof in any form whatsoever. For information address Atria Books, 1230 Avenue of the Americas, New York, NY 10020

ISBN:978-0-7434-5703-3

ATRIA BOOKS is a trademark of Simon & Schuster, Inc.

Manufactured in the United States of America

This novel is dedicated to my daughter Jewell who—
had she still been alive—
would have celebrated her 11th birthday
as I completed this manuscript. Mommy loves you for you
are an angel and angels never die. They never die.

Acknowledgments

Book eight. Wow, it is hard for even me to believe. Never a day goes by when I do not count my blessings. Thank You, Lord, for Your continued blessings and for allowing me to express my creativity and do what I love for a living.

To my parents as I plan their 50th Anniversary Party, thanks for showing me what life really means and how to appreciate the positive and ignore the negative. It takes a lifetime for most people to learn that. Luckily, I learned it early enough to not waste valuable time on the wrong things.

To my hubby, I really don't need to say anything. You hear it every day. You are sitting here on the bed burping our latest one as I type this on my laptop early on a Saturday morning. That says it all.

To my kids, thanks for giving me a reason to succeed.

To my closest friends, Destiny Wood, Pamela Crockett,

Esq., Pamela Shannon, MD, Shonda Cheekes, Karen Black, Janet Allen, Cornelia Williams, Dee McConneaughy (I think I spell your name differently in every book because I can never get it right), Sharon Johnson, Gail Kendrick, Lisa Fox, and the rest of you, thanks for always being supportive and having my back; whether we see each other on a daily basis or for whatever you did for me in the past.

To my family, Carlita and David, Charmaine and Rick, Aunt Rose who just celebrated her 85th birthday earlier this year, Aunt Margaret, Aunt Neet, Miss Bettye, Dr. Edward and Mrs. Joyce Townes, Miss Maurice and Uncle Snook, Aunt Barbara, George and Mary Knox and everyone else, thanks for all the encouragement.

To all the little ones that make life interesting, Arianna, Ashley, Little David, Jazmin, Adam, Brian, Jr., Nicolas, Karlin, Briana, Jeryne, Jahre, and Jerlan, thanks for the memories and allowing me to live my childhood all over again through your eyes.

To my agent, Sara Camilli, thanks for always keeping my best interests in mind and for reminding me to take care of myself first.

Thanks to Tracy Sherrod for originally seeing something special enough about my writing to acquire my books for Simon & Schuster.

Thanks to my editor, Malaika Adero, for your patience and inspiring comments.

Thanks to the rest of the Simon & Schuster family, Judith Curr, Carolyn Reidy, Dennis Eulau, Louise Burke, Karen Mender, Brigitte Smith, Orly Sigal, and everyone else who helps to not only make me a success but helps to make Strebor Books International a success.

Thanks to the Strebor International Staff, Wayne, Charmaine, Destiny, Pamela and the rest of the crew and the Strebor authors for helping to make my publishing dream a reality. We have come a long way in a short time but we will go even further. I would like to encourage all my readers to please check out the Strebor authors. I have hand-selected each and every one of them and feel their work is worthy to be read. Here is the current list: Shonell Bacon *(Luvalwayz: The Opposite Sex and Relationships* and *Draw Me with Your Love),* D. V. Bernard *(The Last Dream Before Dawn* and *God in the Image of Woman),* Laurinda Brown *(Fire and Brimstone* and *Under-Cover),* Shonda Cheekes *(Another Man's Wife),* William Fredrick Cooper *(Six Days in January),* Mark Crockett *(Turkeystuffer),* JDaniels *(Luvalwayz: The Opposite Sex and Relationships* and *Draw Me with Your Love),* J. Marie Darden *(Enemy Fields),* Michelle De Leon *(Missed Conceptions* and *Love to the Third),* Laurel Handfield *(My Diet Starts Tomorrow* and *Mirror Mirror),* Lee Hayes *(Passion Marks),* Allison Hobbs *(Pandora's Box),* Keith Lee Johnson *(Sugar and Spice* and *Pretenses),* Rique Johnson *(Love and Justice* and *Whispers from a Troubled Heart),* Darrien Lee *(All That and a Bag of Chips, Been There Done That,* and *What Goes Around Comes Around),* Jonathan Luckett *(Jasminium* and *How Ya Livin'),* Nane Quartay *(Feenin),* V. Anthony Rivers *(Daughter by Spirit* and *Everybody Got Issues),* Sylvester Stephens *(Our Time Has Come),* Michelle Valentine *(Nyagra's Falls),* A. J. White *(Ballad of a Ghetto Poet)* and Franklin White *(Money for Good* and *Potentially Yours).* You can find out more about them and their books on StreborBooks.com.

Thanks to Carol Mackey at Black Expressions for selecting all of my books for the club. Thanks to the other book clubs that have continuously supported me including RAW-SISTAZ, APOOO, and Book Remarks. Thanks to Karibu Books and all the other bookstores that have helped make me a success. Thanks to the distributors like Culture Plus and A and B Books who have helped to get my books out to the masses.

Most importantly, thanks to all my faithful readers. Without you, this would not be my career. I would still write regardless, but knowing that others appreciate my efforts makes it all worthwhile.

I cannot begin to thank all the authors who have had an effect on my life and I am afraid that I might leave someone important out. If you have been nice to me, you know who you are and thank you. If you have been nasty to me, you know who you are and thank you also for the laughs. I do have to give special shout-outs to Eric Jerome Dickey for being the first author bold enough to give me a blurb and for always encouraging me, to Tracy Price-Thompson, Gloria Mallette, Karen E. Quinones Miller, and Gwynne Forster for always being so kind to me when I run into you guys on a regular basis, to Collen Dixon and Dwayne Birch for always keeping it real, and to Franklin White for being the one to clue me in on how to really get my self-published books out there (welcome to the Strebor family, Franklin). For those who don't know, Franklin White is coming back out strong with *Money for Good,* which will be released around the same time as *Skyscraper,* and *Potentially Yours,* which will be released next summer. Make sure you check them both out.

I have been getting more and more emails from high school and college students seeking biographical informa-tion on me for their school papers. I am flattered. To the young lady whose teacher gave her a B+ instead of an A be-cause she didn't know my real name, tell your teacher that wasn't fair and she should change your grade.

If you have not gotten your copy of my first DVD *Sock It to Me* then you are missing out. Now on with the book. *Sky-*

craper was written to be a fun book but, as usual, I deal with some serious issues as well. This is a lighthearted follow-up to *Nervous.* I enjoy mixing things up with my writing so in the tradition of *Shame on It All,* I hope you enjoy it. For those who want to know, *Shame on It All Again* is still cumming—I mean coming—so look for it in the near future. I have a few surprises in store for you at the end of the book. I hope you like them. They are my Christmas presents to you.

I have to end my acknowledgments with a true story. I wish I could remember the woman's name but I am sure she will know I am talking about her. At a recent signing, a May-December couple approached me and the woman announced out loud that I had sexually liberated her. A lot of the other women standing around agreed that I had done the same for them. She was with a man younger than her who had a backpack full of my books, which he pulled out for me to sign. After getting in line to purchase some of my books for one of his family members, the woman knelt down and said to me, "I hate to monopolize your time but I just have to tell you. An African American woman writing erotica. Do you realize what you've done?" She glanced over at her boyfriend and added, "I'm wearing his young ass out! For a long time, I was too afraid to do certain things but, thanks to you, there is nothing I won't do to satisfy my man!"

Now that was flattering and I appreciated it. People often criticize what I do. Cool. But for every critic there are a thousand people who love what I do. For you ladies and gentlemen, I now present *Skyscraper.*

Peace and Blessings,
Zane

Friday, December 15th

Washington, D.C.

Chico

"Chico, you better get your behind out that bed, boy!" Momma yelled through my bedroom door because she couldn't open it. I always kept it locked because I grew tired of her invading my room without a courtesy knock first. Besides, I was nineteen and that made me a man. Even though I was residing at her crib, a man is still a man. "Chico, do you hear me?"

"I hear you! Damn!" I yelled back at her.

I glanced at my alarm clock. Shit, it was after seven-thirty and I'd slept through the buzzer again.

"Chico, don't you dare curse me, boy! And you have the audacity to do it right here at Christmastime? Don't forget who brought your behind into this world. I brought you into it and—"

"I'll take you out," I said, finishing the tired ass sentence for her.

I hopped out of bed and yanked my door open. Momma took a step back like she'd seen a ghoul or goblin or something. There wasn't a doubt in my mind that I looked jacked up since I'd hung out the night before with Razor and Miceal. We'd kicked back watching a tape of the Felix Trinidad/Fernando Vargas fight. It was a great ass fight, too. Both of the brothers meant serious business. Talk about having heart; they had heart and then some. That tape is one of those things you can watch over and over again to get inspiration to do the damn thing with your own life. Too many people give up too quickly, but not the kid. I'm going to be somebody major and my word is my bond.

"You look horrendous," Momma told me like I wasn't aware of that already. "Chico, have you been drinking again?"

"What if I have? I'm over eighteen. Besides, like you said, it's Christmastime. It's a time for celebration."

"Last time I checked the drinking age in this country was twenty-one. You have no business breaking the law."

"Momma, it's a crying shame that I'm old enough to go to war and get my head blown off for this country but I can't go into a bar and order a beer. If downing a few with the boys is going to get me locked up, then so be it."

Momma smirked and then laughed. "Chico, you wouldn't last five minutes in jail."

I didn't like her implication that I was weak. I didn't like it at all.

Momma straightened up a couple of figures in a Nativity scene she had displayed on an antique table with three legs in the hall. I'd broken the fourth leg off—it was the first thing I could get my hands on—to chase off a bill collector who didn't understand that broke meant fucking broke. Thank goodness Momma had finally stopped mixing secular and religious decorations together. My friends would tease me mercilessly as a child when they'd visit and see a reindeer in the manger, elves chilling with the three wise men, or a statue of Santa seemingly in deep conversation with a statue of a black Jesus.

"God help me! What am I going to do with you? I didn't raise you to hang out at all hours of the night doing horrid things."

"Momma, drinking a beer or two isn't horrid. It's called being a man and relaxing. Going out and robbing banks and jacking cars is horrid. Do you really expect me to sit around acting like a punk while my boys do their thing? Huh? Do you?"

Momma stormed off down the hall toward the kitchen. "You need to start going back to church. That's what your behind needs to be doing. Reverend Stevens has been asking about you every week. I'm sick of making up excuses for your trifling behavior. I don't like nor appreciate having to form my mouth to speak lies to a man of the cloth."

"Then why don't you just tell him the truth?" I asked. "Tell him that I'm not in church because I have better things to do than put on pretenses like ninety percent of the other people there."

Momma looked like she wanted to slap me silly. Instead, she just turned her back to me.

I rolled my eyes at her back—I may be a man but I'm still not stupid enough to roll my eyes at her to her face—and headed into the bathroom. One glance in the mirror and I almost jumped myself. I looked like shit; literally. My curly, jet black hair was kinky as all get out and I was sporting a big ass pimple on my right cheek. That's the only thing I hate about being light-skinned—other than the fact that dark-skinned brothers have suddenly gone back in style. The slightest breakout and the entire world knows about it. I used to try to burst the pimples when I was in junior high but that was the absolute worst. The blotches on my face would run most of the sisters in the opposite direction when they spotted me and you could see the big ass marks they left behind a mile off.

I was attempting to take a dump in peace on my throne when Momma started banging on the door. She definitely had a door-banging fetish.

"Chico, you only have twenty minutes before you need to leave for work. Don't fool around and be late again. You need to keep that job; for both our sakes."

"Okay, Momma." I prairie-dogged a turd, hoping she would walk away so she couldn't hear me drop the bomb.

"I made you some breakfast. Brown sugar bacon, grits, and scrambled eggs. You have to make your own toast because I've gotta run. The elementary school kids are putting on a Christmas program at the nursing home and I promised your grandma I'd be there before it starts."

"Okay, Momma." I could hear her still standing outside the door. I knew what she was waiting on. "Thanks, Momma."

"You're welcome."

She finally made some moves and I was able to finish getting rid of the beer and buffalo wing mixture that was ripping up my stomach. I heard the front door slam a few minutes later while I was climbing into the shower. I didn't feel like going to work that day. Then again, I never did. The only thing righteous about working at Wolfe Industries was that Razor and Miceal worked there also. We had all gone down there six months prior and filled out the applications together. We had been there and done that fast-food gig and it was not the way to live. Shit, I got burned by the fry machine three times at Mickey D's and that crap hurt like all hell.

College was never an option for me. My grades weren't good enough for a scholarship, I was too lazy to play sports by the time I'd hit seventh grade, and Momma definitely couldn't afford tuition. I could've taken out a loan but I have some friends that will still be trying to pay their shit off when they're in their fifties. My grades were fucked up for all the wrong reasons. I was one of those kids who didn't feel challenged and so I didn't do the work; even though I'm smart as hell. As typical in the hood, my teachers didn't care enough to encourage me and I was rebellious against my mother. I wished that I could take it all back because I would have probably been in college on a full scholarship somewhere the hell away from D.C.

My daddy ran off with one of our neighbors when I was eight. She was married also but the sex between them must have been off the chain. Daddy walked away from a wife and one kid, but Dena—the whore in question—walked away from a husband and four kids. Her husband moved away in embarrassment. The entire neighborhood knew the deal but Momma said she wasn't leaving her space. She said people were going to talk whether we left or stayed. She was struggling with this gig as a customer service rep for Amtrak. The pay was mediocre and that was not a good thing. The cost of living in D.C. is so high that most people have to end up living with their parents until they're in their thirties or forties. Shit, sometimes even their fifties.

Miceal, Razor, and I were all hired on the spot at Wolfe and started clocking hours as soon as we passed the required drug testing. Apparently, they had a high turnaround of clerks in the mail room so they were anxious to fill the positions. Two hours after we started on a Monday, it was clear why the turnaround was so high. The supervisor of the mail room, Donald Coleman, thought he was the CEO, COO, or HNIC or something. You ever work with someone that stresses over their job so much that you can see the veins popping around in their head half of the day? That's the way Donald rolled. Damn shame, too, because none of the higher-ups even paid attention to him. I had seen him try to do some serious ass-kissing when the *real* CEO, Tomalis Wolfe, strutted past us in his two-thousand-dollar suits. Mr. Wolfe just kind of waved Donald off every time. I didn't blame him either. Not only did Donald have a fucked-up attitude, he was also in dire need of a bar of soap. No, make that four bars of soap. His ass was just that stank. I mean, damn, soap is about the cheapest thing in a store. Razor, Miceal, and I always talked about his body odor. When he came into the mail room, it was like that movie *Backdraft*. All the air seemed to be sucked out of the room and all you inhaled is stench.

After my shower, I hauled ass down to the bus stop with a bacon and egg sandwich wrapped in a napkin. When I got there, the K-4 had just taken off. It was two blocks away but the exhaust fumes still kicked into my nostrils.

Damn, I missed it again!

I plopped down on the bench and glanced at my watch. Being on time was no longer a possibility. That meant going through some Donald drama. I dug into my sandwich—cold already because the wind was kicking ass that day—and winced when I bit down on something hard. It turned out to be part of an eggshell. Momma couldn't even scramble an egg right. Shame on it!

When I got to the office building, there was a stream of black company cars lined up out front dropping off executives. Those lucky motherfuckers were living too large. Too bad they didn't send a sedan to pick me up every morning. Too many damn freaks on the bus and besides, I could've clocked mad babes chilling in a ride like that.

I was in the mailroom all of two seconds when I smelt Donald behind me.

"Chico, you're late again."

I turned around and stared him in his beady eyes. "I missed my bus. My bad, Donald."

"Your bad? Your bad? What kind of English is that?"

"My kind of English."

"Humph, must be Thug English because it's surely not the kind I was taught in school. You young fools better learn how to speak properly or you'll never get promoted around here."

I wanted to tell him that some of us actually took the time out in the morning to wash our asses but I just ignored him instead and walked toward my station where a ton of mail was waiting to be sorted. I spotted Miceal on the other side of the room trying to push up on this honie named Keisha. She was straight-up hurt in the face but had body for days. I wanted to warn Miceal that I'd heard she preferred to bump coochies but I decided to let him waste his time trying to get up in some puddy that wanted to be licked and not dicked.

The men's room door swung open and Razor walked out with bloodshot eyes. Alcohol had never been good to him.

"What's up, Chico?" Razor asked, slapping me a high five.

Razor was a caramel motherfucker, about six feet, making him a couple inches taller than me. He was what sisters called a "pretty boy" but he wasn't as pretty as Miceal. At six-six, Miceal was damn near a tree. He was dark-skinned with dimples and had a smile that lit up the room whenever he entered. It could be dark as shit in a club but you could always see his bright ass teeth. Women loved his ass.

"Everything is everything," I responded to Razor. "Can't wait until Christmas vacation because I can sure use a few days away from this bullshit."

Razor glared over at Donald for a second and nodded. "You ain't never lied. What I can't wait for is the Christmas party next week. I hear that joint is off the fucking chain."

I couldn't imagine a corporate party being all that but I had heard the same thing from many people so I was curious my damn self.

"Got a hangover from last night?" Razor asked.

"Hell no, I can handle mine." I slapped him gently across the cheek. "But your eyes are redder than a hoe's tampon. You can't handle your shit like me."

Razor chuckled. "Fool, I can outdrink you any day."

"Yeah, right, whatever."

My nose started tightening up, which meant Donald was within breathing distance. I glanced over my shoulder and he was standing there like he was Donald Trump instead of Donald Coleman, raised in a Southeast, D.C., tenement. He didn't think I knew all of his business, but I did. I made it a point to know everyone's business. This honie, Riwanda, had an aunt that used to date him. I couldn't believe that shit when I heard it. Donald getting some ass? I would've believed in the Tooth Fairy before I believed that, but apparently at least one sister was hard up enough to spread them for him.

Let me explain something before you start thinking I'm ragging on Donald for no reason. Donald was about five-four, weighed in at a hundred pounds soaking wet, and was darker than midnight but had the nerve to stick emerald green contacts into his eyes every morning. That was some sick shit! Then there was the body odor problem—I hate to keep harboring on that shit but I might have ended up getting asthma if he didn't discover his bathtub soon—and the yellow teeth problem.

Even with his less than desirable looks—to put it kindly—I could still deal with Donald but his attitude just ruined everything. He talked down to people, particularly his own people like me, and then expected us to look up to and respect him. Please, that was just not happening. Not then. Not ever.

I started my delivery rounds about ten. Like everything else in and about Wolfe Industries, the Christmas decorations throughout the building were at the top of the game. The secretarial pool was always my first stop. That was where all the honies about my age pecked away on keyboards for hours at a time, which was amazing considering most of them had these long ass, fake fingernails. They spent half of the damn day singing along with one of those fools that sings like he has to beg to get the drawers off a woman. Women love it when men seem hard up about fucking them; even when it's imaginary fucking in songs.

I was shocked when they changed it up on me. Someone had the James Brown *Funky Christmas* CD pumping through the air. Now that's what I was talking about. That CD was one of my all-time favorites but it was difficult to find because it was an import. At least one sister in the pool had good taste.

I *loved* the secretarial pool. Anastasia and Shakia—I called them the "Boobalicious Twins"—both had boob jobs a couple months ago. How in the hell they presumed they could take a week off on sick leave and return with double

D's when they left with single A's and not have everyone notice the difference was beyond me. Still, *I liked it!* They wore
these low-cut booty dresses all the time, trying to show off
their new bazookas. At some other corporations, they probably would've been fired with a quickness but the executives
at Wolfe could appreciate admiring tits and ass more than
most.

Without question, some of the other women in the secretarial pool—be they black, white, Latino, or Asian—
weren't feeling Anastasia and Shakia right about then.
Jealousy isn't just a bitch; it's a big bitch! I heard there was a
meeting in the ladies room about the titty sisters that turned
ugly. Apparently, there were even threats of bodily harm. I
didn't know any of that to be fact but, generally, my sources
were straight on the money.

Now I could understand why some of the women were
jealous. If I were female, I would've been hating on Shakia
and Anastasia, too. Shakia was a petite sister. She was about
five feet even with long braids that she switched the colors
up in from time to time, skin the color of dark fudge, and a
gorgeous smile. She had the tiniest waistline I had ever seen
on a grown ass woman, which made her ass look huge. I had
yet to meet a brother who could resist a big butt and a smile.

Anastasia was smoking. There was no other word to de-
scribe her. If she wasn't so ghetto, she might have been able
to be a movie star. She could have definitely been a video
whore. My eyes would have been glued to the screen; that's
for damn sure. She was tall, around five-nine, honey brown
with these dark, sexy eyes and a small gap in between her
two front teeth. There's always been something sexy about
women with gaps to me. Probably because I used to date
this sister named Monie and her gap used to turn me on
big time. I would have tried to push up on Anastasia but I'd

had my share of ghetto girls and I was looking to expand my horizons.

I dropped off the mail in the secretarial pool and made my way over to the executive suites. The sisters in the pool would at least speak to you and even flirt a little from time to time. However, the executive assistants—as they called themselves—thought they were too damn good to even give you the time of day. In their mode of thinking, typing up the shit of one person instead of the shit of a bunch of people made them something special. Not the case, sisters, not even the fucking case.

The only one that was ever polite enough to speak to me was Diana. Now she was one hot babe. About five-eight, somewhere around one-forty, with more junk in her trunk than a station wagon headed to Disney World with a family of five inside, she was all that and then some. What I was really feeling was her intelligence. She was obviously smart and that made my dick hard.

Most of the other men in the building viewed Diana as a stuck-up floozy like the rest of the executive assistants. I kept telling them that Diana was mad cool with me. They always said that was only because she viewed me as a child and didn't acknowledge me as a threat or potential stalker. I say all of that was pure bullshit and Diana just saw me as the cool, laid-back brother that I was.

"Good morning, Diana," I said to her, having lingered a moment for her to finish up a phone call.

"Good morning, Chico. You all ready for Christmas?"

"As ready as I'll ever be."

She looked good as shit that morning. I could tell she'd just had her auburn hair permed. It matched her sienna skin and hazel eyes perfectly.

"I like your hair," I told her. "It's very becoming."

She ran her finely manicured fingers through it. "Thanks, Chico. I went to the salon this morning before I came in."

"Wow, hair salons open that early?" I asked in surprise.

"Chico, if a sister can make money doing some hair and nails, she'll work all night to make ends meet."

We both laughed.

"Well, whoever did it worked magic," I said. "Not that you need a hairstyle to make you beautiful. You've got it going on every day of the year."

Diana blushed. I liked that. She wasn't stuck up like the rest of the executive assistant bitches. I was allowed a bird's eye view of Diana's ass—that magnificent ass—when she got up from her desk. She was wearing a heather gray business suit with off-black stockings and black pumps. I could just imagine the heels of those pumps leaving scratches on my back while I buried my di—

"Chico, are you okay?"

She caught me daydreaming again. *Damn!*

"I'm fine, Diana. I better get going." I didn't want to leave but I was afraid Diana would spot the hard-on that had sprung up in my pants. Like I said, she always made my dick hard. "I still have a lot of mail to deliver so I'll catch you later."

She sat back down at her desk on that ass—that magnificent ass. "Okay, Chico. I'll see you tomorrow."

I hauled my behind out of there so fast that I catapulted right into Mrs. Wolfe. I didn't even see her before my cart caught her in a rib and left her doubled over in pain. I was scared shitless. Being fired was a given after hurting the wife of Tomalis Wolfe. I was just hoping she didn't press charges and have me carted off in handcuffs.

Having no clue what to do, I grabbed one of her elbows. "I'm so sorry, Mrs. Wolfe. It was an accident."

She giggled. I was stunned but happy as hell.

"I'm perfectly fine," she said, standing back up straight. "I'm sure it wasn't intentional."

I'd seen Zetta Wolfe from afar many times, but never close up. She was old enough to be my mother, but my mother doesn't make me almost cream in my pants when she looks at me. That's the effect Zetta had on me when she gazed into my eyes with her black, hypnotic ones. She had the smoothest chocolate skin and no wrinkles for a woman her age. She was definitely hitting somebody's gym on the regular because every inch of her five-seven frame was in shape. She was soft and muscular in all the right places.

She had on this really tight dress that day—really, really tight. I'll never forget it. It was cherry red with pearl buttons down the front. She was showing serious cleavage. She was not huge like Anastasia and Shakia. Zetta had the perfect mouthful. She had her hair pulled back in a bun all the time. It was dark brown with just the slightest hint of gray around the temple.

"What's your name?" Zetta asked me, staring down at my crotch. I'd completely forgotten about the Diana-induced hard-on.

Even in total embarrassment, I wasn't about to punk out and attempt to cover myself up. "My name's Chico. I work in the mail room."

Zetta fingered my cart. "I kind of assumed that. How long have you been working here?"

"About six months."

"That's funny." She played with the collar of my shirt. "I've never seen you before."

I shifted my weight from one leg to the other, willing my

dick to lie down and play dead. It refused to cooperate. It was true that I'd never run into Zetta before but pictures of her and her husband were hanging throughout the building; including a huge portrait of them behind the guard's desk in the entry foyer.

"Well, Mrs. Wolfe, there are hundreds of people that work in this building. I doubt you've met them all."

"But you're so handsome." She pinched my cheeck; the one with the big ass pimple. She was fucking with my emotions—and my "dickmotions"—big time. "What time do you get off?"

"Huh?"

"I said, what time do you get off?"

Was she for real?

"I get off at five, like just about everyone else," I responded, curious to see where she was going with it.

She licked her lips and winked. "At five exactly, there'll be a white limousine out front. Get in it."

"A white limousine out front?" I repeated hesitantly.

"That's what I said."

A few men from the accounting department brushed past us in the hallway, complimenting her on her outfit, trying to earn brownie points with the big man. That allowed me a couple of minutes to ponder over things. On one hand, there was me. Nineteen-going-on-twenty-year-old Chico, son of an overprotective religious mother, raised to know the difference between right and wrong, but willing to suck the ovaries out the woman standing in front of me if she'd let me. On the other hand, there was Zetta Wolfe, old enough to have birthed me, wife of a man that could afford to hire a hit man to take me out with a hollow point bullet, fine as hell, and telling me to get into a limousine after work so she could obviously fuck me. I mean, it wasn't like we had anything else to discuss, so fucking was a no-brainer. She wanted my dick; pure and simple.

"So," she said to me after the men had walked out of earshot. "Should I expect to see you at five o'clock or not?"

"Yea-yea-yeah, you'll see me," I stuttered.

"Wonderful. I'll see you then."

She glanced up and down the hall in both directions and then looked into Diana's office. It was empty. Diana must've been in the inner office with her boss, Bradford Haynes. When Zetta realized the coast was clear, she grabbed my dick like a vise.

"Um, nice size. I think I'm going to enjoy this."

She kissed me on my pimple-infested cheek and then freed my dick.

"I think I'm going to enjoy it also," I replied, getting bold enough to reach out and rub one of her nipples through her dress.

She didn't say another word. Just walked off leaving me there with a big ass grin on my face.

The remainder of my workday couldn't pass fast enough for me. I was glancing at my watch every thirty seconds. I cornered Razor and Miceal outside the loading dock while they were sharing a cigarette. I told them what had happened, about Zetta feeling me up and telling me to meet her later.

"Man, you're tripping," Miceal said, before letting out this horrendous chuckle. "Ain't no way a woman the likes of her is going to give up the drawers to a sucker like you."

Razor chimed in. "Hold up now, Miceal. Why would Chico make some shit like that up?"

Miceal shrugged. "Who knows? Doing horse, maybe."

"I don't do drugs!" I had to resist the urge to pop Miceal in his pretty ass mouth. "I'm telling you that I'm meeting her out front at five. If you don't believe me, walk out with me and watch me get into her whip."

They eyed each other and then all eyes were back on me. They guffawed.

"Damn, Zetta Wolfe!" Miceal exclaimed. "That's almost up there with fucking Toni Braxton or Janet Jackson or some shit like that!"

"Yeah, but they're not on Geritol," Razor chided.

"Fine as Zetta is, I doubt she's senile yet," Miceal retorted. "Hell, I wish she'd come on to me. Chico, you might have to let me make deliveries for you from now on."

"No way, man." I grinned. "There's no way Chico's coming off boob and ass patrol. I get to see the Boobalicious Twins and Diana every day and now this added bonus feature. Hell no, Chico is the man and he's not going anywhere."

The three of us tore out of the building like it was on fire at five on the dot. There was this old dude standing out front ringing a bell to collect monetary donations for the Salvation Army. Miceal almost knocked him flat on the ass, trying not to miss a beat of the action. It was mayhem as always. People were scrambling to get the hell away from there. I quickly scanned the street but didn't see a white limousine, which should've been easy to spot amongst the sea of black sedans and yellow cabs.

Miceal poked me in the arm and went to teasing. "Uh-huh, she's a no-show."

Razor couldn't help but to add insult to injury. "Damn, Chico, she played you."

Pissed and disappointed; that was me. Fucking an older woman had long been one of my biggest fantasies—right behind the threesome—and now it appeared the shit wasn't going to happen.

Razor shoved his hands in his pockets, looking as let down as me. "You might as well just walk to the bus stop with us. The only pussy you're getting today will be between the pages of one of those magazines you're always jacking off with. What's it called? *Black Tail?*"

Miceal and Razor both fell out laughing. I refused to give up so easily. Besides, I wanted to tell them that I didn't use *Black Tail* to jack off; I used *Black Booty.* Zetta had to show. She just had to.

While the two of them continued trying to humiliate me with their comments, I clamped my eyes shut and said a silent prayer. Amazingly, there was a white stretch limo right in front of me when I opened them. It had just pulled up.

Miceal and Razor stopped laughing and stood there with their mouths hanging open as the uniformed driver got out, walked around the car, and opened the back door.

"Time to go to work," I said to them over my shoulder. "Chico has to go lay down some pipe." I waved them off. "You little ones have fun on the bus ride home."

Razor snarled at me and Miceal eyed me with admiration. Yes, I was about to get busy with a rich freak and they were taking their asses home to play video games.

I speed-walked over to the limo and climbed inside. It suddenly hit me that it was the busiest time of the day and I was out in the wide open where anyone could bust me; namely Tomalis Wolfe or one of his cronies. Zetta had a lot of nerve doing that. She should've told me to meet her around the corner.

Speaking of corners, we didn't even make it to the first corner before she was all over me. There was a tinted window so the driver couldn't see us, but I was still ill at ease.

I came up for air, after tonguing the living daylights out of her, and asked, "Are you sure about this, Mrs. Wolfe?"

"Chico, you can call me Zetta now. After all, I'm about to fuck you."

I guess she was sure!

She had my dick out of my pants before I could blink twice and was going down on me. I tried to grab hold of something. I settled on her hair with my left hand and the door handle with my right. I considered the blow jobs I'd had before to be great but I was wrong. The other sisters were mere amateurs.

One thing was crystal clear. I was in for the time of my life. I liked that.

Anastasia

I wouldn't call what Shakia and I did whoring *exactly* because most whores don't get paid like we did. Shakia and I were Entertainment Consultants. All whores get are slaps on the ass, an occasional dinner at a cheap restaurant, and sometimes a broken heart if they are stupid enough to get feelings for the suckers. That's right, I said suckers. That's what most of the men around my way were. They only cared about their cars and jewelry. The only exceptions were street pharmacists; they cared about their dope.

I was not about to end up like my mother, still sitting around the projects when I was forty-five without a pot to piss in or a man to curl up to at night. That's why I didn't hesitate when Bradford Haynes asked me if I might be interested in making a little extra spending money. I'll never forget the conversation.

I was standing by the water cooler getting my gossip on and speculating about which heifer was the probable culprit when it came to the disappearing air freshener from the ladies room. I made it a point to bring in the nice stuff. Not the fifty-nine-cents-make-you-want-to-breathe-through-your-mouth-because-it-smells-too-damn-strong stuff, but the good stuff. Someone was taking it the second I left it in there and I was determined to find out who.

I couldn't stand it when I went in there to brush my teeth after lunch or check my fine ass out in the mirror and it smelled funky, so I brought it in. A few times it was so foul I would've sworn that Donald bastard from the mail room had been in there; if I hadn't known better. Somebody needed to discover the meaning of Summer's Eve. If not that, then that generic Sweet Love they sell at all the dollar stores.

Anyway, I was standing there with Shakia and a couple others when Bradford walked over and tapped me on the shoulder.

"Good afternoon, Anastasia."

"Sup, Bradford?" I answered back.

Even though he was an executive, I knew I could keep it real with him. I'd run into him a few times at Uranus, a strip joint where I used to wait tables. We'd only said hello to each other but he knew I knew the deal with his mere presence. Men that frequented the place had a fetish for looking at women's you know what, which was obvious from the name of the club. I still hung out in there from time to time. I had a lot of friends there and that was the only place I could catch up to them since the majority of them slept all day.

"You have a minute?" Bradford asked.

"Sure." I glanced at Shakia. She was giving me the eye, letting me know she'd be all up in my business later. "I'll be back, ladies."

I strutted off with Bradford, inhaling his expensive cologne and checking out his gold Rolex. While Bradford wasn't the finest thing in the world, he was attractive enough. Early forties, bald head, a little under six feet, mocha skin, and light brown eyes. I couldn't imagine why he was leading me into his office but curiosity can be a mother-fucker.

His assistant, Diana, was at her desk. She eyed me with disdain as we walked by. She was such a bitch. Always looking down on me and the rest of the sisters in the secretarial pool like she was a queen or some shit. I wondered if Bradford was about to kick her ass to the curb and select me as a replacement. After all, I typed more than a hundred words a minute plus I was fine. I knew better though. I'd heard that Human Resources required at least an undergraduate degree for that position and I only had my GED. I also had my DhP; the opposite of a PhD. My Dick Healing Pussy did the job every time.

Bradford shut the door behind us and pointed toward a fine Italian leather sofa against his left wall. I sat down and he did the same, getting so close to me that I could see his tonsils when he spoke.

"Anastasia, you're looking awfully lovely today."

I blushed. Rich men telling me that I look good could never bruise my ego.

"Why, thank you, Bradford."

"My pleasure. Can I get you a drink or something?"

"No, thanks." I thought about taking that back for a second; even though I wasn't thirsty. I imagined him calling Diana in and ordering her to fetch me a cup of coffee. That would've made my day, but I wanted to know what was up with him so I said, "Why'd you ask me in here?"

He cleared his throat and loosened his tie. "I'll be frank. Some associates and I have this penthouse located here in the city where we often hang out."

"Sounds like a winner. You want me to hang out with you?" I asked jokingly.

"Actually, that's exactly what I'd like you to do."

"Word?" I was getting excited. My first high society party. "Can I invite some friends?"

"Only if they're down with the program."

"The program?"

"You see, Anastasia, I'm talking about *special* parties."

Bradford started stroking my hand and eyeing me seductively. That's when I knew the lowdown.

"So you want me to fuck somebody?"

He started laughing. "That's one way of putting it."

"What's another way? Fucking is fucking, right?"

"Yes, that it is."

I would be lying if I said I had never thought about getting with men that didn't mind paying for playing. After all, I did work at Uranus. I had never gone for it because the men down at the club were mostly winos and shit with bad hygiene or breath. Rich executives with fat bank accounts were another story.

"I assume there would be something in this for me."

He grinned, realizing I was considering jumping on his offer.

"Yes, there's a lot in it for you. Money. Nice clothing. A possible promotion."

"Tell me more about this money and nice clothing."

That was how it all started. I went to the penthouse alone the first time to scope things out. After being with Bradford and two other men in one night, I knew I needed back-up pussy to cover for me. That's when I pulled Shakia into the mix. I knew she would be down because she appreciated the finer things in life just like I did. The only problem was that we would spend the money as fast as we pulled it in, which was why we still trudged into work every day. At least we had our new bomb ass titties to show for it.

I had no intentions of being there forever. I had my sights set on the big catch: Tomalis Wolfe. I was just waiting for the space and opportunity to show him my skills. Tomalis was the finest older man that I had ever seen. In his early fifties, he had the body of a twenty-five-year-old. Every bit of six feet, he had a bald head and sported a goatee, which both complemented his almond-colored skin. His smile was perfect. Probably cost a mint, but it served him well. He always dressed nice and he always smelled so damn good. Personally, I think Bradford only went bald trying to emulate Tomalis. He could never be him though. Not in a million years.

Tomalis stopped by the penthouse every once in a blue moon, but never had sex with us. He just sat at the bar off the kitchen, drowned himself in Scotch, and left. Whenever I saw him in the hallways at work, he smiled and sometimes said hello. But fuck all that. I wanted the dick and I was going to get the dick, the money, and the name. Being a second wife was better in my book. You didn't have to be around when the man was struggling to make it. The second wife generally stepped in once the man had "arrived" and that was exactly what I planned to do. The annual Christmas party was coming up in a few days and I had a holly jolly treat for Tomalis Wolfe. One he would never, ever forget.

Tomalis

It all started with a thousand dollars. I wanted that thousand more than I wanted my next breath and it all stemmed from envy. My Uncle Clifford was a cool ass cat: cool house, cool women, and most importantly, cool cars. When he offered to sell me his 1950 cherry red Corvette for a thousand dollars, way below the blue book value, I knew I had to have it no matter what. The only problem was that my parents held true to form and refused to give me a dime. To this day, I believe it was never about the money for Uncle Clifford. He just didn't want to give me the car outright because he wanted to make me a man.

It was 1965 and I was fifteen years old. The car was the same age as me. I made a promise to myself that I would come up with the thousand and purchase the car on my sixteenth birthday. I took every odd job I could find: mowing lawns, cleaning pools, walking dogs. Eventually I wandered into Pop's Electronics and begged Pop—real name Edgar Lee—to let me be his apprentice. Mind you, I knew less about electronics than I knew about ballet dancing but the money was good, so I learned how to fix every single appliance, large or small, that people lugged into the shop.

After a while, my interest turned to more than money and I developed a love of the craft. I started keeping junk parts from various items and began to build things. Invent things. I ended up purchasing my dream car from Uncle Clifford. Even got personalized plates. Thank goodness Tomalis is only seven letters because that was the limit.

Even though I could pull up to the front of my high school at the end of the day and have beautiful girls—including the entire varsity cheerleading squad—vying to get a ride home, all of that became insignificant once I realized how much money I stood to make if I developed something no one else ever had. What I stood to gain if I was the first and the first I was. The first African American man to design and manufacture a line of luxury automobiles. Wolfe Auto is my brain child. I took the love I had of automobiles and the love I had for experimenting with parts all the way to the bank. The cheapest car we make is the GS2 model and it retails at 60K. I accomplished my dream without the benefit of a college education. Just a lot of hard work and a few financially set people that believed in my potential.

I had watched my father work himself to death helping someone else realize their dream and watched my mother die shortly after from the effects of the mental and physical abuse inflicted on her by him. He would bring his stress home and take it all out on her. I told myself that if I was going to work myself to death, it would be for my own corporation and not someone else's.

My parents were gone. My Uncle Clifford was gone. My only sibling, my sister Tamala, was killed in a plane crash when she was thirty-seven. The only things I had left of my childhood were my Corvette—which I still drove on occasion—and Barron, my best friend. Making all the money that I did, it was hard to trust people unless they had been there all along. Barron and I had been to hell and back together and I knew his love for me was as genuine as my love for him.

Like I said, it all started with a thousand dollars. That seemed like a ton of money to me back then. Now that I netted a hundred thousand dollars a week, I had what the deceased rapper used to talk about: mo money and mo problems. We lived on twenty-three acres on the water in Fort Washington, Maryland. Our twelve-thousand-square-foot home had nine bedrooms, ten bathrooms, indoor and outdoor pools, a cabana house, tennis and basketball courts, a home gym with a Jacuzzi and sauna, and a theater room that accommodated twenty. Rarely did I get to kick back and enjoy the amenities. I generally lived in five rooms: the family room, kitchen, master bedroom, office, and the master bathroom. I did get in my weekly swim every Saturday morning. That was the one luxury I demanded. It relieved a great amount of stress.

I had a twenty-three-year-old daughter that was doing great in medical school grade-wise, but emotionally, she was a basket case. Since Heather lived in Chicago, she didn't think I knew about her little recreational drug habit. That was where she underestimated me, where they all underestimated me. I was well aware of the comings and goings of my family.

That included my seventeen-year-old son, Jonah, who needed to stop having unprotected sex before he had fifteen children before he turned twenty-five. He already had two definites and one possible. Sure, I'd had the proverbial bird and bees chat with Jonah—at least a million times—but you could talk until you were blue in the face and Jonah still wouldn't hear you. Money and the wicked ways of his mother had destroyed Jonah's sense of principle. He thought that money, power, and respect were the only three things he needed to leave his mark on the world. I could bequeath him the first two when I died, but the third he would never have. How can others respect you when you don't respect yourself?

Speaking of respect—or the lack thereof—my wife Zetta regarded me as more of a fool than everyone else. She was the real fool if she thought I didn't know about her numerous affairs. I never confronted her about them because I didn't care. As long as one of her young studs was servicing her, I didn't have to be bothered with her overactive sex drive. If I could have just done something about her overactive mouth, life would have been a dream.

"Long day, Tomalis?" Zetta asked snidely as she whisked into the family room of our mansion. She collapsed into the armchair directly across from my favorite recliner where I was seated.

I was trying to enjoy my daily *Wall Street Journal* in peace and had been praying that Zetta would pull an all-nighter someplace else, anywhere else but home.

"Why do you ask that?" I finally replied after she'd taken about three heavy sighs, letting me know that she wasn't budging until I acknowledged her presence.

"Well, you look like shit and you're sitting there with an entire bottle of Scotch beside you."

"My day went okay. Longer than some. Shorter than some. How about yours?"

"I'm exhausted. Julia and I went to Arundell Mills this afternoon to do some last-minute Christmas shopping. I picked you up some wonderful neckties."

I wondered when Zetta had possibly had time to shop, being that she had stopped by my office earlier. Thank goodness I was in a board meeting because I didn't want to be bothered. It was bad enough that I would have to see her at home. Then there was her little sexcapade with her latest victim from the mail room. Zetta didn't think I knew her whereabouts but I always did. She forgot that her chauffeur Phil was on my damn payroll; not hers. He had phoned me while she was inside her little apartment on Wisconsin Avenue. Something else she didn't think I knew about. She would often threaten Phil with being fired if he told her business, but Phil knew which side his toast was buttered on.

Phil and Barron were about the only two men on the planet Zetta could never seduce; they both knew they were risking having their dicks fall off if they boned her. Zetta didn't realize the amount of ammunition I had against her, but she would when the time was right. There was just one last missing piece to the puzzle. Besides, as long as she was fucking someone else, I didn't have to worry about her trying to fuck me.

I was sitting there wondering if one of the ties she had bought me could be used as a strangulation device when Zetta continued to get on my nerves.

"By the way, that *fool* called here earlier."

"You mean Barron?"

"How many *fools* do you know?"

"Barron isn't a fool."

"Humph, that's debatable. Case in point. You have an office, a cell phone, a pager, parachutes falling from the sky with messages on them, and he calls here: the *one* place you're least likely to be on a weekday morning. What kind of sense does that make?"

So Zetta wanted to get nasty. Two could play that.

"Just so you know, Zetta, I've invited Barron to spend the holidays. It'll be just like old times."

For a moment, you could have heard a piece of toilet tissue falling in the toilet three flights up if you had listened hard enough. Zetta took about three deep breaths and asked, "Here?"

"No, I invited him over someone else's house for the holidays," I said defiantly.

"You don't have to be so nasty, Tomalis."

"You don't have to be . . ."

"What?"

"Forget it."

I was going to tell her that she didn't have to be such a skank ass hoe, but it wasn't even worth the aggravation. Besides, I wasn't ready to spill all the beans and show my trump card just yet.

"Tomalis, I wish you'd be more considerate and discuss these things with me beforehand. Momma's flying in from France and you know she can't stand Barron."

Zetta's mother, Zora Mason, was the biggest bitch in the world. I gave her a quarter of a million a year just so she would travel the majority of the time and leave me the hell alone. She came from the ghetto and to the ghetto both she and her daughter would return before I was through with them. She could not stand Barron, but that was a personal problem. I could not stand her. Barron was welcome into my home before she was any damn day.

"That's unfortunate," I said with disdain. "However, as long as I can stand Barron, he can come and go as he pleases."

"But Momma's family. She's blood."

"Your blood." I downed my glass of Scotch in one gulp and poured myself another one. "Barron's family to me. He's all the family I have left. If Barron wants to move in here, he can. If he wants a job at Wolfe, he can be the vice president. Barron's welcome to anything and everything I have. I'd advise you to remember that."

"Don't you dare talk down to me like I'm one of your subordinates, Tomalis. I won't allow it."

"Allow?" I chuckled. "Zetta, I think you're the one who needs a drink. Why don't you grab a glass and share this bottle of Scotch with me?"

"I never drink before dinner, you know that."

No, you only suck other men's dicks before dinner, I thought to myself.

The phone started ringing and neither one of us moved a

muscle to get it. Zetta was too busy rolling her eyes at me and I was too busy formulating my escape plan for the night. There was no way I was staying there with her and had hoped she'd stay out with her young stud until the wee hours of the morning. He probably had to get home to Momma or something. I couldn't help but laugh at the thought.

Our housekeeper, Marguerite, entered the room. "Mr. Wolfe, Heather is on line three."

"Thanks, Marguerite," I said. Marguerite had been with us for more than a decade and was the only person in the house I felt had my best interests in mind at all times.

Before I could make it out of my chair and over to the phone, Zetta had pounced onto it.

"Heather! Darling!" Zetta glared at me like she would have wrestled me down to the ground to get the phone if she'd had to. "How are things in Chicago?" She paused and rolled her eyes. Obviously Heather wasn't elated that she'd picked up. "I realize you called to speak to your father, but . . ."

I could hear Heather's voice from three feet away. She must have been laying into Zetta something fierce. My daughter and wife didn't get along. Mostly because Heather had long been aware that her mother was a whore. Both of my kids recognized that fact. Jonah pulled me aside when he was ten and asked if he was really my biological son. I assured him that he was, but to this day, I honestly don't know.

"Fine, I'll give the phone to your father but it would be nice if you would call here and ask for me every once in awhile."

Zetta handed me the phone; more like tossed it at me. I told Heather to give me a moment, put her on hold, and retreated into my study so I could talk to her in peace.

•   •   •

"So what did Heather say?" Zetta asked me after I reluctantly joined her at the dinner table half an hour later.

"About what?"

"About anything. About everything. The two of you were on the phone for quite some time."

"Heather's fine, Zetta. She just needed to discuss something personal."

"She needs money, doesn't she?"

That was a stupid ass question in the first place considering that Heather had a twenty-five-thousand-dollar-monthly trust fund. It didn't surprise me, though. Zetta was infamous for asking stupid questions.

"No, she doesn't need money."

"Is Heather coming home for Christmas?"

Not if she has a lick of sense, I thought to myself.

"She's not sure yet. She's dating a bit seriously right now and she's thinking about going home to Arkansas with the young man. Homer, I believe."

"Homer from Arkansas? You can't be serious." Zetta tossed her fork on her plate of beef Wellington, egg noodles, and asparagus and pushed it away. "My appetite is ruined. He sounds like trailer park trash. Please tell me he's at least in medical school with her."

That did it. I'd had enough of Zetta's attitude for one day. Jonah wasn't at the table so I assumed he was out utilizing his sex organ. Like mother, like son.

I took the napkin off my lap and placed it back on the table. The beef Wellington looked great, but Zetta had managed to spoil my damn appetite as well.

I stood up. "I'll be back."

"Tomalis, where do you think you're going?" Zetta jumped up from the table like she was contemplating blocking the door.

"I'm going out."

"Out where?"

"Zetta, I'm fifty years old and I'll do as I damn please."

Zetta looked like she had been slapped. She did not realize how close she was to the real thing. I went into the foyer, opened the key compartment hidden in the wood panel underneath the staircase, and got the keys to my baby: my Corvette.

Diana

Another late night. I was sick to death of working overtime. Bradford Haynes had no concept of family life. He had no wife. He had no kids. I had a set of rambunctious, demanding twin boys: Darren and Dean. They had just turned thirteen in November and while I spoiled them rotten because it was such a landmark, I still wanted to give them an extra special Christmas. That was the least I could do, considering their daddy had pulled a disappearing act shortly after I had gone through the labor from hell to bring them into this world. Dean was breeched and Darren had the umbilical cord tied around his neck so there was no question that they were cutting me open to get them out. Every time I looked at them, I appreciated the C-section because they both had perfectly shaped heads, unlike some kids that have to struggle to get down the birth canal.

Stephen, the sorry ass babies' daddy in question, and I were undergrads together at the University of Maryland. I saw his eyes before I saw anything else. They were simply divine; as black as pure diamonds and just as mesmerizing. From the second I laid eyes on him in the student union, I knew we would end up making love. At least, that was what

I called it and Stephen called it that for two years until I turned up pregnant three months before our graduation. Then what we had been doing all that time suddenly switched to "knocking boots" and "slapping skins." Stephen started ignoring me and treated me like shit. I would call and he would hang up. I would approach him on campus and he would curse me out in front of his frat brothers. I would go over to his dormitory and he would toss water balloons from his window so they would splatter all over me. Stephen went from what I viewed as a mature, driven gentleman to an immature, complete asshole.

I won't even attempt to sugarcoat the facts. I considered all options including adoption and abortion but, in the end, I couldn't live with the repercussions of either. Thus, I swallowed my pride and drove home to Philadelphia to tell my parents about my disappointing behavior face-to-face. I just knew they would be heartbroken but, surprisingly, they were extremely loving and helpful. My mother wept at first but later convinced me they were tears of joy and not dismay. She had recently been diagnosed with breast cancer and becoming a grandmother before He called her home was a blessing in her eyes. My father told me how proud he was of me for being the first member of the Cannon family to get a college education. Since my graduation was already a done deal, he didn't stress over it.

I promised both of them, right there on the spot, that I would do right by my child and wouldn't allow motherhood to negatively affect my career goals. That much was true. Even after I got the results of the sonogram revealing twins, my determination never failed. If anything, I became even more career driven. My only regret was that I wouldn't be able to attend graduate school as I had planned.

Mommy lived long enough to see my sons celebrate their

third birthday and then she succumbed to the excruciating pain. I missed her terribly but I realized that she was in a better place. I often talked to her late at night when the boys were sleeping and I was lying in bed alone.

Daddy moved to South Carolina, the state of his birth, to spend his golden years fly-fishing. The twins and I visited him four times a year but he had made plans to spend Christmas in the Bahamas with his new soul mate. Personally, I did have a problem with it, but Pearl seemed like a sincere woman and who was I to begrudge my father his happiness. It was bad enough that I didn't have any of my own. I take that back. My boys made me happy but it still would have been nice to have a warm body to curl up next to from time to time.

Most of the men at Wolfe considered me to be a bitch. *The bitch,* in fact. That was because I got sick and tired of men trying to draw me into their sex games. Professionalism was extremely important to me. Whenever I attempted to explain that to Bradford—who definitely wanted to jump my bones—he ended up piling more and more paperwork into my in-box. Some of the things I didn't even know how to do and most of them weren't in my job description.

Bradford thought that if he pestered me enough, I would either have sex with him or quit. I didn't plan to do either. For the past four months, I had been secretly recording conversations between Bradford and me. I was seriously contemplating bringing him up on harassment charges. I hated to use the term because it was so unladylike but Bradford didn't realize who he was fucking with. He was about to find out, though.

Edmund was another one. He worked in the parking garage and never missed out on the opportunity to comment about my looks. While I could appreciate compliments just as much as the next woman, hearing the same thing from the

same man on a daily basis became a source of major irrita-
tion. Don't get me wrong. Edmund was quite handsome but
after struggling to make ends meet the way I had and relying
on my education to get me that far, I could not afford to mess
things up by dating below the standards I had set for myself.

A man that directed people where to park and kept an
eye on vehicles—mostly Wolfe vehicles since we got a major
discount—was not the type of man I wanted my sons to have
as a role model. They needed a man of substance to spend
quality time with. A man who would take them to the *real*
theater instead of these mindless and trifling films that were
hitting movie theaters lately. How much martial arts and gun
violence did they need to display across the screens to realize
that violence begets violence and sexual promiscuity does
the same? We were living in an age when more rappers were
movie stars than professionally trained actors. That in itself
spoke volumes.

I'm not trying to come off as a virgin or anything with
the promiscuity comment; even if I was a recycled one.
That's a term I made up. A recycled virgin is a woman that
realizes that sex isn't worth the drama or the trauma; especially in such a disease-ridden age, unless a man is about
more than just getting his rocks off. If, and this is a big if, I
met a man that could truly spark my interest and he already
had his career and future on the right track, I could envision
myself taking the risk to see what could develop. Stephen
had truly hurt me and while I realized that I shouldn't spend
the rest of my life trying to figure out what I had done wrong
and dreading the prospect of opening my heart to someone
else, that was easier said than done. I used to be offended by
those shirts and key chains that said "I wasn't born a bitch!
Men like you made me this way!" Now I was truly digging
the statement and owned two of each.

• • •

"Hello, Diana."

I was so startled by Edmund's stealth tactics that I dropped my purse and the contents tumbled to the asphalt of the parking garage.

"I'm sorry. I didn't mean to surprise you," he said, bending down to pick up the items.

"That's okay, Edmund. I've got it." I gently pushed him out the way so I could collect the remaining items. While I was not feeling Edmund in a romantic sense, I definitely didn't want him to see the tampon and feminine spray I kept in my purse in case Aunt Flo paid a surprise visit while I was out and about. I had one of those strange cycles; her ass showed up whenever. Sometimes, even twice a month.

"You look great, Diana." Edmund licked his lips and eyed my cleavage; even though it was completely covered.

"Thanks, Edmund."

I suppressed a laugh because Edmund reminded me so much of Chico, this little fellow from the mail room that was always complimenting me and lingering around my office a little longer than necessary when he dropped off Bradford's mail. Chico had it bad for me but hopefully he knew better than to ever make a serious play. Edmund had no qualms about it.

"How old did you say you were again?" Edmund asked me after I'd recovered everything and unlocked my car door.

I giggled. "I've never told you how old I am."

"Okay, then how old are you?"

"Don't you know it's impolite to ask a lady her age?"

"Hmm, but if I don't ask, how will I find out?"

He did have a valid point.

"I'm thirty-five, Edmund, and you?"

"Twenty-nine."

"Aw, you're just a baby," I stated teasingly.

"Twenty-nine isn't a baby." I could tell by the expression on his face that he was offended or embarrassed; possibly both. "I'll be thirty on February twelfth and, besides, I'm very mature for my age."

I wondered how many times I had heard that same tired line since I had turned thirty. As soon as I hit the magic three-o, the only men attracted to me were three or more years younger and that was still the case. The only exception was Bradford and that was a joke.

"February twelfth. Lincoln's birthday."

"My birthday. I'm still alive and kicking so it's my birthday."

Another valid point.

"Well, in case I don't get around to it when the time comes, happy birthday."

"Are you going to the Christmas party, Diana?"

"The one here?"

"Yes, the corporate one next Friday."

"Of course; I always go. It's the only opportunity to get to break bread and hold conversations with the crème de la crème who strut past me like I don't exist the other three hundred sixty-four days a year."

I laughed. He didn't.

"Kind of the way you strut past me like I don't exist, huh?"

What nerve! I couldn't believe Edmund went there with me.

"Edmund, I always talk to you whenever you speak. I can't understand you insulting me that way."

"Sure, you speak, but you don't feel I'm good enough for you. Just because I don't come to work in Brooks Brothers suits doesn't mean that I'm any less of a man."

I took a good look at Edmund, standing there with his

hands pressed inside the pockets of his polyester uniform, and felt guilty for some reason.

"Edmund, it has nothing to do with you being good enough for me."

"Then what does it have to do with? I'm extremely attracted to you, Diana, and I know you're single."

"How do you know that?"

He shrugged. "Okay, maybe I don't know it for a fact but I get that impression."

I really didn't want to hurt his feelings but saw no other options. "It sounds like you're making another assumption as well; that the attraction you feel for me is mutual."

"Isn't it?"

I sighed and glanced at my watch. It was almost nine and I needed to get home before the twins went to bed. I hated the fact that they came home to an empty house every day; at least they had each other. The last thing I wanted was a set of latchkey kids but I had no choice but to work. Maybe one day I would get the type of job—or better yet start my own business—that would allow me to be there when they got home so I could cook a healthy meal, help them with homework, and spend more quality time. Plus, they were at such an impressionable age where their hormones were jumping off and I dreaded them having sex with fast ass girls in my home. One of my neighbors even warned me that her teenaged daughter and her friends had the hots for my sons.

"Well?" Edmund asked.

"Well, what?"

"Is the attraction mutual?"

"No, it isn't," I responded and got into my cherry red Wolfe coupe. "I really have to go, Edmund."

I tried to shut my door but he held it open. "One last question."

My eyes had already reflexively rolled before I could prevent them from doing so. "Yes, Edmund?"

"Would you like to go to the party with me?"

That was one laugh I didn't even attempt to suppress. After I'd had a good chuckle, I replied, "Didn't you just hear me say that I'm not attracted to you? I'm sorry, Edmund, but you're not my type."

"Fine. Whatever." Edmund slammed my car door so hard that I was surprised the window didn't break.

He stomped away with his hands balled into fists. I started my car and exited the garage as fast as possible.

I got home to find Darren and Dean glued to the usual: Darren to the music videos on BET and Dean to his computer monitor, checking out the latest ridiculously priced athletic shoes to hit the market.

Dean was the first to actually acknowledge my presence. "What's up, Momma?" he asked, glancing away from the screen just long enough to see how downtrodden I appeared. "Momma, you look tired. Why don't you go take a long, hot bath?"

"I have to get you boys some dinner first." The volume on the television was up way too high and the last thing I felt like dealing with was loud, gold-toothed rappers on a Friday evening. "Darren, can you please turn that racket down?"

"Yes, Momma."

My sons were gorgeous and that was not just my biased opinion. Everyone said so. They were tall for their age and had been playing basketball since third grade. We wouldn't find out for sure until the next month, but I was hoping they would both get full athletic scholarships to St. Vincent's High School. I wanted them to have the best education, but I couldn't afford private school unless they got financial aid. I might have been able to come up with the money for one of them but I could have never made such a choice. I could barely afford my mortgage most months. I was purchasing my three-bedroom house, which was more financially savvy than throwing away thousands on rent every year. It was a huge sacrifice to scrape together enough money for the down payment and closing costs but I somehow managed and I was five years into my thirty-year loan. Thirty years is a long damn time.

Dean got up and hugged me. He was always the loving one. Darren tended to be withdrawn and didn't let me kiss him or hug him in front of his friends. He got the most evil look on his face. I knew both my babies loved me, though. They just expressed it in different ways. Every once in a while—when no one else was looking—Darren would cuddle up underneath me like a baby craving attention.

I returned Dean's hug. "So, what do you feel like for dinner?"

"We're cool, Momma. I already made us some grilled cheese sandwiches and we had a few chips left."

A twinge of guilt shot up the middle of my spine. This wasn't the way it was supposed to be. I should have had salads and fresh vegetables on the table every night. Instead, they were using a plug-in sandwich maker to eat greasy grilled cheese sandwiches. Somehow, I was going to find a way to be a better mother. Somehow.

I promised the boys I would take them to the mall the following day. We would hang out at the mall most weekends, even though I couldn't afford to splurge on them like I would have liked. All of the malls would be packed, considering it was ten days before Christmas, but I needed to pick up something for my father and ship it to him before he left for the Bahamas. I would buy the boys' things at the last minute and I already had several things on layaway at Wal-Mart. I just hoped they liked the clothes I had picked out. They were not designer by far, but they were neat and that was what counted. At least, that was what should have counted. That was one reason why they needed to attend private school so they could wear uniforms instead of trying to keep up with their peers.

We had the worst water pressure, which was my only gripe about my house. I think it had something to do with the development because we were set off by ourselves and I was not sure how many pipes were servicing the more than a hundred homes. It took me about fifteen minutes to run a tub of water and while I sat there flipping through the pages of my latest issue of *Today's Black Woman* magazine, my mind wandered to Edmund. I still couldn't believe he had accused me of being stuck-up. He was one of the few men I actually talked to at Wolfe, with his fine self. Yes, hell yes, I was attracted to him but he would never know it.

The majority of employees at Wolfe came to work, minded their own business, and went home. All they wanted were paychecks. However, there was some downright trifling behavior going on behind closed doors around there. I didn't know the exact names of all those involved—I had my suspicions—but I was convinced that Bradford was dead center in the middle of it.

The mysterious phone calls that would come in forcing him to close his office door so he could engage in hush-hush conversations. The continuous references to some penthouse that I had heard Bradford and a handful of other executives mention. Then there was Anastasia and her sidekick Shakia. I didn't know what the hell was up with them. All I knew was that they—Anastasia in particular—needed to cover up their behinds before they showed up at work in the mornings.

I took my bath, surrounded by the cheap scented candles I always purchased from the dollar store since I couldn't afford the good stuff, crawled into bed, and passed out as soon as my head hit the pillow.

Saturday, December 16th

Chico

I heard someone banging on my bedroom window and glanced over at my alarm clock. It was seven in the fucking morning. I jumped up and went for my bat. Surely whoever was ignorant enough to wake my bed-hugging ass up on a Saturday morning was expecting a beatdown.

I inched my curtain back and didn't see anyone. I fell back on my bed when Razor's two-hundred-pound Rottweiler sprang out of nowhere and started breathing its stank breath on my window, fogging up the glass.

"Damn!" I hissed.

I slipped into my bedroom shoes, threw a robe on top of the boxers and tee I had on, and tiptoed down the hallway past Momma's room so I wouldn't wake her. When I made it to the front door, Razor and Miceal were chillin' in

Momma's white wicker furniture like it was the middle of a summer afternoon instead of cold as shit in the dead of winter.

"What the hell are you fools doing here?" I asked irately, not even trying to mask my anger. "It's seven o'clock in the damn morning."

"We know what time it is, fool," Razor came back at me.

Brutus, Razor's monstrosity of a pet, was doing laps around my front yard with a big ass radial tire attached to a chain around his neck.

"Man, you're going to fuck that dog up in the head doing that," I told him.

"Hey, I'm training Brutus to be a gladiator. You never know what kind of shit will go down in the hood."

"True, but tire or no tire, his ass can't stop a bullet."

Miceal and I slapped each other a high five.

"Whatever, fools. I know my dog is the shit."

Razor had serious issues. His parents—both habitual prisoners—had raised him to be a hard-ass. That's why they named him Razor. They wanted him to be tough and while he thought he was a rough rider and often talked mad game, he really wasn't even equipped—mentally or otherwise—to confront real danger.

"Hey, ya'll keep your voices down," I warned them. "Momma's still sleep."

"All these Jehovah Witnesses around here, your momma should be used to early visitors. Hell, a set of four came past my house this morning at six while I was getting ready to come over here," Razor said.

"Damn, they rolled through at six?" I asked.

"Yup. It just boggles the mind, doesn't it?"

"It boggles the mind and then some."

"That may be, but can we get to the real reason we came

over here?" Miceal stated sarcastically. "What happened yesterday with Zetta Wolfe?"

I fell out laughing. "Hold up! You two fools came over here at this time of the morning to find out about my sex life?"

The two of them eyed each other and responded in unison, "Hell yeah!"

I sat down on one of the steps and watched Brutus run around looking stupid. I wanted a few seconds to get my thoughts together. What happened between Zetta and me was the shit but I wanted it to sound even better than the shit so they would be weak in the knees by the time I finished.

"Okay, I'm going to open up with you two, even though it's against my regular policy," I said.

"What policy?" Miceal asked.

"You see, son, when a boy becomes a man and starts dealing with grown women, he has to stop putting all his business out in the streets. After all, men who really get pussy on the regular don't have to brag."

Razor crossed his arms and smacked his lips. "Chico, who are you trying to fool? You know good and damn well you ain't getting pussy on the regular. Hell, you can't even get any from your baby's momma half the time."

I cringed when he made reference to McKenna, the mother of my two-year-old daughter Gina. McKenna and I didn't get along. In fact, we hated each other's guts. I knew that I had to go past her house later that day and I wasn't looking forward to seeing her. I just wanted to see my precious little girl.

Miceal said, "Razor, you're a stupid fuck sometimes. Don't bring up McKenna when we're trying to get the 4-1-1. You're only going to piss Chico off and then we'll never know shit."

"Naw, I'm cool," I said. "Razor's just mad because that honie Judy won't even look his way."

We all got quiet because we knew Judy was a touchy subject. Razor had been trying to get in those drawers for years and the sister just wouldn't give him any play. Personally, while fine, she wasn't that damn fine and he should have moved on ages ago.

"That's a low blow," Razor finally responded. "I came over here to give you props for getting with Zetta Wolfe and this is how you do me."

I laughed. "You came over here to see if she's as good a fuck as she looks."

Miceal leaned forward in his seat, closer to me. "Well, is she as good a fuck as she looks?"

"Naw," I said. "Hell naw!"

"Don't tell me someone as fine as Zetta can't get down in the sack?" Miceal asked.

"What I mean, man, is that she isn't as good as she looks. She's ten times better." We all laughed and slapped high fives. "Yo, brothers, Zetta worked me over. As soon as I got into that fly ass limo, it was on. Tongue action everywhere. First we kissed and then she went for it."

"Went for it how?" Razor asked.

"She sucked me off, man!" I boasted. "Sucked me like I had the tastiest dick in America. Naw, fuck that, the world."

"Damn!" Miceal exclaimed. "Did you bust a nut in her mouth?"

"Man, did I? I came so hard that I ended up cockeyed for a minute."

"Shit, that must've been some good ass head," Razor said.

"Razor, I'm telling you. We always hear that sex gets better with age but it's nothing like living the actual experience. I'm not even trying to fuck another sister anywhere near my age again. I want some more of that seasoned, marinated pussy."

"Okay, yeah, let's move on to the pussy," Miceal urged. "When, where, and how many times did you hit it?"

"We went to this apartment over on Wisconsin Avenue. It was fucking awesome; the way the place was laid out. Zetta told me that she rents the place behind hubby's back. Just somewhere she can go and chill. You know, take a load off."

"Hmm, you sure about that?" Razor asked.

"Sure about what?"

"That she just keeps the place to chill out in. Sounds like she has her own private fuck palace to me."

"Naw, man," I said. "Zetta told me that I'm the only man she's been attracted to—other than Tomalis—in years."

"Hell, as rich as Tomalis Wolfe is, I might fuck him my damn self," Miceal said. Razor and I both eyed Miceal suspiciously. "Shit, I'm just kidding. The only booty I'm trying to push up in has two lips in front."

Razor glared at Miceal. "Don't even joke about that shit, man. I'm not trying to fall asleep over your crib one day and wake up with a dick all up in my grille."

Miceal looked pissed but changed the subject. "So what happened after you got to the apartment?"

"She gave me a bubble bath, sucked *everything* on me, including my toes, and then fucked me. . . . Shit, let me think. It was at least five times; maybe as many as seven or eight. All I know is that I was dehydrated like a motherfucker but loving every minute of it."

Both Razor and Miceal yelled out "Damn!" at the same time and Brutus started barking. It was only a matter of seconds before Momma was stomping out onto the front porch.

"Razor! Miceal! What you boys doing over here this time of morning? You all ain't got work today, do you?"

"No, Mrs. Grayson," Miceal said politely. "We're off. We just wanted to drop by to see Chico for a moment on our way to . . ."

All of us waited for Miceal to finish the sentence. He took forever and a damn day.

"On your way to where?" Momma finally asked.

"On our way to, uh, church."

"Church?" I asked, trying to suppress a laugh. It had been at least a year longer since Miceal had stepped inside a church than I had.

"Yes, church. My mother's having a bake sale to raise money for the new parking lot and Razor promised to help me carry the cakes, pies, and shit. Um, I mean, and the other items to the cars for people."

Momma grimaced. It was obvious she wasn't buying it. "Well, I'm still trying to get some rest. You boys get on from around here."

Razor was already off the porch retrieving Brutus. "Yes, ma'am, Mrs. Grayson."

They both knew Momma didn't play and they were ready to disappear before she asked them anything else.

"Chico, we'll catch you later, man," Miceal said.

"Aight, I'll call you when I get back from seeing Gina."

"Cool," Razor said. "We'll be at the fish fry over at the church."

Miceal slapped him on the arm and whispered, "Bake sale."

Momma shook her head and reminded them, "God don't like ugly!" With that, she went back in the house and slammed the door.

• • •

I took a deep breath before I knocked on McKenna's apartment door. I really should have downed a few beers before I showed up but I didn't want to be drunk when I saw my daughter. I only got to see her once every two weeks—for three hours—and I didn't want to jeopardize that.

McKenna had gone to court and spoke all kinds of lies, trying to make me out to be an unfit parent. None of the shit was true. She said I was a drug dealer. I had never dealt drugs, done drugs, or any such thing. That in itself was admirable considering the neighborhood I grew up in. Southeast D.C. is infamous for drug dealing and while most of my friends had at least dabbled with them, never the kid.

McKenna also told them that I was irresponsible when it came to sex. She lied and said I had been with all these chicks from high school. Now that much I wish were true but, unfortunately, I'd only fucked two other girls from our school. I wanted to fuck the top fifty but they weren't having it.

So anyway, she just went on and on with her lies to the point where the court decided I could see Gina but only in McKenna's presence and only for six hours a month. I fully intended to do something about the situation as soon as I could figure out my best course of action.

McKenna was only mad because I wouldn't marry her after she tried to trap me with the pregnancy. I couldn't prove it but if one of us was a whore, it surely wasn't me. She was playing her game well because I had never caught another fool over there. Then again, she knew exactly what days and times I would be there so she could have been running a brothel the rest of the time without me knowing it. I did have a little spy on her floor—a ten-year-old boy named Danny—who let me in on some of her comings and goings.

But Danny had to go to school and his bedtime was nine-thirty so even he wasn't privy to everything. I paid him twenty dollars a month to tell me whatever he did know. Twenty dollars is a lot of cheddar to a child whose mother is on welfare.

When I knocked on the door, I could hear a bunch of scrambling about inside.

What the fuck is up with this, I wondered.

McKenna knew I was coming. Twelve to three. Twelve to three. Same time every time.

"McKenna," I finally said. "Open the door so I can see Gina."

"I'm coming," she screamed from the other side. After another two minutes, she swung the door open with much attitude. "Chico, you can't come over here acting all nasty toward me. You better recognize."

"You better recognize that you better have my daughter ready to see me when I get here. I wasn't early. I wasn't late. I was right on time."

I started inspecting her place. As usual, *nasty*. "McKenna, you could at least keep a clean home for my child. I pay you child support, you sit on your ass all day collecting aid, and there's no excuse for this."

She had Section 8 housing so it was up to code but you would have thought it wasn't from the way she kept shit lying all over the place. Dirty dishes were always in the sink, the floor was always caked with grime, and I didn't even want to talk about the bathroom.

"Where's my daughter?" I asked, not seeing her rushing from one of the two bedrooms into my arms.

"She's sleep," McKenna announced with pleasure. "I just got finished breast-feeding her."

I sighed. "McKenna, Gina's two. She's too damn old to

be breast-feeding. Here's a clue, if a child is old enough to fix her own bottle and heat it up in the damn microwave, she needs to get off the bottle and she definitely needs to get off the damn titty."

"Breast milk is the most nutritional food for babies. It's a medically proven fact."

"Gina's two; she's not a baby." I eyed her with disgust. "Go wake her up."

"But she just went to sleep," McKenna protested.

"I don't care. I only get three hours and you're already cutting into that. You shouldn't have let her fall asleep; knowing I was coming over."

"Look, you trifling excuse for a baby's daddy, don't come out your mouth at me like that. I am not the one to be fucking with like that, aight!"

I just stared at McKenna, willing myself not to open a can of whup ass on her. I left her standing there in the middle of the floor pouting while I went into the bedroom to wake Gina up. Dealing with McKenna wasn't worth losing another precious minute of my three hours.

Gina and I had a great time, despite McKenna giving up snide remarks and smacking her lips every five seconds. I taught her how to count and we went over the alphabet; all the things her sorry ass mother didn't do for her. I refused to let my child grow up thinking that two plus two equalled twenty-two.

What was so upsetting about the entire thing was that McKenna used to be such a nice girl. She used to take care of herself, her surroundings, and have goals. Now she was just a shell of a woman who had already given up on her hopes and dreams and she was only nineteen. Granted, neither one of us was prepared to have a child but life doesn't stop because of it. You have to use what you've got to work with and do the best you can. That was exactly what I planned to do.

I was going to make sure Gina's Christmas was off the hook that year. Last year, her first Christmas, I was still struggling with that fast-food gig. I was barely able to buy her a stuffed teddy bear and a couple of outfits. This year, I had been saving up, and plus, I would be getting a Christmas bonus from Wolfe right before the holiday. It was going to be all good. Speaking of all good, it was time for me to leave and get ready for my night with Zetta. We had made plans to hook up again. This time, I planned to blow her spine right out her back.

Tomalis

I was doing laps in the pool when I spotted Zetta's legs from underneath the water. I wished I could hold my breath long enough for her to just take a hint and walk away but I eventually had to surface.

"Good morning, Tomalis," Zetta said as I started floating on my back away from her.

"Good morning, Zetta. You know this is my private time. What can I do for you?"

"Tomalis, don't worry." She crossed her arms and rolled her eyes. "I just want to inform you that I will be out late this evening. I'm going to a benefit fund-raiser with Abigail."

"Thank goodness," I mumbled.

Zetta leaned over closer to hear me. "What did you say?"

"Nothing, Zetta. You go ahead and have a good time," I replied. "Fund-raisers are always important."

She cleared her throat.

"Is there something else?" I asked.

"Can you get out the pool for a few minutes so we can talk?"

I hesitated but figured she wouldn't leave until I let her have her way. As far as the fund-raiser thing, I already knew she was lying. Zetta wouldn't get caught dead at a benefit fund-raiser and neither would Abigail—her whorish best friend. They were obviously up to something and using each other as alibis, as usual. I often wondered if I should have educated Abigail's husband about the comings and goings of his wife. Jeff seemed like a cool brother; he was just naive. Then again, maybe he wasn't naive and knew everything she was up to. He just might not have given a fuck about it like me. Jeff was a film producer and probably got thrown more ass than most men because women will do just about anything for a movie role, small or big. I would just worry about my situation and leave his to him.

After I got out the pool, I sat beside Zetta at one of the pub tables surrounding it. Jonah used the pool area more than anyone. He invited his wild ass friends over so they could try to screw the little sluts from his school. I told my pool cleaner all the time to make sure he used extra chlorine because heaven knows what went on in my pool.

"What is it?" I snapped at Zetta after we were seated.

"You don't have to be so nasty!" she snapped back at me. "I just want to talk."

Don't you have a dick to go suck or something? was on the tip of my tongue. Instead, I said, "So talk."

"Momma will be here tomorrow," Zetta announced. "I expect you to be on your best behavior."

I laughed. "Zetta, don't talk to me like I'm your child. I'm sick of telling you that and I don't plan to speak on it again. Understand me?"

It seemed like she was trying to decide whether to try me

or not. I gave her the I'm-not-in-the-mood-to-take-shit-off-you look.

"Okay, Tomalis, I apologize if you think I'm talking to you in the wrong manner. I'm just concerned because every time Momma shows up, there are arguments between you two. This is the holiday season and I want it to be a pleasant one."

"Then tell Zora not to come." I eyed Zetta with disdain. "Zora's living high on the hog off me. Why can't she just go someplace else for Christmas? In fact, why don't you join her? It would be fun for the two of you to get away and spend time alone."

Zetta started tapping the tabletop with one of her manicured nails. "Tomalis, I'm going to ignore that suggestion. Now, listen, she'll be here about one tomorrow and I thought it would be a good idea for you to pick her up at the airport."

"Me?"

"Yes, you. That way the two of you can do some bonding and get to know each other better. If you just give Momma a chance, you really will like her."

I laughed again. "Zetta, you and I didn't just get married last year. Our daughter's twenty-three, for goodness sake. If I don't know Zora by now, I never will. Quite frankly, I know more than I care to know and I won't pretend. I can't stand your mother."

Zetta rolled her eyes. "Just consider picking her up."

"Zetta, I'm a businessman. I run a corporation and to-morrow is—"

"Tomorrow's Sunday, Tomalis, and the *corporation* is closed."

A lightbulb went off in my head. "You did say tomorrow at one?"

"Yes, she's coming in to gate D-4 at BWI."

"Fine, I'll go get her," I said, devising a plan in my head. "It'll be my pleasure."

Zetta got up, walked over to me, and kissed me on the cheek. "Thanks, hubby. You're such a sweetheart."

I got up and headed back to the pool. "I trust that's all."

"Yes." As I was getting back into the water, she added, "Tomalis, the fund-raiser is down near Richmond so Abigail and I might just stay overnight in a hotel. You don't need me here tonight, do you?"

The slut was planning to spend the night with one of her male whores; probably the fool from the mail room she had fucked the day before.

I grinned. "No, I don't need you here. You go ahead and have a wonderful time. Tell Abigail that I said hello."

"Certainly." Zetta smiled. She was a stunning woman. Too bad she was no damn good. "I love you, Tomalis. See you tomorrow and don't forget Momma."

"Oh, I could never forget her," I said. "See you tomorrow, Zetta."

I decided to stay around the house that Saturday; especially since Zetta's ass was gone and wouldn't be bothering me. I went up to Jonah's room and he was snoring up a storm. I was going to wake him to ask if he wanted to watch a movie with me in the theater room—something I had probably done less than ten times since we'd had it—but he seemed so exhausted that I decided to let him rest.

Marguerite was off on Saturdays. It was the only day of the week she got to spend with her young son who lived with her parents. He was twelve and I felt guilty about the fact that Marguerite rarely saw him since she lived in with us. I tried to encourage her to bring him by the house but she shied away from it because Zetta was always telling her that it was not professional. That was one reason why Zetta had really lost respect with me—other than her whoring around. To tell a woman, any woman, that she shouldn't be around her own child was just plain old mean.

Marguerite was widowed and because of a lack of education, she was forced to become a domestic. Don't get me wrong. I adored her and more importantly trusted her, but I would have liked to have seen her do something more with her life.

We lived in a gated community so I decided to do something I hadn't done in ages. I drove over to the country club and scoured the cigar room for someone to play golf with. Most of the men who were there were all phonies. I ordered a Scotch—even though it was only midmorning—and sat at the bar. I was elated when I spotted Ben Constantine coming through in a golf outfit. He was a Greek who had made a ton of money in real estate development. He and I had known each other for quite a few years and I loved the aura he had about him. Ben loved life and everyone recognized that.

"Ben, how's it going?" I yelled out to him, waving him over.

He came toward me and took the stool next to me. "Tomalis, it's been a long time."

"Yes, it has." I pointed to the wall of premium brand liquor behind the bar. "Can I buy you a drink?"

"It's a little too early for me. I'm trying to cut back somewhat."

He seemed uncomfortable as he spoke the words and I suddenly remembered hearing somewhere that Ben was drying out after a bout with alcoholism.

"I need to give Scotch up myself," I admitted. "So, how's the development business going?"

"Great! This is the perfect time. This area is really building up, with them planning that new harbor on the Potomac."

"Yes, I plan to hang on to my land. I figure it will double in value over the next few years."

Ben shook his head. "With the acreage you have, more like triple in value."

"From your mouth to God's ears," I stated jokingly and glanced up at the ceiling.

"I don't have to ask how business is going for you," Ben said. "I see Wolfe automobiles everywhere and that new commercial you're running is incredible."

"Thanks. We're holding our own."

"Holding your own?" Ben smirked. "From what I hear, Wolfe is on the brink of putting some major players in jeopardy. That new SUV you're debuting next year is nothing short of amazing. What's the retail on that?"

"About ninety," I said. "Some people, mostly athletes, are paying up to one-fifty to get one of the first ones off the plant floor."

"Damn, I'm in the wrong business."

"Do you love what you do, Ben?" I asked.

"I love the hell out of it."

"Then you're not in the wrong business."

We both laughed.

"Say, Tomalis, did you just come here to hang out or are you looking to play golf?"

"I brought my clubs with me. They're out in the car. I was just hoping to find someone tolerable to play with."

"Well, I'm available and ready for action if you can tolerate me."

I punched Ben playfully on the arm. "Then let's do this. Give me a minute to get my clubs."

Ben got up from the bar. "I keep mine in a locker. I'll grab them and meet you out front in a cart."

"See you in a few."

Ben and I had a great time. At least we were having a great time. We were on the ninth hole and running neck and neck, which made for an interesting game, when I heard someone yelling out my name.

I turned around and saw Bradford riding down the greens in a cart with a caddy driving him. He was waving at me and I wanted to scream. I didn't feel like dealing with Bradford on a Saturday. It was getting to the point where I didn't want to deal with him period.

"Someone you know?" Ben asked me after his stroke had been thrown off by Bradford's yelling.

"Yes, unfortunately. He's one of my employees."

"Must be a mighty dedicated one to track you down on a golf course. I hope everything's all right." Ben genuinely seemed concerned.

"Ben, I'm sure it's nothing. Can you give me about five minutes to see what he wants?"

Ben shrugged. "Take your time. I've got all day."

It was nippy out but we had on insulated golf jackets to break the wind. Bradford, on the other hand, had on a pin-stripe suit and was probably freezing. The idiot.

I walked about ten yards to meet the cart so I could talk to Bradford away from Ben's range of hearing.

Bradford jumped out and the caddy asked him, "Should I wait, sir?"

Bradford said, "No."

I yelled out, "Yes! Can you wait right over there? We won't be long."

Bradford looked offended. "Tomalis, this is going to take some time."

"No, it's not. Whatever you want is going to take five minutes or less because I fully intend to finish enjoying my game of golf. How'd you find me anyway?"

"I went past your house first and Jonah said you weren't there so . . ."

"Jonah was awake?"

"Actually, I think I probably woke him up."

I sighed. "That still doesn't explain how you found me. I didn't tell anyone I was playing golf today."

"I know and you aren't answering any of your voice mails or pages either. I've left several."

I shifted my weight from one leg to the other and leaned on my putter. "That's because it's Saturday and I'm trying to relax. Where's the fire?"

"I was leaving and as I was driving by the country club, I spotted your Corvette out front. There's only one of those beauties, especially with Tomalis on the license plate, so that's how I found you."

I made a mental note to park behind the building the next time. "Okay, now that you've found me, what is it?"

"I need you to come to an emergency meeting this evening," he said.

I laughed in his face. "Whatever it is can wait until Monday."

"No, it can't. We have a crisis."

I shifted my weight again. "Hmm, I'm listening." As much as I hated my private time being interrupted, I was not about to let my corporation end up in any sort of jeopardy.

"Mr. Tanaka's here from Japan and he wants to meet with you."

Tanaka was the head of one of my largest competitors:

Prism Motors. They could make vehicles so much cheaper in Japan because of the low cost of labor but I still say my cars were better designed.

"Meet with me about what?" I asked.

"He says that since Wolfe has become publicly traded, he plans to take over the controlling shares."

I picked my putter up and started walking back toward Ben.

"Tomalis, this is serious."

I swung around to face him and grinned. "Tanaka can't take over the controlling shares of Wolfe, Bradford. I own the majority of them and I'm not selling mine so what the hell is he talking about? Better yet, why are you acting like a scared little bitch about it? I certainly hope you're not encouraging the fool by acting like that around him. Don't be an idiot."

I realized that I was a bit tough on Bradford at times but he didn't have me fooled. Bradford would have cut my throat to get ahead if necessary. He wouldn't hesitate for a second and I knew it. Bradford held an MBA from Princeton and thought he owned the world. Well, he was wrong; I owned it. At least I owned the world he currently resided in and I didn't ever want him to lose sight of that fact.

"Tomalis, I'm nobody's idiot and I would appreciate being shown a certain level of respect."

"Then respect yourself," I told him in anger. "Speaking of which, now that you've tracked me down, I do want to make mention of something that's been troubling me."

Bradford seemed like he was trying to control his temper. "What's troubling you, Tomalis?"

"That penthouse activity. It needs to stop."

Bradford grinned. "Tomalis, you can't be serious. The penthouse serves a very important purpose."

"It serves no purpose. We shouldn't have to provide men

with sexual favors to get their business and I no longer care to have my name or my corporation's name tied to such nonsense."

"No harm, no foul, Tomalis," Bradford said. "Those bitches knew what they were getting into from day one and they are paid very well for their services."

"Yet and still, I manufacture cars, not whores."

"I understand where you're coming from, Tomalis. I really do. But, I've got something important lined up for later tonight and a few things for the end of the year. At least let me go through with those and then we can talk."

I glanced over my shoulder at Ben who had to be growing impatient. The caddy was over on the side with a pair of headphones on listening to his CD player.

"Bradford, you do these last few things and then that's it. There's nothing to talk about. Comprende?"

"But Tomalis—"

"Do we understand each other, Bradford?" I dared him with my eyes to challenge my orders. He knew better.

"Yes. Tomalis, we understand each other."

"As far as Tanaka, tell him to take his idle threats back to Japan. I have better things to do than deal with the likes of him."

Bradford sighed and looked away from me. "I'll deliver your message."

"Fine."

Bradford echoed my "fine" and then went to get back into the golf cart.

The nerve of him. Cleaning out my closet was long overdue and I intended to clean it out completely.

Diana

"Diana, I know you're home!" I heard Pinky yelling through my front door.

Dean and Darren had left early that morning to go spend the night with their friend, Pryor. I was relaxing in bed, trying to catch up on some much needed sleep, when she started banging.

I got up and yelled, "I'm coming, Pinky! Hold your horses!"

I opened the door and she was grinning from ear to ear. She always did that. I had never seen someone so happy in my life. Pinky was always happy.

"What's going on, girl?" I asked after she was inside my foyer.

"Diana, I came over here to snatch you up. We're hanging out today."

"Girl, I'm worn out. I need some rest."

"Puleeze! I already heard your boys are gone for the day. Red told me. We're going to scoop her up after we leave here, so go get dressed."

I looked down at the gray sweats and burgundy turtle-neck I had on. "I am dressed."

Pinky waved her finger in my face. "Uh-uh, you ain't dressed. Not to hang out with me and Red."

Let me explain something about Pinky. The word "trip" didn't do her justice. I had met both Pinky and Red during my freshman year at the University of Maryland. Their real names were Susan and Leandra, respectively. Both of them were from the Bronx and sometimes their accents drove me crazy; especially when they got to talking loud out in public. I could always understand them—since I was used to them— but other people had to often ask them to repeat themselves.

Their nicknames were Pinky and Red because you would never catch them wearing anything outside of those colors. Pinky was about five-three with a pink weave going halfway down her back. She was dark skinned with this gigantic smile and she wore ice blue contact lenses to finish out her look. In the summertime, she would wear the skimpiest pink outfits she could lay her hands on. She might as well have been butt-ass naked. Pinky worked at an art gallery, which was about one of the only places she could get a job other than a strip club.

Red was taller, light skinned—what the brothers called "red-boned"—and had natural light brown eyes. Her hair was reddish brown. She wore everything blood red, including her lipstick. Red did dress slightly more conservatively. She had no choice because she was a bank vice president.

Pinky had on a tight leather pink outfit when she came over that day. The skirt was so short that if she had sat down the wrong way, her coochie would have been exposed to the world. It was so tight, I wondered if she could even sit down in it. But she had driven to pick me up, so somehow she had managed.

"You and Red have a good time," I said. "I really just want to stay home and chill out."

"Diana, you're my girl and all, but I have to keep it real. How often do you have a Saturday to yourself?"

"Not often," I responded. "The boys usually demand all of my time."

"Exactly. That's why I'm here, sistergirl. Red schooled me on them being gone so we are going to show you a good time."

"Actually, I got my Christmas bonus yesterday. I begged them to let me have it a week early so I could buy the boys something nice. I'm going to go shopping a little later."

Pinky spread her manicured pink fingernails on her hips. "Diana, now you know shopping is my middle name. I know just the spot. I have a teenage nephew and he's into the same things your sons are into. We can have a ball shopping."

I debated. *Was I really up for a day with Pinky and Red?* "Then what?" I asked. "After we go shopping, then what?"

"Let me break it down for you while we pick out something else for you to wear." She started pulling me toward my bedroom. "We want to take you out to lunch, then we want to take you to this cocktail party one of the Redskins players is having out in Mitchellville, and then we're going to a cabaret."

"Pinky, you had me going until the cabaret. A sister has to eat, so lunch is cool, and I love the houses out in Mitchellville, so that's cool, too. But the cabaret; I'm not feeling that."

"Why not?"

"Most cabarets are dead. That bring your own bottle nonsense is for the birds. Who's having it anyway and where is it being held?"

"One of my sorors is having it to raise money for her church and it's being held at a fire station out in Bladensburg."

"A fire station?"

"Yeah, some of them have nice dance halls. Look, Red and I went last year. It was fly. I wouldn't lie to you."

I smirked. "Yeah, right, Pinky."

"Let's just hurry up and get dressed. Red's waiting and you know how impatient her ass is."

I actually had a good time hanging out with Red and Pinky, after all the people at the restaurant got finished checking out Pinky's hair and outfit. We went to this new soul food restaurant in Upper Marlboro called Flossie's. The food was delicious and the small atmosphere was classy and cozy. They also had incredible service. I was thoroughly impressed.

We waddled out of there after eating too much and piled back into Pinky's car: a pink Monte Carlo.

We got to the Redskins player's home—no, make that mansion—in Mitchellville and there were people everywhere. Of course, Pinky had men lined up waiting to talk to her and Red wasn't doing so badly herself. Even though I had put on a pair of black leather pants and a tight white sweater, I guess I wasn't quite hoochie enough to get a lot of attention. I did engage in a conversation with one player who had just been traded from the Cardinals. He was way too young for me—as most of them were—but he was extremely nice and had good manners. He wasn't that attractive but surely he could've gotten a woman at the party to leave with him. Professional athlete meant he was making money and some sisters would do anything for money. Women like Anastasia and Shakia from the office. I was hoping the rumors about them weren't true but knowing the way they carried themselves and knowing Bradford, the rumors were probably as factual as they come.

Even though I didn't meet a man who interested me—not that I was looking—I still had a wonderful time at the cocktail party. Mostly, I just admired the layout of the house and the expensive furnishings. One day I hope to have it like that. But, if I do, it would be on my own because I would never allow a man to define me. Once a woman does that, she might as well be a prisoner in her own home because if he leaves, so does her level of comfort. I wouldn't put myself in that position. But, I did want a man that was at least on the same level as me.

We dropped back by my place for a few minutes to freshen up and so I could drop off my packages. I had bought the twins several outfits and matching leather jackets. I had also bought them gift cards for Best Buy so they could pick out whatever video games or computer software they wanted. I was not on top of the latest "hot picks" so I decided to leave that up to them.

I decided to make a last-ditch effort to get out of the cabaret without hurting their feelings. "Sisterfriends, I'm kind of tired. It's been a long day," I said. "Why don't you two just go to the cabaret and have a good time?"

Red glared at me. "Oh, no, if I'm forced to go, so are you."

Pinky hissed. "Forced to go? Didn't you have a good time last year?"

"Um," Red replied. "It was aight but nothing to write home about. Ain't no happenings around here as hot as shit in the Bronx."

"You ain't never lied," Pinky said. "But the cabaret's cool and we're all going. It's been agreed upon."

Pinky went into the kitchen to get something to drink. Red walked over to me and whispered, "Hey, I gave up some super hot sex to go to this damn thing tonight so you better go, too."

"Who are you having super hot sex with?" I asked, being nosy.

"We haven't had it yet but one of the players today was making all kinds of promises in my ear. His rap alone almost made me cream in my pants but I put him on the back burner to make Pinky happy."

"Okay, okay, I'll go." I hated myself for giving in so easily. "But I need a bottle of Moët if I'm going to make it through tonight. You make more money than me, so how about it?"

"You're going to make me bribe you? You heifer!"

We both laughed.

"Hey, I get a bottle of Moët or I'm coming down with the menstrual cramps from hell. She'll believe me, you know she will, because it's a well-known fact that I have messed up menstrual periods."

Red smiled. "Deal, heifer. Now when Pinky comes back in here, act all excited and shit about tonight."

"I'll try. But don't forget our first stop is the liquor store."

We got to the fire station and I cringed when I saw the people walking in. Most of the women looked old enough to be my grandmother and they were all wearing fake minks. Their men looked like old school pimps.

Pinky was acting all excited about being there. "Ladies, it's on now. Look at all these big ballers rolling up in here."

Red and I just stared at each other as we exited Pinky's Monte Carlo. I could tell she was ready to go home—or hook up with the player she'd met earlier—and I was damn sure ready to go home.

Pinky had our tickets already and handed them to the ancient sister collecting them at the entrance to the hall. I was clutching on to my bottle of Moët. I was going to need it big time to make it through the night. Once inside, it was actually kind of a nice spot. It was much larger than I had expected and they had it decorated well. Still, I wasn't feeling the entire scenario and would have preferred to be at home watching the latest DVDs. I had heard Zane's *Sock It to Me* DVD was all that and a bag of chips. Plus, I wanted to see *National Security*. That Martin Lawrence was hilarious.

We found some vacant seats at a table with some people

that were only twice our age instead of three times our age. Just as I had figured, the night was boring as hell.

The DJ was so-so. He mixed it up between old school and new school. People stayed on the dance floor but I refused to dance with the men who approached me. I just sipped on my champagne, trying to stretch it out. Pinky and Red were drinking hard lemonade. Pinky loved dancing so she got her groove on quite a bit. Looks didn't matter to Pinky; money mattered and she obviously smelt some up in there because she was strutting her stuff.

Red was turning men down right and left just like me. She kept looking at her watch and sneaking off to the hallway to use her cell phone. After her third disappearance, she came back, sat down next to me and whispered, "You think Pinky will get upset if I cut out early?"

"How are you planning on doing that?" I asked. "We all came together."

"That brother I was telling you about earlier said he'd come scoop me up."

I leered at her and then squeezed her hand so tightly that she started trying to yank it away. "I don't know if Pinky will be upset but I will. You aren't leaving me here to deal with this boring ass party alone."

I let her hand go and she picked up her bottle of hard lemonade to take another swig. "This is messed up. Why should I have to stay?"

"Why should I?"

She snickered. "Good point. Okay, aight, shit! I'll stay."

I hugged her and kissed her on the cheek. "Thanks, Red."

"You owe me, Diana."

"Why do I owe you? I wasn't the one who invited you."

"No, but you're the one insisting that I stay up in this

bitch. I already gave up more than forty dollars for the bottle of champagne. What more do you want?"

We both fell out laughing.

"Red, let's just make the best of this. It'll be over in a couple hours."

"Cool, but after that, I'm going to get me some dick action."

"Hey, I ain't mad at you."

"So what's up with you, anyway?" she asked, having to raise her voice a bit because the DJ went from a slow jam— "Sexual Healing" by Marvin Gaye—to a fast song—"Word Up" by Cameo.

"Nothing's up with me," I replied. "What do you mean?"

"Who are you fooling around with these days?"

"I don't believe in fooling around. I just go to work, take care of my kids, and try to make ends meet."

"Your boss still coming on to you?"

"Not as much as he used to. I set his ass straight and he knows better."

"That's good, but why not date? Life's too short to be alone."

"I'd rather be alone for all the right reasons than be with someone for all the wrong ones," I said. I pointed to Pinky on the dance floor, shaking her ass with a toothless man with a velvet green suit on. "Check Pinky out, for example. Do you honestly think she's even remotely attracted to that man?"

"No. We both know the deal with Pinky. She's attracted to his money."

"Exactly, but that's not me, Red. I want more than that. If I just wanted a man with money, I could hook up with Bradford because he's getting paid. But he's an asshole and I want a real man."

Red smiled. "Now this I've got to hear. What's your idea of a real man, Diana?"

I paused to think about it. "A man who has goals in his life. A man who has a college education and a good job. A man who is a gentleman and knows how to cater to a woman's needs."

"I was wondering when you were going to get to the sex part."

I rolled my eyes. "Those aren't the kinds of needs I was referring to."

"Well, those are the kind you should be referring to. Diana, are you sexually liberated?"

I sat up in my chair, offended. "Of course I'm sexually liberated. What makes you think I'm not?"

"I never said I thought you weren't. I was just asking a question," Red stated sarcastically. "I've only recently become sexually liberated, believe it or not."

"Red, you've been getting your freak on since I've known you."

"That's the vibes I've been giving off, but I just used to let men get their nuts and not worry about myself. As long as they were wining and dining me, it didn't matter. Now I insist on having an orgasm. Otherwise, the sex isn't worth my time or effort."

"I heard that."

The music suddenly stopped and Pinky returned to the table. She got a business card out her purse and handed it to Pimp Daddy. "Make sure you call me, Boo," she said, fingering his lapel and winking at him.

"I'm going to call your fine ass tomorrow," he replied. "Maybe we can have dinner."

"That sounds good." Pinky noticed the way I was glaring

at her. "Well, I need to spend some time with my friends since I dragged them in here. You take care."

Red jumped up as soon as some of the overhead lights were raised. "Oops, they must be ending the event early. We need to hurry up and get the car so we don't get stuck in a line trying to make it out the parking lot."

Pinky pulled her back down in her chair. "Red, relax and release. They aren't ending it early. They have something special this year."

I beat Red in asking the question. "What?"

Pinky giggled. "You'll see in a moment."

The lady that had been collecting tickets at the front door got on the stage and announced, "It's time to really have some fun. While I realize tonight is to benefit the church, we wanted to make it extra exciting this year. Now everyone in here is over eighteen so I'm sure you can handle the heat." She pointed to a door on the right. "Men, we're going to have something just for you a little later but ladies, right now welcome The Heat.

All the females' heads snapped around toward the door; even mine.

The DJ put on "Do Me Baby" by Prince and there was a collective sigh. That's a classic fucking song. Out came a fine specimen of a man wearing a Santa Claus outfit, complete with a white wig and beard. Even with all that on him, you could tell he was holding something underneath. He was about six-two with ebony skin and these intriguing eyes. There was something about the eyes but I couldn't place them.

"Now, ladies, Santa wants to know if you've been naughty or nice this year," the same woman said on the microphone.

A bunch of women started yelling out that they'd been

nice. Pinky stood up and screamed, "I've been naughty, Santa!"

The woman pointed at Pinky. "There's one for you, Santa. Santa told me in private that he's looking for the naughty girls tonight. With all that pink on, you look naughty," she said to Pinky.

Pinky yelled out, "I'm very naughty and I have something else on me that's pink. Wanna guess what it is, Santa?"

I covered my forehead in shame. Pinky was out of fucking control when she got some liquor in her system.

Santa came over to our table, taking his time and shaking everything God gave him on the way. He picked Pinky up and she didn't hesitate to clamp her ankles behind his back.

Red started laughing. "Pinky's a nut!"

I had to see what was going to happen next so I stood up like everyone else was doing; just in time to see Pinky being placed in a chair in the center of the room.

Santa was singing to her and doing all the hand motions for the song while she sat there with her legs spread wide open, giving him the "come here" gesture with her finger. He unbuckled his thick black belt and pulled it out the loopholes, inch by inch.

Just then the song switched up and "Booty Call" by Guy came on. All the women really got hyped up and started doing the line dance right there by their tables. Santa started getting undressed with the help of Pinky. She was all into it as she lowered his jacket off his muscular shoulders, exposing his thick arms and tight abs. Then she got up from the chair while he sat down so she could pull his black boots off.

Pinky started shaking her stuff so much that if someone had entered at that moment, they would have had to guess which one was the stripper and which one was an audience member.

Santa got back up and started doing the Booty Call with Pinky, lowering his pants a little each time he made a ninety-degree turn. Soon, his thong was exposed and I gasped. "Long Dong Silver" didn't have a damn thing on him.

He still had on the wig and beard and I was curious to see his face. Something came over me; I was hornier than the Devil. It had been ages since I had yearned to fuck a particular man but I wanted to fuck Santa's ass; *bad!*

Pinky did what I was hoping she would and yanked off his wig and beard. I was weak in the knees when I whispered his name: "Edmund."

Red tapped me on the shoulder. "You know him?"

I giggled. "I can't believe this. He's the garage attendant at my job."

Red asked, "The one you said is always sweating you?"

"Yeah, the one and the same."

Red smirked. "Diana, he wouldn't have to sweat me. That man is fine. Girl, you are a damn fool. You mean you've been coming home alone every night when you've got that kind of brother hanging out at your job? You've got serious issues!"

"He doesn't look like that at work, Red," I said in defense of my actions. I had to admit she was right, though. I had been blind.

Pinky finished freaking all over Edmund and then several other women took a turn. I really didn't want him to see me because I was at a loss for words and needed to think. If Edmund stripped on the side, he must have been getting mad pussy so why would he want me? Maybe he just viewed me as a challenge and planned to dump me by the wayside the second he got the drawers.

I shook my head in dismay and sat down at the table, burying my head in my hands. The Moët had made me tipsy and now this. I was shocked when I felt a pair of strong hands on my shoulder. I knew it was him before I even looked up. He was right on top of me, staring down at me. "Hello, Diana."

"Hello, Edmund."

He turned my chair around and gave me a lap dance. Then he leaned down and whispered in my ear, "See what you missed out on. Your loss."

He moved away from me with a thong full of bills and exited the room. The woman was back on the microphone asking, "Did you ladies enjoy The Heat?"

They all screamed. I didn't. I was ready to go.

She announced the female dancer and Pinky was suddenly ready to go. "I'm not trying to watch some hoochie. Let's roll."

I was the first one to jump up. "I'm ready."

Red teased me all the way home and Pinky joined in after she found out the stripper was the same brother that I was always complaining about. They both said that if I didn't fuck him by the end of the year, they would.

"You're both so damn nasty!" I lashed out at them.

"Hey," Pinky said. "I'm just telling you like it is. The brother is slamming and I'd slam him in a heartbeat."

"Hell, you almost slammed him on the dance floor." Red giggled. "I thought you were going to give some of those old fogies in there an eyeful."

"You heifers are just jealous," Pinky said.

Pinky was right about one thing. I was jealous but not of her. I was jealous of whoever Edmund was screwing every night. I wanted it to be me.

Anastasia

Shakia is such a bitch! She pissed me off when I called her Saturday night and she tried to pull the "I've got the flu!" shit. That whore wasn't sick. She just didn't feel like whoring. She could've been honest and just said, "Anastasia, I don't feel like being a whore tonight!" Why lie?

Anyway, Bradford had requested both of us to be present in the penthouse that night. I wasn't trying to go alone but I didn't have any options. All the other whores I knew were already out whoring.

I was glad when I got there and Bradford had found someone else to fill in for Shakia. She was flat chested and had a fucked-up grille but she would do as a substitute for Shakia. As long as she could give up the ass and suck a mean dick, it didn't matter to me. I wasn't the one who'd have to fuck her.

Her name was Whitney and it was obvious we weren't feeling each other from the second we were introduced. She was probably jealous of me—who wouldn't be—and I thought she looked mighty skank. I wanted to ask which street corner Bradford found her on but there were more pressing matters when I noticed the men who were chilling on the leather sectional in the living room.

"Um, Bradford, isn't that man's last name Tanaka?" I pointed to a Japanese man sitting in the middle of four other Japanese men.

"Yeah, what of it?" Bradford responded.

"So, isn't he like Tomalis's biggest competition? I may not be an executive but I know he owns Prism Motors."

"That he does." Bradford gave me this evil sneer. "You have something against screwing Japanese men?"

"No, please, dick is dick and fucking is fucking but why would you be entertaining him and his friends?"

"That's my business," he said nastily. "You handle your business and I'll handle mine. I don't pay you to ask questions." Bradford handed me an envelope. "It's all there. Now you're a seductress so go seduce somebody."

"I don't feel comfortable about this."

Bradford grabbed my elbow and pulled me into one of the three bedrooms. He tossed me on the bed and slammed the door. "Listen, Anastasia, I don't have time for your shit! Either you're going to do what I pay you for or you're not! Whores are a dime a dozen so just let me know if I need to replace you."

"Calm down, Bradford! Shit!" I adjusted the shoulders of my dress. "I'm just curious, is all."

"Curiosity is not a good thing around here. You follow me?"

"That may be, but I do have one other question?"

"What?" he practically screamed at me.

"Does Tomalis know that man is here?"

"He knows that Mr. Tanaka is in town. I tried to get him to take a meeting with him earlier. Any other fucking questions?"

"I take it that he didn't want to have a meeting. So why are you still hanging out with the man."

"Because I'm minding my fucking business." Bradford came closer to the bed, grabbed my ankles and spread my legs. "I think you need a little reminder of who and what you are before we go back out there."

I tried to pull my ankles together. "No, I don't think so."

"I just handed you an envelope full of cash to fuck for the

rest of the night. I want you to fuck me first. Are you down or not?"

I laid there thinking. Christmas was right around the corner and I needed the cash badly. I couldn't afford the shit I had planned to buy for my family and friends without it.

"I'm straight, Bradford." He released my ankles and I stood up on the bed to get undressed. "What about Tanaka and them?"

Bradford smirked, beginning to unzip his pants. "They'll get their turn. Meanwhile, Whitney will keep their asses in check."

After Bradford was finished with his "grudge fuck" I went out into the living room where Whitney was going down on two men at the same time. I had to admit that the shit was impressive. She was moving her mouth from dick to dick like a starving animal and the other three men—including Tanaka—were sitting there looking nothing short of amazed.

Bradford slapped me on the ass. "Get to it!"

I walked out into the middle of the floor, in my birthday suit, and said, "Okay, who wants some of this black pussy?"

All five men raised their hands. I turned around to see Bradford with his hand up as well; greedy motherfucker. It was going to be a long ass night. I had my own plans, though. After they were done doing the do, I intended to get Bradford drunk as a skunk and find out what course of action I needed to follow to seduce Tomalis. It was time for me to push that bitch of a wife of his to the curb.

Sunday, December 17th

Chico

"I love you!" I sat up in the bed suddenly, not believing I had just mouthed those words.

Zetta squirmed beside me and then sat up as well. "Chico, I'm flattered but don't you think you're rushing things."

She smiled and I smiled back. *What the fuck was I doing?*

"Zetta, I know this is crazy but I've never felt like this before. It has to be love."

She laughed. "Or lust." She ran her fingers through my hair and then massaged my right shoulder. "Chico, you've never been with an older woman before, have you?"

"No, but that doesn't mean anything."

"It means a lot."

She let go of me and got out of the bed. I watched her

walk into the bathroom and could hear her urinating. Even that shit turned me on. She came back out in the buff and climbed back into bed next to me.

"Want some breakfast?" she asked me. "There's this fantastic deli on the entry level that delivers."

"No, I'm not that hungry," I said. "I'm still full from last night."

On Saturday night, Zetta had treated me to dinner at Morton's where the steaks started at thirty bucks and then you had to pay extra for the side dishes. I'd never had a dinner that expensive before but she didn't blink an eyelash when they presented her with the bill. Shit, it wasn't her money anyway so I guess she wouldn't care.

After dinner, we had headed back to her apartment in her limousine. I kept having this uneasy feeling about the driver. She claimed everything was cool with him but I didn't like the way he stared at me. He knew everything we were up to—short of watching us actually fucking—and he could have easily sold us out to Mr. Wolfe.

"Where did your husband think you were last night?" I asked her.

She giggled. "He thinks I'm in Virginia with a female friend. I told him that we were going to a benefit fund-raiser and it was going to run late so we planned to spend the night."

"What if he calls your friend?"

Zetta smacked her lips. "Tomalis isn't about to go hunting for me and besides, Abigail's not even home so she can't tell him anything. She never does."

She never does? What the hell! "You make it sound like you do this often."

"Do what often, Chico?"

The tone that she addressed me with suddenly made me

feel like she was my mother. Momma; she was going to be pissed. I didn't plan on being out all night and I didn't call her to let her know. Even though I was a man, she expected me to let her know when I wouldn't be there so she wouldn't be worried.

"Do what often, Chico?" Zetta repeated.

"Stay out all night and have to use your friend as an alibi."

"No, not at all," she said. "I told you before. You're the first man that I've been attracted to in a long time." She pinched my cheek. "You're so cute!"

"Little boys are cute," I said with disdain. "I'm a man, Zetta. I'm a man."

She ripped the covers off my crotch and started fingering the head of my dick. "Oh, Chico, I'm well aware of the fact that you're a man."

Zetta started giving me a hand job and I threw my head back in ecstasy. She had mad skills. She stopped right before I came—my toes were curled up and everything—and then climbed on top of me. When her pussy slid onto my dick, I almost screamed like a bitch. The pussy was just that damn good.

I grabbed onto her hips while she rode me for what seemed like forever. Every time I was about to explode, she would stop and wait for my heart rate to return to normal and then start riding me again.

She finally let me come and I don't think I had ever come so hard in my life. She collapsed on top of me and I caressed her spine. I whispered it again. "I love you."

Zetta didn't respond but for a brief second, I thought that I heard her laughing.

Diana

It was so strange; my dream. I was standing on the balcony of an oceanside hotel and I had on nothing but a red bra and matching panties. There were a lot of people on the beach but they were all nude and most of them were engaged in some form of sexual activity. Oral sex, vaginal sex, anal sex. Sex period. I just stood there, eyeing couple after couple as they pleasured each other. What was so strange about it was, at first, I couldn't see the features of any of the men. The faces of the women were all crystal clear. I even recognized a couple of them: Pinky and Red.

Suddenly all the men looked up at me and they were all the same person: Edmund. He was fucking all these women at once. How was it possible?

"Momma, are we still going to church?"

I heard the question but it took me a moment to open my eyes and find Darren standing beside my bed. I sat up, yawned and stretched. "What time is it?"

He looked at my alarm clock—something I could've just as easily have done—and said, "It's ten after nine."

Church started at ten so we would be pushing it but it was important to attend.

"Sure, baby, we're still going. Is Dean up yet?"

"Yeah, he's on the phone with his girlfriend."

"His what?" I asked in astonishment.

"His girlfriend, Brandi."

"Dean has a girlfriend?"

"Yeah, they've been dating for a couple months now."

I frowned; immediate visions of teenage sex went rushing through my mind. "What exactly do you mean by dating?"

"Talking on the phone, walking from class to class together at school, kissing, hugging, going to the movies to-gether, and—"

"When has Dean been to the movies lately?"

Darren seemed like he didn't want to give up any more information. "Why don't you just ask him all that?" He started for my bedroom door. "I'm going to get dressed."

"Tell Dean to get off the phone and get dressed, too."

"Okay, Momma."

Darren eased my door shut behind him and I felt a shud-der run through me. I wasn't sure what caused it. It was a toss-up between finding out that one of my sons was in-volved with a girl or fantasizing about Edmund. Both were equally disturbing.

The twins and I went to church and then decided to go have pancakes afterwards. When we got home, there was a mid-night blue Lexus coupe parked in front of our house.

"Who's that, Momma?" Dean asked.

"Bad car," Darren added. "I wonder who it could be."

We pulled into our driveway and got out of my car. I stared at the Lexus. It had tinted windows. I couldn't see if there was even someone in the car.

"Probably someone visiting one of the neighbors. I'm not expecting anyone," I said.

"Neither are we," Dean said.

I had the front door unlocked and the boys were already inside when I heard someone yell out my name.

I turned to look and the window of the car was lowered a bit. I couldn't imagine who it might be. Then my mind flashed to Edmund. Could he afford a car like that? If he made enough money as a stripper, he could. But if he was making cash like that, why would he be working as a garage attendant at Wolfe?

I walked down the sidewalk and got closer to the car. "Yes? Can I help you?"

Dean and Darren were inside peeking out the living room curtain. Normally, I would've been upset because they were being nosy but not this time. In case something crazy happened, I needed them to either protect me or be witnesses.

The person in the car didn't say anything else so I got even closer. I fell backwards a few steps when I recognized the person inside.

"Stephen, what are you doing here?"

"Diana, I need to talk to you. Get in."

Fifteen minutes later Stephen and I were sitting down in a Starbucks with two cups of coffee. I had gone inside and told the boys that an old friend had popped in and that I would be back shortly. There was no way I was going to spring their father on them out the blue. They might have jumped him and whupped his ass for being an absentee parent for so long.

"Diana, I know this must come as a shock. My showing up and all." He had an expression of concern on his face. "I just had to see you."

"For what?" I got loud with him and people started looking. "The twins are thirteen, Stephen. Thirteen damn years old, teenagers, and you pick now to show up."

"I know the boys probably hate me."

I smirked. "Humph, that's an understatement. Of course they hate you. They've watched me struggle all their lives to make ends meet while you were somewhere living in the lap of luxury."

"It hasn't exactly been all that," Stephen said. "Diana, do you mind lowering your voice a bit?"

"Hell, yeah, I mind. I will be as loud as I damn please, you trifling Negro."

Stephen sighed in disgust. "Maybe this isn't such a good idea after all."

"You come rolling up to my house after all this time in a fancy ass car, and you expect me to pretend like everything is everything?"

"No, I don't expect that, Diana. I was hoping we could at least be cordial to each other; for the sake of the boys."

"Huh, you're sick." I got up from the table. "I'll take a cab home. You stay the hell away from me and the twins."

He stood up to face me. "You can't keep my boys from me. I'm their father."

"You donated some sperm. That's it."

He grabbed my wrist. "You can't keep them away from me. I have rights."

"Then take me to court but you'd better be ready to pay me a shitload of child support."

I had him and he knew it.

"Yeah, that's right. Thirteen years of child support for two kids. You add it up and don't forget to tack on interest and future payments. Once you have my money, give me a call. Until then, stay the hell away from me and them."

Stephen followed me outside. "Diana, you're really not being fair. Making this all about money. At least ask the boys if they want to see me. I won't press the issue if both of them are against it. But how can you feel right about yourself if you don't give them the option." He took a business card out of his bag and scribbled something on the back. "I live in Atlanta now but I'm in town for the holidays visiting my cousin. My cell number is on the back. Please call me."

With that, he walked away. If the idiot really wanted to

earn brownie points, he would've insisted on taking me back home; even if I didn't want him to.

It took me almost an hour to hail a cab. I was pissed, depressed, confused, and horny. Damn both Stephen and Edmund.

Tomalis

Every once in a while, something good did happen in my life. Waking up without Zetta in the bed with me was a blessing. I lingered in bed longer than I normally would. Most of the time I would hurry and get up before her so I didn't have to hear her whining about this, that, or the other.

I fell back into a deep sleep without realizing it and was startled awake by my cell phone.

"Hello," I said, after locating it on the nightstand and flipping it open.

"I hope your ass didn't forget about me!"

"Barron, my man!" I was so excited that I jumped up. "Where are you?"

"At the airport waiting on you, fool!"

I looked at the clock. "Oh, shit! I'm sorry, Barron. I'll be out the door within ten minutes."

I could hear Barron huffing and puffing into the phone. "Forget it. I'll just grab a cab."

"No, I'm coming to get you personally. Not sending a limo for you. Not letting you take a cab or shuttle. I want to pick you up."

"Damn, you almost sound like you have a hard-on for my sexy ass or something!"

"First off, you aren't sexy and secondly, I'm not gay." We

both laughed. "I just want to get you so we can talk on the way back. Plus, I'm up to something."

"I'm relieved to hear you say you're not a booty bandit. If any woman can turn a straight man gay, it's that bitch wife of yours."

"Don't mention Zetta. I'm trying to enjoy my day." I was already in the bathroom putting toothpaste on my toothbrush. "Hold tight. I'll be there in a flash."

"Okay, but hurry up. These two flight attendants are staring at me like they want to jump my bones."

I chuckled at the thought. "You wish. In your damn dreams."

I hung up, brushed my teeth, washed my face, and threw on some clothes so I could go pick up the one and only person I truly regarded as a friend.

When I got to BWI, it was one-thirty. Barron's flight had landed at twelve-fifteen and I knew he was probably pitching a fit by then. That was just his nature. He was overly dramatic about most things. He was also funny and had missed his calling as a stand-up comedian.

Zetta didn't rear her ugly head before I left. She was still laid up in her apartment on Wisconsin Avenue with that little boy from the mail room. She was beyond help and so was our marriage. I had promised that I would pick up her mother so she probably wouldn't show up for at least another couple of hours.

Zora Mason was standing there with her hands on her hips and with much attitude as I slowed down in front of where she stood on the curb. "Tomalis, it's about time," she hissed. "Why'd you bring this tiny ass car? Will my luggage even fit?"

I grinned at her from the driver's seat of my Corvette. "You know what, Zora? You've got a point. I don't think your luggage will fit. In fact, you won't fit either."

With that said, I pulled off and left her stupid ass standing there.

"Tomalis, you get back here!" she screamed after me. "What nerve!"

I came to a halt about four airlines down where Barron was standing. I could see Zora stomping my way in my rearview mirror.

"Hurry up, man!" I said to Barron. "She's coming!"

"Who's coming?" Barron asked. Then he turned and spotted her. "Aw, hell!" He threw his duffel bag in the trunk quickly and hopped in the car. "Let's get out of here while we can still make a run for it."

I almost burned rubbing pulling off. Barron waved bye to Zora. I could still see her in the mirror. She had fumes coming out her stuck-up nose.

"Man, we'll never hear the end of this shit!" Barron said.

"Good. I'm trying to stir up something."

"Hot damn! Well, all right! You know you can count me in. I wasn't looking forward to another boring holiday anyway."

I winked at him. "Barron, boring is the one thing this Christmas definitely won't be."

Barron and I were sitting in my study smoking cigars and laughing our heads off when we heard Zetta come in calling for her mother.

Barron whiffed the tip of his Cohiba. "Damn, man, we've come a long way from smoking rabbit tobacco out in the woods."

"That was a lifetime ago."

"You hear her out there, don't you?" he asked.

"Yeah, I hear her. Let the games begin."

I sat back in my fine leather chair and waited for Zetta to follow the scent of the cigar smoke.

"Tomalis, there you are," she said as she entered my office. Barron stood up and eyed her up and down. "What are you doing here?"

"Zetta, I told you Barron was coming for the holidays," I said.

"Welcome home, Boobie," Barron said jokingly.

Zetta looked like she wanted to slap him. "Where's Momma?"

I glanced at my watch. "She should be here any minute."

"What do you mean? Didn't you pick her up?"

"No, I picked up Barron." Barron and I both snickered. "We did see her, though. She had to get another way here. I was in the Corvette and had to keep my priorities straight."

Zetta came closer and hovered over my desk. "Are you telling me that you stranded Momma at the airport?"

"I wouldn't call it stranded. She's not in the middle of nowhere. She's at the airport with tens of thousands of other people."

"You know what the hell I mean, Tomalis. Don't insult my intelligence."

"Like I said, Zora should be pulling up here any minute."

Zetta stormed out; probably to go call her mother on her cell phone. I called after her. "How was the fund-raiser?"

"Fund-raiser?" Barron inquired.

"That was the lie she used for not coming home last night. Going to a fund-raiser in Virginia with a girlfriend."

"How do you know she was lying?"

"She's always lying. The only thing being raised last night was Zetta's ass in the air while this young boy hit it from behind."

"Oooh, you are rough." Barron chuckled. "So Zetta's robbing the cradle again, huh?"

"Big time." I put my cigar out and decided to save the rest of it for later. "Let's get out of here before Mommy Dearest shows up. I'm not trying to deal with her shit tonight."

"And miss the family dinner?" Barron asked sarcastically.

"Humph, what family dinner? Heather's in Chicago, probably thanking her lucky stars she's not here, Jonah's out doing whatever it is that Jonah does, and I'm not trying to eat with the two hoochies from hell."

"Now that you put it that way, I'm not either." Barron put his cigar out. "What's open around here on Sunday?"

"Plenty. Let's just ride around, grab a bite to eat someplace, and then get into some dirt."

Barron gave me some dap. "My man, just like old times."

Anastasia

I still have no idea how I ended up at Uranus on a Sunday night. There wasn't really anything else to do and I didn't want to sit in the house since Sunday was about the worst night for watching television; especially during football season. I was into football players but not into the game. I just wanted to fuck them for their money.

That was growing old. So was what I was doing with Bradford. The night before had made me sick to my stomach and that was rare. It wasn't the sex exactly; it was fact that I knew something was shady about the entire thing. For some reason, I felt protective of Tomalis Wolfe; even though he barely acknowledged my presence. Bradford was definitely up to no good. I just couldn't figure out what his deal was.

My girl, Mickey, was doing the damn thing on the center stage when I came in. She was dancing to some song I had never heard but it was tight. I was going to have to ask her the name later on so I could buy it to put on repeat in my car. I had a tendency to play the same song over and over again for days, if I was really feeling it.

There was a decent crowd for a Sunday, football games on or not. It really picked up after the games had gone off, though. Freaks are freaks seven days a week. I couldn't help but wonder how many of the men had their wives thinking they were at a sports bar kicking it with friends. How many men are likely to say, "Honey, I'm going to go watch the game over Robert's house and then we're going to a titty bar?" Not many; that's for sure.

I was sitting there chilling at the bar with Mickey and this new dancer who called herself Honor. While I failed to see what was so honorable about getting butt-naked in front of a bunch of strangers, I still thought it was a cool name.

Mickey asked, "Anastasia, when you gonna finally become a dancer? We need some flava here at Uranus!"

"Mickey, you know dancing was never my thing," I responded. "I've done a few private dances but I'm not shaking it up on stage. You go 'head and do your damn thing, sis."

"Humph, private dances, huh?" Honor inquired with a smirk. "I think I get your meaning."

I rolled my eyes at her. "Honor, I was thinking you were aight but now I don't know. You need to watch what you say and who you say it to around here. Some of the sisters will kick your ass."

Honor stood up. She was a tall bitch. She flung her

weave—as much as it was possible to fling one—behind her back and put her hands on her hips. "Ain't nobody gonna kick my ass! I'm from the hood. I will beat a chick down and not bat an eyelash."

I laughed. "This is D.C. We're all from the fucking hood."

Honor couldn't help but laugh also.

Mickey was sitting there like she was afraid something was about to jump off. "Anastasia, Honor didn't mean to insult you or anything. She was just making a comment."

I took another sip of my Screaming Orgasm. "Whatever, I just didn't like the implication."

Honor sat back down and if I could read minds, she was probably thinking that I shouldn't have been offended by her question unless she was right. Yeah, I was getting paid to fuck but the whole world didn't need to know it.

I had just ordered another drink when my luck changed for the better. I couldn't believe my eyes when Tomalis Wolfe strolled into the place looking like a million bucks. He was with this other dude who was kind of sexy also, but Tomalis was damn right fine—as always.

They took one of the tables closest to the stage—I was surprised one was vacant—and then ordered some drinks. I sat there staring at them and watching their every move.

Mickey tapped me on the shoulder. "You still with us?"

I glanced in her direction. "Huh?"

"Are you still with us?" She pointed to Honor. "Honor was asking you something."

"Oh, what?" I asked Honor.

"I was asking if you think I could get a day job where you work. I'm just now getting into this strip thing and it's going to be a minute before I start making serious ends. I just got my own place after my old man threw me out so I gotta make my bills."

Honor didn't seem like she would fit in at Wolfe. She was cute and all but she had this sleaziness about her. I didn't want to insult her, though—even though she had damn sure insulted me earlier. "You can check with Human Resources and see what's up. Can you type or you looking to do something else?"

"I went to business school for a hot second so, yeah, I can type."

"Then check it out. I believe their office hours are nine to four. You gotta have a resume or they won't give you a chance at all."

Honor giggled. "That ain't a problem. This little geek I've been stringing along is good at those things."

"Little geek?" Mickey inquired.

"Yeah, I met his ass at the movies down at Union Station. He ain't the kind of brother I usually let push up on me but there was something kinda hot about him. He can't fuck worth a damn, though."

We all laughed.

I asked, "So why you fucking him then?"

Honor shrugged. "Just feel sorry for him, I guess."

"Well, he ain't feeling sorry for himself if you're giving it up to his non-fucking ass," Mickey stated jokingly.

"True that," I added and Mickey and I gave each other a high five.

I started staring at Tomalis and his friend again. Mickey must have followed my eyes. "Yo, now that's what I'm talking about. Those older men—especially the ones that look and smell like money—are who I need to be hooking up with." She paused and then added, "I've seen that one dude before. The really fine one."

While I didn't really want to divulge the information, I didn't see any real reason not to. "That's Tomalis Wolfe."

Mickey almost sprang up out of her chair. "The Tomalis Wolfe? The billionaire?"

"I don't know if he's a billionaire but he's damn near there."

"Shit! I seen his ass on the cover of that magazine when I was getting my hair did. What's that joint called?"

I cringed at Mickey's broken English. She could never get a job at Wolfe but since Honor could halfway talk, it might work out for her.

"It was *Black Enterprise*," I said, well aware of the article because I had the tattered cover under my pillow at home. That's how I knew it was to the point where I needed to make a move. That was some serious obsessive shit, for me to have his picture under my pillow. I didn't even do that with Ronny's picture—my boyfriend from high school and my senior prom date—and he was the first one I ever let hit it. Ronny and I could've had something major together but he got locked up for some stupid shit and wouldn't see the streets for at least five more years.

"Yeah, that's that joint," Mickey said. "So he's your boss? Girl, I'd be at work early every day."

"He's not my direct boss so I don't see him all the time. He just owns the corporation."

Honor jumped in. "Shit, from what I hear Tomalis Wolfe owns the world."

"Definitely half of D.C.," I said.

Mickey sucked on her teeth. I hated that shit. "I bet a man like dat there could fuck me blind."

Honor nudged her shoulder. "Then go for it."

Mickey said, "You know his ass gotta be married."

"So, he's up in here," Honor replied. "He can't be too damn married if he's in Uranus on a Sunday night."

"Point taken." Mickey started giving off some vibes that I wasn't feeling; like she was about to try to get with Tomalis. To confirm my suspicions, she added, "I might have to just rock his world before the night is through."

It was time for me to mark my damn territory. "Forget it, tramp. He's mine."

They both glared at me but didn't say a word.

I got up and started walking toward the two of them. They were laughing hard as shit and not even really paying attention to what was happening on the stage.

"Excuse me," I said when I reached their table. I eyed Tomalis seductively. "Hello, Mr. Wolfe."

He grinned at me with that perfect set of teeth. "Hello yourself."

His friend jumped up, grabbed my hand, and started slobbering all over it. He was drunk as shit. "Now who might you be, with all your fineness?"

I was irritated but attempted to be friendly. "I'm Anastasia."

"Damn, that's a pretty ass name," he said. "I'm Barron, Tomalis's best friend."

"Nice to meet you." I pulled my hand free and looked back at Tomalis. "Are you having a good time?"

He shrugged. "Yes, it's very nice. My friend just arrived in town and he wanted to do something *different*. We were driving past and he asked me to stop." He surveyed the room. "Quite an interesting place. Do you work here also?"

I shook my head. "No, I just work for you."

His friend, Barron, collapsed back down into his seat. "I think I need another drink, Tomalis."

Tomalis chuckled. "You can think that but you're not getting one."

I really wanted to tell Tomalis how much he meant to me and how I would make a better wife for him than that Zetta bitch. I wanted to ask him to give me a ride and make a detour to an upscale hotel so we could get to know each other in the physical sense. I wanted to make a ton of promises about how I would treat him in and out of the bedroom. Instead, something totally stupid came out of my mouth. "You look very nice tonight."

He cleared his throat. "Thank you. So do you."

I couldn't tell whether he meant it or was just being pleasant.

Barron grabbed my hand again. "You know, I don't know any nice young ladies here in D.C. Maybe I can take you out to dinner."

"Thanks but no thanks," I replied, never taking my eyes off Tomalis. "Mr. Wolfe, have a nice evening and let me know if there's anything, *anything at all,* I can get for you."

"I thought you said you don't work here," he said.

"I don't but I know everybody." I didn't want to admit that I used to work at Uranus, but he was not a dummy and probably realized that was about the only way I could know everyone there. "Just let me know if you need *anything.*"

He gave me a quick two-finger salute. "Will do." He pulled Barron's jacket collar. "Let the young lady's hand go, man."

After Barron obliged, I said, "Enjoy the rest of your evening," and walked away.

Mickey and Honor were sitting there snickering when I got back over to them.

Honor said, "Looks like his friend was trying to take you in a back room and get some ass."

Mickey added, "Yeah, I thought you said Tomalis Wolfe was yours? Didn't look like it from over here."

"Bite me, bitches!" I lashed out at both of them and then stormed out.

I got to my car and sat behind the steering wheel fighting back tears. Shit was getting too serious. First his picture underneath my pillow and now crying. I was going to get with him if it killed me.

Monday, December 18th

Diana

"Diana, I need to see you in my office."

I could tell by the tone of his voice that Bradford had much attitude. I had just walked into the door and was still getting situated on a Monday morning and he was on me already. "Sure, Bradford. Just give me a moment."

He was standing in the doorway of his office with his arms folded across his chest. "I don't have a moment. Get in here now."

Bradford disappeared into his office so he missed the expression of anger that I couldn't possibly hide. It was bad enough that I had to deal with Stephen the day before. I was trying to deal with the fact that he had suddenly appeared after pulling a vanishing act thirteen years ago. Then there was the Edmund issue. Just thinking about him was driving me crazy. I didn't see him when I had parked in the garage but to my knowledge, he didn't come in until midmorning or early afternoon. I wasn't quite sure since I left my car parked for the day once I arrived. If I went out to lunch, I would go someplace within walking distance or catch a cab.

Bradford never came in so early; especially on a Monday. Yet there he was, making demands and acting like he was royalty.

I took my time going into his office. It was a matter of principle. He wasn't going to order me around like that. When I finally did make my way in there with a note pad and pen in hand, he was sitting at his desk on the phone.

I waited patiently for him to get off. He was speaking in Japanese. I had to give that to him. He was fluent in many languages and that was good in his line of work.

"Yes?" I asked the second he hung up the phone.

Bradford eyed me with pure disdain in his eyes. "Didn't I ask you to finish that proposal for Tomalis and have it on his desk by this morning?"

I ran all the recent conversations I'd had with Bradford through my head and could not recall him asking me to do a proposal. "Which proposal?"

He picked up a globe paperweight he had on his desk and slammed it back down. Only a miracle prevented it from shattering to pieces. "Shit, if you have to ask, you obviously haven't done it."

He was getting a bit too hostile for me. It had been a while since he had shown violent tendencies but he had shown them before. Once I could have sworn he was trying to sneak up behind me to choke me after we had gotten into it over something ridiculous. It all stemmed back to the fact that I would not sleep with him.

Attempting to maintain some composure, I calmly

stated, "Bradford, you never asked me to do one. I would've remembered and I would've done it; just like I do everything you ask of me."

Bradford clasped his hands behind his head and leaned back in his chair. "We both know you don't do *everything* I ask of you."

He got up and walked around his desk, approaching me. He started playing with my hair and placed his face so close to mine that I could smell the mint in his mouth. I started trembling when he lowered his index finger to the spot at the cusp of my breasts. There was silence as we both contemplated our next move.

I swiped his hand away and moved away from him. "You do realize that you're sexually harassing me, don't you?"

He chuckled, walked back over to his desk, and sat down. "It's your word against mine and mine comes with more clout."

Humph, that's what you think, you filthy bastard, I thought.

"As far as the proposal, can you please give me more information?" I sighed and waited for him to respond. He did not. I added, "I'll be glad to complete it right away."

He started opening and forcefully closing his desk drawers. "Forget it; I'll do it my damn self. But I'm sick of being humiliated because you don't know how to do your fucking job. I told Tomalis it would be on his desk and it's not there. That makes me look awful."

I did not feel like being in there one more second so I lied and said, "Well, I apologize if it is indeed my fault."

"Yes, it is indeed your fault." He grinned like the cat that ate the canary. "Diana, I'm not sure this is working out. You may want to start seeking employment elsewhere."

"Is that right?" I asked. *Fucking prick!*

"Hey, I'm just trying to warn you about the future. I need someone dependable all the time; not just some of the time."

"Bradford, need I remind you that Wolfe Industries has a Human Resources Department and there are certain rules and regulations that must be followed in order to terminate someone's employment? Particularly someone who has seniority and has never been written up."

"You're right," he snarled. "Go back to your desk and get Human Resources on the phone for me. Then you can just consider yourself written up."

I stormed out of his office. He wasn't just going to push me out without a fight. I had too many responsibilities and three mouths to feed. I pulled out the voice-activated recorder I had hidden under my shirt in the small of my back and pressed the off button.

The rest of my workday was stressful. Bradford—the asshole—did write me up and I was called down to Human Resources to be reprimanded. He and I both knew he was lying about the "imaginary proposal." There never was one. In all my time as his assistant, I had never neglected to perform a task. I purposely wrote everything down so I wouldn't ever forget even the smallest thing.

When it was time to get off, Bradford tossed a pile of paperwork on my desk and told me it had to be done before I left. I didn't utter a word. I called the twins and told them I would be late, then rushed through the bullshit work he'd come up with at the last minute.

Once I got down to the garage to get my car, I did something that I had never done before. I searched for Edmund. I didn't see him. I was disappointed. That sexual fantasy that I had about him sexing all those women at once still had my mind reeling. I was ashamed of the way I had been treating Edmund. Even though I didn't think he was my type—until I saw him shaking that big dick of his—it was still inappropriate for me to have behaved the way I did whenever he had approached me.

I wondered if an apology at that point would seem fake. It didn't appear that I would get the opportunity to find out so I started to get into my car. Suddenly I heard a pair of keys hit the ground behind me and I spun around.

"Edmund!" I had to struggle for my next breath. Not so much because he had startled me but because my coochie had soaked my panties just that quickly. "You snuck up on me."

"I'm sorry. I didn't mean to scare you, Diana." He bent down and picked up his keys. "It's late and I just wanted to make sure you got into your car safely."

I blushed. "Thanks. I appreciate it."

He watched as I unlocked the door, tossed my briefcase across the gear shift onto the passenger seat and got in. I looked up at him. "Edmund, about the other night."

"What about the other night?" Edmund shrugged. "I performed and it was what it was."

"I didn't know you danced."

"You don't know anything about me except what you see here in this garage. I've been trying to get to know you better for a long time but you're just too good for me. At least, that's what you think."

I felt like crap as the words left his mouth. "I deserved that. It's just that I haven't had a lot of luck in the relationship department. The father of my twins left me hanging when I got pregnant and it's been hard for me to open myself up to men ever since."

Edmund's left eyebrow went up in the air. "I didn't realize you had a set of twins. Are they girls or boys or one of each? How old are the babies?"

"They're boys—Darren and Dean—but they aren't babies."

"Then how old are they?"

"They just recently turned thirteen."

"Wow, they're teenagers. You look great to have kids that old."

"Thanks."

Edmund paused like he was doing some heavy thinking. "You made it sound like your heart was broken recently. You're still harboring on something that happened thirteen years ago?"

I was so uncomfortable. It did sound preposterous.

After I didn't answer, Edmund said, "Diana, it wasn't me that hurt you. It wasn't me or any of the other men who've probably tried to pay you some attention or show you some affection since then. It was one man. Why should all of us have to take the blame for the actions of one stupid brother?"

"Edmund, you're right. I couldn't agree with you more."

I hesitated, hoping he would ask me out like he had a hundred times before. Instead, he just said, "Have a nice evening."

Edmund tried to shut my car door but I held it open. "Hey, what time do you get off?"

He grinned at me and chuckled. After glancing at his watch, he replied, "In about an hour."

"Well, I really need to get home but the boys are probably okay. How about a drink? I could meet you at that little neighborhood pub down on Pennsylvania Avenue."

"Diana, I don't know quite how to put this. When you continuously dismissed me and my feelings, it hurt. I've moved on."

"Moved on?" I asked in disappointment.

"Yes, moved on."

"But you just came on to me last Friday. That was only three days ago."

"A lot can happen in three days. I actually met a nice young lady at the fire station."

I laughed. "Yeah, right. She only wants you because of the strip show you put on. She only wants your body."

"And what do you want?" he inquired. I didn't answer. "Exactly. Before you caught my little performance, I was just a garage attendant who was beneath you and not worth your time. Now all of sudden you want to go have a drink."

"Things change, Edmund."

He smirked. "Yeah, they sure do. I'm not into shallow women, Diana. I was into you but I couldn't see past your beauty to the real you. Now that you're all gung ho to bed me after an exotic dance, it just shows me what type of woman you truly are."

"You've got me all wrong, Edmund. I just told you that it's been a long time since I had a man."

"Maybe that's the reason you don't know a decent one when you see him. I'm going to see what happens with the sister that I just met. If things don't work out, who knows what might happen. Anything is possible."

"Uh . . ." I wanted to say something in my defense or beg him to give me a chance and boot the other sister to the curb but I realized that I was simply getting a taste of my own medicine. I hated the aftertaste.

"I need to go patrol the garage and make sure everything's secure," Edmund said before turning and walking away.

I closed my car door and started the engine. I didn't pull off right away. I just watched him and wondered how I could have been such a fool. Especially after my encounter with Stephen. He was such an asshole and I had a good man in front of me the entire time.

I was heated—in more ways than one—and before I knew it, my right hand was inching down between my legs and moving the elastic aside on my panties. I never took my eyes off Edmund as I fingered myself into a quick climax. *Damn, I just had to have that man!*

Chico

Zetta had told me to meet her after work at Pentagon City Mall. That was a long ass way from my hood but I would've traveled to the moon for Zetta's fine ass.

It was already seven-thirty and she hadn't shown up. I sat on a bench outside a jewelry store and watched people walk by. Rich white people are a trip. They act so differently from us. These two women had sat down on the bench next to me and started talking about some stupid shit. They were planning to have a home party to learn how to make creative scrapbooks. Hello, we are talking *scrapbooks* with "scrap" being the operative term. Black people just slap their shit into a photo album and call it a day. Most of us just stack pictures in empty boxes and pull them out whenever we want a good laugh. White people had to get fancy with their shit.

I had gone into the jewelry store for a hot minute but after scoping out the prices, I damn near fainted. The only jewelry I had ever purchased came from a street corner or a pawn shop. I knew there had to be some rich motherfuckers up in that mall after I saw what they were getting away with. Shit, some of those damn rings cost more than I was making in a fucking year.

I was getting worried but had no way of getting in touch with Zetta. I tried to get her to come up off her cell phone digits but she claimed it was too risky; that hubby might find out. I didn't exactly fall for that one. As busy as Tomalis Wolfe was, he damn sure didn't have time to scan over her monthly bill or check her call logs. I couldn't picture it.

By eight I realized she planned to stand me up. There had to be a good reason, though, because she would never do that to me. She cared about me; she had told me so. I slapped myself in the forehead when I remembered her saying something about her mom coming into town from one of those damn countries overseas; someplace I'd never been and would never go to because my ass wasn't about to get on anybody's plane. I wasn't putting my life in the hands of one man. What if his ass was drunk or high or—fuck it—sleepy? The entire plane would just be ass out.

Long ass boat rides were out also. I would get seasick from fishing along the Potomac River. I had tried that shit with one of my cousins a few times and it was boring as hell. No way the kid was going to spend a week or two on the water. Not in a million fucking years.

I don't know why my dumb ass sat there for another hour but I did. Just holding out hope that she'd show, let me tag along with her shopping as planned, and possibly let me even get a whiff of her pussy. She didn't have to fuck me every day; I wanted to make that clear to her. I didn't want her to think sex was all I wanted her for because it had gone way beyond that. I loved her. It was still scaring the shit out of me that I felt that way, but I did.

I started walking through the mall. Most of the stores were way out of my league. I couldn't afford a pair of socks; rather less an outfit.

One store did catch my eye. It was a toy store. Now

while I would never want Razor or Miceal or anyone else in the world I knew to catch me in there, I loved toys. They had this beautiful wooden dollhouse in the window that I wished I could have afforded for Gina. My little girl deserved it. The intricate details were spectacular and I couldn't help but admire the architecture. I had always loved building things. I had dozens of ships and other items that I had spent countless hours putting together. That was common knowledge. I was always fixing stuff for my friends as well. They'd buy shit from the thrift store and expect it to work like it was brand new. By the time I messed around with the damn things, they usually did.

I went inside to see the price of the dollhouse. It was eight hundred bucks. Well, that left my ass out for sure. There was a young sister behind the counter counting out the cash register. It must have been nearing closing time. I moved my head from side to side to see if anyone else was around. I could tell it made her uneasy. She might have thought I was about to pull a heist.

I walked closer to her and she threw all the money back into the register and slammed it. "Can I help you, sir?"

I shook my head. "Every black man is not a thief."

She eyed me uncomfortably. "I wasn't thinking that."

"Yeah, whatever. Anyway, I was looking at that dollhouse in the window."

"Would you like to purchase a kit?"

"A kit? It doesn't come assembled?"

"No, you have to put it together."

Damn, for eight hundred bucks you still have to do all the damn work.

"Would you like one?" she asked again.

"No. I wanted to know if you thought it would be on sale after Christmas."

She shrugged. "I have no idea. A lot of the things we have overstocked will be on sale if we don't get rid of them before next week. I'm just a seasonal employee but I think that dollhouse might be the same price all the time."

"Damn!"

She looked more relaxed after she understood that I wasn't there to hold her up. In fact, she started looking like she wanted to jump a brother's bones.

"So, you live in the area?" she asked. "I go to college here but I'm originally from Virginia Beach."

Shit, I knew she wanted the dick! She wasn't getting it, though! I was about to have Zetta's name tattooed on my johnson.

I decided to lead her on a bit to see what I could get out of it. "I live in D.C. What school do you go to?"

"Howard."

"Aw, so you're a Bison."

"Uh-huh and you? You in college?"

"Naw, I'm a hardworking man. I take care of my mother so I have to do what I have to do."

That was partially true. Momma could take care of herself—if push came to shove—but I did help her out as best I could.

"That's way cool," she said. She extended her hand. "I'm Carrie."

"I see that on your name tag." She laughed as I took her hand and shook it. "I'm Chico."

"Chico and Carrie, they sound good together."

Carrie wasn't a bad-looking sister. A week earlier—hell, three days earlier—and I would've been trying to mack her big time. Zetta had me turned out, though. I couldn't wait to see her again and was sure she would call me at some point to make plans.

I stood there talking to Carrie until closing and walked

out with the instruction manual for the townhouse. I tried to get her to hook a brother up with the real deal but she was afraid she'd get fired. I refused to give Carrie my number but I took hers.

Miceal only lived a few blocks from me so I stopped by his place to see what he was up to. He lived in the little apartment above his parents' garage. I saw a car in his driveway so I knew he had company. His ass was like me; carless and catching the METRO everywhere. I wondered if it was a hoochie and if he was getting some. Miceal had been kind of quiet about who he'd been doing the nasty with lately. Razor swore he wasn't getting any, but I knew Miceal better than that. Two weeks—a month tops—without fucking and Miceal wouldn't be able to function in society.

I knew which two steps creaked when you stepped on them so I hopped over them so he wouldn't hear me sneaking up. I got to the top of the stairs and peeked through the window. There were smudges and fingerprints all over it so I couldn't make everything out clearly. I could make it out enough, though. This whore was going to town on Miceal's dick like she hadn't had a meal in forty days and forty nights.

Miceal's eyes rolled up into his head when he came and he grabbed the back of the sister's head to keep his balance. She kept on sucking him off and then he started trying to get her mouth off him. Women don't realize how much it hurts when they keep sucking after we cum. Women are always complaining about contractions during labor. Well, getting your dick sucked after you just busted a nut is right up there in the pain department.

I hissed, "Damn!" under my breath when the sister finally freed Willy. It was Judy. The same sister Razor had been trying to get with for heaven knows how long. That was some fucked-up shit Miceal was pulling. He could've gotten his

dick sucked by a dozen other whores—with his pretty ass—
but he had to be dick-feeding Judy of all people.

My first inclination was just to turn and walk back down
the steps. Instead, I marched over to his door and started
banging on it. He didn't say anything for a minute but I could
hear them scrambling around inside.

"Miceal! Open up! It's Chico!" I yelled out.

About three minutes later, Miceal opened the door
halfway and poked his head out. "Chico, what's up, man?"

"What you up to?" I asked, pretending like I didn't know
the deal. "I came over to see if you wanted to watch the tape
of that fight again."

"Uh, not tonight, but you want to borrow it?"

"No, that's okay."

"I'm about to go to bed." He faked a yawn. "I'll catch you
tomorrow at work."

I pressed my left palm against the door when he tried to
close it. "Can I come in? I think I left one of my watches over
here the other night."

"I haven't seen it," he said uneasily. "If I come across it,
I'll bring it to work."

"It's kind of special to me. Momma gave it to me and you
know how she is. If she ever asks me to wear it, I'm going to
be in serious trouble."

Miceal laughed. "Yeah, your momma don't play." He
glanced behind him briefly and then opened the door wider.
"Come in, but make it quick please. I really am tired."

Judy was nowhere in sight when I entered. I knew
Miceal's crib like the back of my hand. Hell, it was my second home. There were only a few places Judy could've been
hiding. She couldn't have climbed out of a window because
there were no ledges and it was about a twenty-five-foot
drop to the ground.

I went into Miceal's bedroom. Fitting under his bed was out of the question because he had a waterbed. I looked in his closet and she wasn't there.

Miceal was shadowing me like crazy. "Why would your watch be in my bedroom? Especially in my closet?"

"I'm just covering all bases," I answered.

"Then why are you overlooking the obvious places like the coffee table in my living room or between the seat cushions?"

I was being way too obvious. I decided to just come on out with it. "Where is she, Miceal?"

"Where is who?"

I had to hand it to him. He was playing it cool.

"Man, you're busted. I saw Judy giving you head through the window."

He threw his hands in the air. "Aight, aight, I won't front."

I laughed. "You can't front, my brother. I saw it all. That's fucked up. You know Razor's been trying to get with her."

"Hey, she has a right to make her own decisions. Isn't that right, Judy?" he yelled out.

We went back out into the living room and Judy crawled out from behind Miceal's big-screen television. *Damn, good ass hiding place! I hadn't even thought of that one!*

"I'm sick of this shit, Miceal!" Judy lashed out as she got up off her knees. "I'm not trying to sneak around anymore. Fuck this! We're a couple and we need to just throw that shit on out there."

Miceal gave her this odd look. "A couple?"

"Yeah, a couple." She came over and poked me in the chest. "You need to mind your fucking business. What are you? A peeping tom? That's some foul ass shit, for you to be peeping us through the window. You're just jealous."

I swatted her finger away from me. "You need a reality check. I'm fucking a goddess right now. A *rich goddess.* Nobody wants your skank ass."

"That's right," Miceal said. We both stared at him. "I don't want your skank ass, either. You were just a piece of pussy to me. Razor's my friend. Pussies come a dime a dozen. Friends don't."

I had to admit that I was proud of my boy right then. It took a real man to choose friendship over a roll in the hay.

"You tell the bitch, Miceal," I exclaimed. "Razor's more important."

Judy cursed and slammed shit around in Miceal's crib for the next ten or fifteen minutes. We both just sat on the sofa and ignored her, watching the sports highlights on ESPN. She finally left and I was right behind her. I had only stayed to make sure she didn't try any violent shit with my boy. She was angry enough to try to chop his head—or both heads—off.

When I got home, Momma had fallen asleep on the couch watching her videotape of *The Preacher's Wife.* She used to play that tape over and over. She said it was the perfect combination of religion and Denzel. Denzel even had my momma sweating him. Now that's what you call motherfucking sex appeal.

I stared at the phone in my room, waiting on it to ring. I wasn't one for praying much since I had stopped going to church but I prayed that Zetta would call me. I whacked off to *Black Booty* and passed out with my dick in my hand.

Anastasia

There's a lot of shit I might have skimped on but my hair and nails weren't two of them. When it came to looking ghetto-fabulous, I only dealt with one salon. Now Hair This was in Fort Washington, Maryland, and I had never been in there when there weren't at least twenty to thirty sisters getting hooked up at one time.

The owner was this chick named Bambi. A black woman named Bambi? Puleeze, that shit couldn't have possibly have been her real name. But if she wanted to be known as Bambi, it was cool with me. She could do the damn thing with some hair. It was time for me to get a new rinse to match my smooth as a baby's ass honey skin.

I got there about six and there were wall-to-wall women waiting to get hoochified up in there. I switched right over to Bambi and told her that I had to get out of there as soon as possible because I had something to do that night. I really didn't have a damn thing to do but I hoped creating a sense of urgency would speed things up for me.

Bambi, who did kind of favor a deer, suggested that I go in the back and get my nails done first so I could get that part out of the way. She promised me that I could slide right into her chair once my nails were straight.

I went in the back where the pedicure seats were located and Aimee ran the water for me to soak my feet. She turned on the massage chair and I felt so relaxed.

Aimee and I went way back. She and I attended high school together. So when she asked me, "What's going on with your love life?" I was happy to spill the beans. I needed someone with an unbiased opinion to vent my frustration to anyway.

"Aimee, I'm in love."

She gave me this serious look for a second and then fell out laughing. "Anastasia, you, in love? Get the fuck out of here!"

"I'm serious." I splashed a little water at her with my

right foot as she pulled it out to start buffing it. Aimee had told me once that a woman had come in with feet so rough that they refused to service her. I hollered.

"Girl, you can't be in love. You love sex too much for that," Aimee said.

"That statement makes no sense."

There was an older woman climbing in the chair next to me. She had on tons of perfume but looked like she was rolling in dough. Karen was going to do her feet.

"Aight, I'll bite. Who you all up in love with?"

"Girl, he's all that. Tall, handsome, rich, se—"

"I knew rich was in the mix someplace," Aimee said, interrupting me.

I splashed her again. "Do you want to know the deal or not?"

"Yes, I want to know. Is he famous?"

"Hmm, in some circles, he definitely is."

"Ooh, is he a rapper?"

Aimee had a one-track mind. All she ever wanted to do was hook a rapper. I could relate but there were other kinds of men out there also. Ones with some intelligence.

"No, he's not a rapper. Actually, he's my boss."

"Girl, stop!" Aimee grabbed her chest like she was about to have a heart attack. "You're kidding, right?"

I shook my head. "I'm dead serious. He's the one for me."

Aimee eyed the woman next to me, who had her eyes buried in a magazine.

"We'll talk about it later," Aimee said.

"Girl, we won't be talking about jack later. I'm going to get my hair hooked up and I'm out of here. I have some major scheming to do if I'm going to have Tomalis Wolfe in my Christmas stocking this year."

Aimee sighed. "Damn, I was trying to save your ass!"

"What do you mean?" I quizzed. The woman next to me flung the magazine at my head and it ricocheted off my earring. "What the fuck?" I screamed out.

She glared at me. "I happen to be Tomalis's mother-in-law, you huzzy!"

Oh, shit! Zetta's mother!

"And you'll have him in your Christmas stocking over my dead body!" she continued. "What rock did you crawl out from under, anyway? You look cheap!"

Aimee and Karen jumped up and went to stand in the doorway to the pedicure room. They wanted to be a safe distance away but not too far; they wanted to hear everything. Some of the other sisters, including Bambi, were standing beside and behind them in a matter of seconds.

"Look, I have no beef with you, aight?" I told her. "I didn't realize you were Zetta Wolfe's mother but I'm not sorry about what I said. I'm the better woman."

She started maneuvering her way out of the chair, wet feet and all. "I've got your better woman, bitch!"

Bambi came and stood between her and me. "Oh hell no, I'm not having fighting in here. Not today; not any day. I worked too damn hard to get this place and everything in here is expensive. If you two want to fight, take that shit outside."

I just stayed seated in the chair. "Aimee, you going to finish my feet or what?"

"Um, Anastasia, that might not be such a good idea."

"Anastasia?" The old biddy stared me up and down. "What kind of name is that?"

"The one my momma gave me," I replied.

When it became obvious that Aimee wasn't going to come back in there, I got up and dried my feet off.

"Aimee, you know you're wrong. We go *way* back and

you're going to play me like this? Fuck you, heifer. I never could stand your ass anyway."

"I never could stand your ass either." Aimee was suddenly trying to get to me and Karen had to hold her back. "You were a whore in high school and you're a whore now."

"Takes one to know one, bitch!" I yelled. I got as close to Zetta's mother as they allowed me and pointed my finger at her. "Your daughter's days are numbered. Tomalis will be mine. Take that shit to the bank because you won't be taking his money to the bank any more. I will."

"You crazy slut!" Zetta's mother yelled back at me. "That'll never happen. I'm going home to get to the bottom of this bullshit right now. You're obviously some low-class want-to-be hooker and Tomalis would never get involved with the likes of you."

I pushed my way out of Now Hair This and got into my car. I cranked up my music as I pulled off with a screech. That bitch knew my name and was going to start all kinds of shit. Now that the cat was out the bag, the stakes had been raised and I wasn't about to lose.

Tomalis

I got home from the office early about four. Barron was snoring up a storm on the leather sofa in my office. I had tried to sleep there a couple of times—to escape from Zetta—and it was far from comfortable.

I lifted Barron's left leg and shook him awake. He struggled to open his eyes.

"Man, are you still hung over from last night?" I went over and opened up the blinds to let some sunshine in.

Barron took his time sitting up. "Why do you ask?"

I planted my behind in my office chair. "Well, let's see. I've been to the office, worked all day, come home, and you're still lying in the same spot. Have you even been up to the guest bedroom where you're *supposed* to be sleeping yet?"

Barron sat across from me at the desk. "Hey, those drinks we had were strong as shit."

"You just can't handle it." I laughed. "I don't know when you're going to realize that you can't hang with the big boys."

"Tomalis, I'll drink your ass under the table any damn day." Barron grabbed his nutsack. "As for big boys, if I whip my nuts out, you'll have an inferiority complex for life."

"Maybe, but I can still get up the next day." I had zero interest in seeing Barron's nuts but had no doubt he would be crazy enough to whip them out if I had challenged him. "Your ass is practically comatose."

He yawned and chuckled. He got up and went over to the minifridge I kept behind a file cabinet on the left and got himself a bottle of spring water. After popping it open and sitting back down, he asked, "Hey, what's up with that chick that was all over me last night?"

"I must've missed it because I didn't see anyone all over you."

"You know who I'm talking about, fool." Barron downed the entire bottle of water in one chug. "The one with that sexy ass gap between her two front teeth. The one who knew your name."

"Oh, that's Anastasia. She works at Wolfe. In the secretarial pool, I believe." How Barron interpreted her actions as being all over him was beyond me. She had always had a thing for me and I knew it but that was a joke. By utilizing her *services* in the penthouse, Bradford had somehow given her the impression that she was something special. There was no way I was leaving the arms of one whore for the arms of another one. At least Zetta didn't get paid to fuck. That was just downright nasty.

"She can be my secretary any damn day," Bradford said. She was right up his alley. He had always loved sleazy looking women. "I'm telling you, Tomalis, the few times I've been over to your building, I've seen nothing but major tits and ass. Why you don't partake of the goodies right under your nose is beyond me."

Even though I didn't need to defend my actions, I asked, "Have you ever heard the term 'don't shit where you eat'?"

"Yes, but I'm not talking about taking a shit. I'm talking about fucking." Barron got his second bottle of water and downed it just as quickly. "Besides, it's your corporation. You can't get fired."

"No, but I can get sued. Ever heard of sexual harassment?"

"You just have to be careful during the selection process, but you need to get up on at least one of those sisters."

"Not my style." I had never been a cheater. I always felt that if I needed to cheat on a woman, I had no business with her in the first place. In all the years Zetta had been messing around with her male toys, I had never stepped outside of our marriage. Not once. "Anyway, if I were to do something like that, I couldn't be sure who to trust. No one is ever what they seem. Look at the whore I married."

"True." Barron nodded his head. "I can't argue with that one."

"Barron, you're the only person I truly trust and that's pathetic because you're a fool."

"Hey, I've got your fool. You're the fool because you keep letting Zetta use you for your money."

"Well, the time has come to do something about it."

"You mentioned something to that effect before. So what's the plan?"

"The plan is simple. It's time for Zetta and Zora to get the hell out of my life. I'm going to be rid of them by the time New Year's Eve comes around."

Barron sat on the edge of his chair. "How so?"

"I'm still thinking on that one. Zetta's done a lot of dirt but she's cautious. She never does anything in the open so I can get a private detective to get photos. She does shit in the limo but never lets Phil actually see it."

"Yeah, but can't you get photos of her hanging around various men?"

"Hell, I have those already but they're not enough. She could always go into court and claim they're all just friends. Without intimate photos, it's too risky."

"So what are you going to do?" Barron asked.

"I'm going to have to beat her at her own game."

Barron jumped up, came around the desk and put me in a bear hug from behind. "Tomalis, I have to tell you that I'm so damn proud of you."

He smelled like a brewery. I pushed him gently away and asked, "How so?"

"I've been waiting decades for this moment."

I sighed. "Humph, you and I both."

"Seriously. I've stood by and watched that huzzy play you for a fool all this time and felt completely helpless to do anything about it. After all, she is your wife and the mother of your kids. It's not my place to insist that you get rid of her or make any demands."

"I understand." I stood up and faced him, placing my hand on his shoulder. "Barron, the proverbial shit is about to hit the fan. I've had enough and you know me. Once I set my mind to something, it shall be done."

A seriousness came over Barron's face. "I just hope I'm around long enough to see you find a woman that truly loves you for you."

"I'll probably never find true love." I was about to walk away from Barron when the implications of his last statement dawned on me. "Wait a second. What do you mean; you hope you're around long enough?"

Barron shrugged. "Nothing."

"Barron, I've known you all my life. What's wrong, man?"

"It's nothing, Tomalis." He started for the door in a hurry. "Listen, I'm going to finally head up to that guest bedroom and grab a shower. I must reek by now and the alcohol all over me can't be helping."

"Oh, no. You're not getting off that easy." I pulled him by the elbow and swung him around. I pointed to the sofa. "Sit down, Barron."

"Tomalis, I don't want to discuss this. Not now. Possibly not ever."

As I watched Barron walk away, a fear came into my heart. Barron was all I had left. I couldn't imagine losing him, too.

Dinner that night was pure insanity. I only stayed home because I didn't want Zora to think she could run me out of my own home night after night. Besides, Jonah was there for a change and I cherished the rare, brief periods I was allowed to bond with my son.

Zetta, Barron, Jonah, and I were already seated and having a surprisingly interesting conversation about Jonah's experiences at school. He was a brilliant child and his grades were the only things I could never find fault with. I just wished he would cut down on having so much sex.

"Jonah, I understand you speak other languages?" Barron

inquired after taking a bite of his chicken Marsala and wild rice.

"Yes, I do, Uncle Barron. I speak Spanish and—"

"He's not your Uncle," Zetta interrupted. "He's not related by blood.

Well, the conversation had been going good!

"Zetta, Barron is my blood," I stated with disdain. "If my son wants to refer to him as his uncle, I have no problem with it."

Zetta placed her fork on her plate. "Well, I do, and he is not your blood."

Jonah decided to raise the bar on the drama when he asked Zetta, "Am I his blood, Mom?"

Zetta was stunned. "Excuse me?"

"I want to know if Dad is really my father or just the one you're blaming me on."

Barron cleared his throat and I suppressed a laugh.

"Actually, I'm interested in hearing the answer to that myself," I said. "I've been wondering that for years."

"Yeah, we all have," Barron added.

The three of us sat there glaring at Zetta while she tried to pick her phoney ass face back up off the floor. "I can't believe you all. Of course Jonah is your son, Tomalis. What do you take me for?"

I threw my cloth napkin on top of my plate. "Do you want an honest answer or a polite answer?"

Before Zetta could choose, Zora came bursting into the dining room like a tornado. "Who the fuck is Anastasia?" She hovered over me and the amount of perfume she was wearing made me nauseous. "Who is the bitch, Tomalis? Have you fucked her already?"

Jonah practically fell out of his chair, he was laughing so hard. "Way to go, Dad."

Zetta got up from the table and came to stand beside her mother. "What's this all about, Tomalis?"

I got up and stared them both down. "I'm still waiting on an honest response to my question. Is Jonah my son or is he the result of one of your numerous affairs?"

Zora must have gotten weak because she stumbled into the nearest chair. "Goodness, what have I walked into?"

Barron took much pleasure in filling Zora in. "You see, we were sitting here and Zetta got nasty—as usual—when Jonah called me Uncle Barron. She was going on and on about how I'm not related to Tomalis by blood. That's when Jonah asked if he was related to Tomalis by blood—something we've all been dying to know—and Zetta came out her mouth with the same old bullshit trying to play that innocent and virginal role when all of us in this room know she's the whore of the damn century. Then you came in talking about Anastasia—who is one hot number—and the rest is history."

"Who is this Anastasia bitch?" Zetta demanded to know.

Zora replied, "She was in Now Hair This talking about being in love with Tomalis and when I confronted her, she said your days are numbered and she plans to steal him away from you."

"Actually, there must be some mistake," Barron said. "Anastasia wants me. She was all over me last night. I almost gave her my boxers to take home to make a shrine."

"You fucked her?" Jonah asked.

Zetta yelled out, "Jonah, watch your mouth! You're still a child."

That's when I stepped in. "Jonah may be under eighteen but he's not a child. He has two kids, Zetta, so he definitely knows what the term 'fucked' means. As for Anastasia, she works at Wolfe but I have no interest in her. However, that doesn't change the fact that you are a slut."

Zetta slapped me. "I'm not a slut, Tomalis. I'm your wife."

Zetta left out the room with Zora right on her tail. Barron and Jonah were both bowled over with laughter. I joined them.

Tuesday, December 19th

Diana

I arrived at the office early the next morning, having witnessed the break of dawn. I was a mixing bowl of emotions, worried about both Stephen and Edmund. The twins had already been asleep when I had arrived home the night before and for once I was glad. I didn't know how to face them after I had just been embarrassed more than I had ever been before in my life.

I sat up most of the night and then got in about two hours of tossing and turning. My issues stemmed from two men: one from my past that I was still allowing to regulate my present and one from my present that I had ignored because of my past.

Bradford was holding true to form that day, unlike the

previous one, and did not get in until midmorning. That gave me plenty of time to do what I had to do. I had made one stop on the way to work. I had purchased two more voice-activated minicassette recorders from Wal-Mart. I put the batteries in them and stuck one behind a copy of *Think and Grow Rich* on his bookshelf and once he got in, I bided my time for him to go to the restroom and then I stuck the other one in his laptop case in a small zippered section that was empty. He never went anywhere without his laptop so I knew it would capture all his dirt sooner or later.

He thought he was cute with the Human Resources stunt he had pulled the previous day. I could have whipped out my taped evidence then but I decided to go for the gusto and not only salvage my employment but also destroy his.

No, Wolfe Industries was not my corporation and I was going to get the same salary regardless of whether I kept my mouth shut or not. But Bradford was the type of man that I could no longer tolerate and he deserved to learn an extremely valuable lesson. No matter how educated or successful a woman gets, there will always be men with the mentality that we are only placed here on this earth to suck their dicks. Bradford was one of those men and I planned to send him packing on the same horse he rode in on.

I had just gotten back from taking a file down to the third floor when my telephone rang. We had caller ID at work but I didn't recognize the number; not even the area code. I assumed it was one of Bradford's business associates looking for him. I was wrong.

"Hello, Bradford Haynes's office."

"Hello, Diana."

"Stephen?" I couldn't believe it. "What are you doing calling me at work? How did you get this number?"

"Didn't you read my business card? Finding people is how I make a living."

I rummaged through my purse and pulled his card out. It said he worked for some company called The Human Tracker.

Damn! I mumbled under my breath.

"So it seems," I finally said after listening to him snicker on the other end of the line. "What do you want?"

"I want to know if you thought about what I said. Are you going to let me see my sons or are you going to continue to deprive both them and me from having a relationship?"

"Stephen, I never deprived you of anything until two days ago. *You* deprived them. *You* made the decision to let them be fatherless. *You* moved on with your life as if nothing had happened. *You* left me here to struggle alone when we could have accomplished so much more together. It was not me and don't ever say that shit to me again."

"Ooh, feisty! I like that!"

Just then Chico came in to deliver the mail. He waved and set the stack on my desk. It seemed like he had no intention of leaving until he could tell me how good I looked so I told Stephen, "Hold on!" I lowered the phone from my ear. "Good morning, Chico. Thanks for the mail."

"You're welcome." He paused and just stood there staring. "You look great today, Diana."

"Thank you, Chico. Listen, I hate to be rude but I have an important call. I'll see you tomorrow."

"Okay, see you tomorrow, Diana."

He took his little sweet time exiting my office. I put the phone back up to my ear. "I'm back."

"So I'm important, huh?"

"What?"

"You just told whoever that was that you were on an important phone call."

I clucked my tongue. "That was just a figure of speech, Stephen. For the record, you are not important. Not anymore." My mind did a quick replay of my conversation with Edmund and how ridiculous I made myself appear when I said that I had not really dated in thirteen years. "You did mess my head up for a long time as it pertained to dating and relationships but I have moved on," I lied. Edmund had moved on, though. That's what he had said to me and I still was upset about it.

"Of course, you've moved on," Stephen said. "That was more than a decade ago. We both moved on. Hell, I've been married twice already."

Did he just say he'd been married twice?

"That's one reason why I want to get together with the twins. They have five younger siblings—between my two ex-wives—and I want all my kids to grow up knowing each other."

It took all of thirty seconds for me to catch my breath and will myself not to start screaming in my office. He had been off knocking other women up and—from the sounds of it—supporting their kids while Darren and Dean had suffered.

"Stephen, this is a lot to swallow. I'm going to have to call you back."

"Diana, when should I expect to hear from you?" he asked.

"Later today or tomorrow."

"Promise?"

"Don't go there, Stephen. Unlike you, I tend to keep my word. I said that I'll call you back and I will. Now I have a job to do so I must go."

I hung up before he could say anything further.

• • •

Bradford was in and out of the office and acting nasty whenever he got the chance. He was still making up lies about me not performing my job duties. I started to just ignore him. At noon, I informed him that I was taking a lunch break. He was shocked because in the five years I had been his assistant, I rarely took lunch.

He acted like he wanted to say something smart but I beat him to the punch and said, "Since we're being so particular about the rules and regulations imposed by Human Resources, I think it's about time I start taking the two fifteen-minute breaks and hour lunch I am entitled to every day." He bit his bottom lip in anger. I added, "See you at one," and walked out the door.

I went down to my car and retrieved the picnic basket from my back seat. More than likely, I was about to make a fool out of myself once more but I had to try. I walked over to the booth where Edmund was sitting and pretending like he didn't see me.

"Ahem, Edmund, have a minute?" I asked.

He looked up from the *Sports Illustrated* he was reading. "Yes, Diana. What can I help you with?"

"I was wondering if you would like to have lunch with me." I held the basket up so he could get a better view of it. "I got up early this morning and prepared some sandwiches and a fruit salad in hopes that we could eat and get to know each other better."

He tried to cover up a blush but I saw it. "Hmm, I don't know. My lunch break is really not for another hour or so."

I looked around the garage. "Who's going to notice?"

He shrugged. "No one, I guess."

"Cool."

"Cool."

There was an uncomfortable silence. Then he asked, "So where do you want to eat?"

"How about the park around the corner? I hate to admit it but I've never once been there."

"Really? Never?"

"No, not once."

"Then we must go. It's time for you to see the world," he said jokingly.

We found a vacant bench and sat down to eat. I had made peppered turkey breast and Swiss cheese sandwiches with chipotle mayonnaise and a mixed salad of seasonal fruits. I also had two bottles of sparkling cider and some kettle corn.

"This is different," Edmund commented about five minutes into our meal.

"How so?"

"I'm used to bologna or ham sandwiches with American cheese slices and mustard."

"I'm sorry," I said apologetically. "I just have a certain taste."

"Oh, no, don't get me wrong." He took another bite of his sandwich and rinsed it down with some cider. "This is very good. I could get used to this. It's just that like most kids who grew up *financially challenged,* I've had my share of fried bologna sandwiches."

I laughed. "Who hasn't? I grew up on them as a kid. Fried bologna sandwiches and Vienna sausages."

"Vienna sausages. Now those bring back memories."

We both chuckled and then eyed each other seductively.

"Edmund, this woman you just started seeing. Is it exclusive already?"

"No, nothing that deep. But, I feel like it could be something major."

"Oh." I'm sure the disappointment was written all over my face. "Well, if things don't work out, maybe we can see what happens. Until then, I would really like for us to be friends."

"Why?"

I wasn't expecting that question and felt like I had been put on the spot. "Why?" I asked back, stalling for time.

"Yeah, why? Why do you all of a sudden want to be my friend?"

"Okay, here goes nothing." I took a deep breath. "I've always found you attractive, Edmund. I just never wanted to admit it. I felt like you and I couldn't possibly have enough in common to make any sort of a relationship work. I was stupid and way ahead of myself. The other night, when you were dancing, it aroused me and . . ."

Edmund grinned from ear to ear. "Aroused you?"

"Yes, it made me horny. I'm a grown woman and have teenage kids and I'm confident enough about my sexuality to be able to say it. For a long time, I've been what I call a recycled virgin. The man who fathered my kids really did a number on me but I should have just let live and let go. Instead I buried myself in the pain. He recently resurfaced demanding to see Dean and Darren. Then came the clincher this morning. He called me at the office and told me that he's been married twice and he has five other children by two women. Now he thinks we can all be some sort of big happy family."

"He sounds like an idiot," Edmund said with a frown. "I have zero respect for any man who turns his back on his children."

Edmund said that with such animosity that I just had to ask, "Do you have any kids?"

"No, not now."

I touched his hand. "I'm sorry."

"Hey, there's nothing for you to be sorry for. It's not your fault and we are here to get to know each other. My pain is a part of me just like yours is a part of you."

"Boy or girl?"

"Girl. She had congestive heart disease and died when she was five months old."

"I'm so sorry." Edmund gasped. "I mean, that's unfortunate," I said, correcting my mistake. "Were you and her mother married?"

"No, we hardly knew one another but that didn't mean I was going to neglect my responsibilities. I saw her every chance I got and supported her financially as much as I could. God just had other plans for her, I guess."

He grasped my hand tightly.

"Edmund, He has plans for all of us."

It was getting close to time for me to get back and I didn't feel like hearing Bradford's mouth or giving him another excuse to write me up.

"I have to get back, Edmund."

"Yeah, me too." He stood up and helped me gather everything together. "Maybe we can do this again sometime. Next time, I'll bring some bologna sandwiches and a couple cans of Vienna sausages."

We both laughed.

"Sounds great."

Chico

Miceal and Razor were getting on my last nerve at work. I hated them. No, I hated myself for being such a fool. They kept asking me about my latest sexual escapade with Zetta and I was ashamed to tell them that she hadn't called me again since I'd last seen her on Sunday afternoon. I damn sure wasn't going to tell them that she'd stood my ass up at the mall.

I knew that I'd run into her sooner or later and like Ricky would always say to Lucy, she had some "splaining" to do. If push came to shove, I planned to smooth-talk one of the hoochies from the secretarial pool into giving me the Wolfes' home address or phone number. At least one of them had to know the information.

I had gone home the night before full of anger. McKenna called me to ask for money for Gina. I told her that I would give her some—in addition to what I already was ordered to pay by the courts for child support—if she'd let me spend Christmas Day with my daughter. She said, "Hell no," but I finally convinced her to let me have Gina for Christmas Eve. I was so excited about that. I was going to show her a great time.

Momma was happy to hear about it, too. She always complained about not seeing her grandbaby enough. McKenna was a trip. She would let Momma come over all the time at first—even though I was banned—but once she got mad at me, she took that shit out on Momma. I would never forgive her for that.

Momma and I decided that we would wait for Gina to trim the tree and bake homemade gingerbread cookies and make mugs of hot chocolate with whipped cream. Momma always believed in going all out for Christmas. I knew Gina would love it because McKenna was just downright trifling.

After getting over the excitement of having my baby with me for Christmas Eve, I shut myself up in my room and stared at the ceiling. What the hell was Zetta thinking? She'd told me how much she wanted me. She'd even used the word "adore." Now that shit turned me on. I'd never had anyone say they adored my ass.

I came to the conclusion that there had to be a logical explanation. It had to have been because of her mother hitting town. But that didn't explain why she hadn't called me. I fell asleep thinking everything was cool and that the hellified sex would break back off the next day.

Come to find out I was right. The hellified sex did break back off the next day. It just wasn't between Zetta and me. It was between—

Hold up, let me back it up for a second. Any story worth telling is worth telling right. So there I was at work trying to dodge Miceal and Razor as best I could. I did my regular rounds and tried to buy some time by hanging out in Diana's office talking to her. She was on the phone and it was clear that she didn't want me around eavesdropping so I left.

I decided to do something I rarely did—can't say never because I had done it once or twice. I was going to leave the building without anyone knowing it. That was the one good thing about making rounds. You could goof off if you wanted to and no one would really know it unless they were trying to track you down. The key was not to be gone a long ass time. Then it would be way too obvious that you weren't on the job.

I just needed to get away for a few moments and think. I still felt guilty about Miceal doing Judy behind Razor's back—even though it was over and even though Judy was never remotely involved with Razor. Wrong is just fucking wrong and Miceal was wrong for that. Then again, who was I to talk? I was boning the hell out of another man's wife. Then again, again, I wasn't hanging buddies with Tomalis Wolfe. Surely, he didn't even know I existed, so Zetta was fair game.

In order to sneak out the building I couldn't use the front entrance. Too many motherfuckers try to earn brownie points by getting someone else in trouble. The security guards all knew me and knew I worked regular hours and it was too early for me to be taking lunch. They reminded me of those slaves that used to whip the other slaves for the massa so they wouldn't get an ass-whupping themselves. I can't really say what I would have done if I had lived back then. I always hear people saying they would have killed the massa or run away or just kicked ass all over the place and gone out in a blaze of glory. That's all bullshit because unless you lived it, you don't know what the hell you would have done.

I took the elevator down to the basement, planning to hide my mail cart in a cleaning supply room that nobody ever used. It was down this long ass hallway that smelled like ammonia day in and day out. When I got to the door and had my hand on the knob about to turn it, I heard some noises coming from inside. *Sexual noises!*

I placed my ear on the door and listened, thinking this was the second time in as many days that I was getting in on someone else's booty action. But there I was; listening like a motherfucker. Moaning and groaning, dick slapping into pussy, sucking and licking, it was all there. Now someone else—especially someone who was up to no damn good himself—would have just turned around and went about his business. Not the kid. From doing mail drops, I knew most of the people at Wolfe and had heard many rumors about who was fucking who. I had heard about men fucking women, men fucking men, and women fucking women. The dick slapping into pussy sound was a definite so that narrowed the shit down.

I figured what the hell because even though I was trying

to play hooky for a few, I wasn't fucking in the building, and I yanked the door open.

The two people were going at it. Fucking like animals. Because of the dim lighting in both the hallway and the supply room, I could only make out forms but they were fucking big time. They were fucking so hard that they didn't even realize the door was open.

Then I heard it. The motherfucker yelled out, "Oh, Zetta! Oh, damn! I'm cumming!"

I recognized the dude's voice and wanted to vomit. I also recognized his smell. "Ew, this is disgusting!" I yelled out and slammed the door back.

I backed up against the wall in the hall and started hyperventilating. *What the hell is this?* I thought.

A minute or so later Zetta came out the room with her clothes halfway hanging off and her makeup smeared all over the place.

"Hello, Chico," she said like the shit had not just happened. "I've been meaning to call you. I mean, I was going to call you later on this afternoon. How are things?"

"How are things?" I had to resist the urge to strangle her. I pointed to the supply room. "You're in there fucking Donald—the nastiest, skankiest, foulest motherfucker in the free world—and you want to know how things are?"

She straightened up her shirt some more. "I can explain. It's not what it looks like."

I laughed my ass off. "Come on, now. You can't go better than that? Of course it's what it looks like. Damn, you must really be a whore if you fucked Donald. I don't think there are five women on earth that would fuck him. Maybe some chicks in their nineties that can't see straight and don't give a fuck who they're fucking as long as they're still getting some, but you? That's just nasty!"

Donald came out next, zipping up his pants with one hand and lighting a cigarette with another one. He had this triumphant look on his face and I couldn't blame him. Getting Zetta Wolfe to fuck a troll must've been like getting a nun to give it up. It was fucking amazing.

Still, I just couldn't go out like that without putting up a fight. "There's no smoking in this building, you fuck. Take it outside."

He grinned at me. "I'm your boss, Chico. Remember that and keep your Ebonically inclined mouth shut so you can keep your job."

"I don't need this fucking job!" I yelled out without thinking. I had promised McKenna some money and Christmas was coming up so I needed it more than ever.

"So that means you're quitting then?" Donald asked.

"Hell no, I won't give your ass the satisfaction. You can't make me quit and I dare you to try to fire me. I triple dare you."

Donald was about to say something but Zetta pushed him away. "Donald, just put the cigarette out and go back to work. We'll talk later."

Donald grimaced. "Then you come with me. I'm not about to leave you here with this . . . this ghetto trash."

"Ghetto trash?" I asked. "Donald, you grew up less than ten blocks from me. If I'm ghetto trash, then you're old ass ghetto trash." Donald seemed like he wanted to fight me. He balled his hand into a fist. I said, "You wanna fight, motherfucker? Then act like a frog and leap."

Zetta stepped farther in between us. "Donald, I can handle Chico. You go on back upstairs before you're missed. You're a supervisor so someone might be looking for you."

Donald straightened his collar and boasted, "Yes, I am a *supervisor* with *major responsibilities.*"

"Okay, Tomalis, Jr.," I said with sarcasm. "Go on up there and make your, what, thirty a year?"

"Hey, that's more than you make, idiot," he came back at me. He turned his attention to Zetta. "Why do you need to talk to Chico, anyway? He's nothing to us."

Finally, the fool was about to catch on. I was wondering if he rode the short yellow bus to school as a child. Zetta didn't reply so I did it for her. "Donald, let's put it this way. Those boots you just smoked; I was smoking them less then forty-eight hours ago."

His eyes almost popped clear out of his head. "Excuse me? I must be hearing things. Zetta, what is the meaning of this?"

Again, she said nothing.

"Like I said, Donald aka Funky Skunk, Zetta and I are doing each other also. At least, we were. Now I'm too disgusted to even think about it."

Zetta grabbed my arm. "Chico, I meant what I said. You are very special to me."

I yanked my arm away. "Zetta, for you to fuck him," I said, pointing to Donald, "even once, is repulsive."

"Well, if you think once is repulsive," Donald said, "try so many times that I've lost count. Zetta and I have been fucking for more than a year."

I couldn't take it any more. I hadn't had lunch but Momma had fixed me breakfast and it ended up all over my cart—eggshells and all—when I hurled. *A year? A year of Funky Skunk? Yuck!*

Zetta asked me, "Are you okay, Chico? Come on, baby, let me take you someplace and get you fixed up."

"Get the fuck away from me!" I told her. "Both of you!" I started pushing my cart down the hallway. "I'm taking the rest of the day off and I dare either one of you to say something about it."

Out of all places, I found myself pacing the aisles of Home Depot less than thirty minutes later. I knew that Razor and Miceal were probably wondering what happened to me when I didn't return from my rounds. I didn't care, though. Let them ask Donald's skank ass. Damn, just thinking about him almost made me hurl again in the lightbulb aisle.

I had stuffed the directions for that dollhouse into my back pocket before I left home and decided to get everything I needed to build it. I sure nuff couldn't come up off eight big ones; especially since it looked like I would be out of a job soon. While I had no intention of quitting, I knew Donald would come up with some reason to have me fired. I hadn't been there long enough to even protest it. Then again, I had some serious blackmail material in the palm of my hand. I could easily go to Tomalis Wolfe and tell him that his wife was fucking not only me, but Funky Skunk as well. Then again, again, he could kill my ass if I went to him with that bullshit. *Naw, hell naw, not the kid! I wasn't about to get taken out at the age of nineteen over some pussy!*

Anastasia

Tomalis. Tomalis. Tomalis. He was all I could think about. I called in sick the next day. I had an important mission to handle. I camped out in the coffee shop across the street from the Wolfe building and waited. Tomalis's limo—the phattest one of the bunch—was parked out front so I knew he was already there. Now I just had to bide my time until he came out.

I hit Shakia up on her cell phone about ten and asked her had she seen him anywhere in the building. She said no and asked why I wasn't at work. She wanted to know what kind of illness I had. I started to tell her the deprived pussy disease but just said I had come down with the flu. She didn't need to know all my business. While Shakia and I both had the penthouse connection in common and while we both got new tits together, the fact remained that she had a big ass mouth. My own mouth had already landed me in enough trouble at Now Hair This. I didn't need her mouth causing any more damage.

I wasn't a coffee drinker but I did order a vanilla bean frozen contraption and a sticky bun. I wasn't the least bit hungry or thirsty but time was moving awfully slow just sitting there.

I was about to doze off right there at the table by the window when a bypassing trucker blew his horn at someone who had pulled out in front of him. Thank heaven for small favors. If that trucker hadn't done that, I would've missed out on getting my chance with Tomalis.

I saw him come out the front of the building just as the truck cleared my path of vision. He was talking to Bradford. *Shit!* That was all I needed. I got up from my table and stood by the door, waiting to see if Bradford would go back into the building or get into the car with Tomalis. I started whispering, "Go back in. Go back in."

This older woman glared at me as she pushed her way past me to get out the door.

I felt like popping her on the head. "You ever heard of saying excuse me?" I asked her.

"You shouldn't be blocking the entrance, young lady. That's not polite," she said.

"Oh, and pushing me aside is polite?" I was about to lose my train of thought and switched my eyes back over to the building. "I don't have time to deal with you, you old heifer. Consider yourself lucky and have a great day."

She hissed something underneath her breath and left. She was lucky. On any given day, if someone came off at me like that—especially a female—I would've been ready to pull a WWE Smackdown on them.

Bradford shook Tomalis's hand and then headed back into the building. I wanted to yell out, "Yippee!" but didn't. I rushed out of the coffee shop and across the street just when his driver was opening up the back passenger side door for him. Tomalis got in and I jumped right in behind him.

"Miss, you need to get out the car," his driver said as I tried to pull the door shut. "This is a private vehicle."

"I know that," I told him with much attitude. "I work for Mr. Wolfe and I need to talk to him *in private.*"

Tomalis's driver leaned down and asked, "Mr. Wolfe, would you like for me to call security?"

Tomalis eyed me and smiled. "That won't be necessary, Lavar. Close the door but don't pull off yet. This won't take long."

"Yes, sir, Mr. Wolfe." Lavar shut the door and stood by the side of the car on the curb.

"Mr. Wolfe, I mean Tomalis," I said, nervous as shit. "I know this is gonna sound strange but—"

He held his hand up toward me. "No need to explain. I already know."

"You already know?" I crossed my legs—to expose some skin—and touched his hand. "Oh, I guess your mother-in-law filled you in on what happened yesterday."

He chuckled. "She filled me in on enough."

"So . . . what do you think?"

"About what?" he asked.

"The fact that I'm head over heels in love with you."

He scooted away from me on the seat and folded his hands on his lap. "Anastasia, I barely know who you are. You're one of hundreds of people that I employ and I can't imagine why you'd think I would have an interest in you."

That hurt. It really did. Now I knew what it meant to be pimp-slapped. "Tomalis, while part of me can understand that, the other part is craving to have you inside of me." I moved over to him and had him trapped in the corner. I started fingering his thigh and moving my way up to his dick area. "I could make you feel so, so good. If you'd give me a chance, I could show you things you have never dreamed of."

He burst out into laughter. "Anastasia, do you have any idea how much play a man of my stature gets? I have been approached by some of the most beautiful women in the world. Famous women, rich women, women you probably wish you were. Yet, I have never slept with even one of them. I won't say that I'm not flattered but I will say that I'm definitely not interested."

This couldn't be happening. I was going to be the second Mrs. Tomalis Wolfe. I had to be. If not, what was I going to do with my life? I had it all planned out and my plan was going to work, dammit!

That's when I really went for it. I tried my best to kiss Tomalis. He pushed me away. I tried to get to his belt buckle. He pushed me away again. I told him, "Just let me suck your dick and if you don't enjoy it as much as I know you will, consider it a freebie."

He replied, "Thanks but no thanks. I don't know where your mouth has been." He paused. "I take that back. I do know some places it has been. Like on Bradford and numerous other people at the penthouse."

"You can't fault me for that," I said. "I'm just a young sister trying to make ends meet."

"And that's admirable to an extent but there are a lot of young sisters trying to make ends meet who don't sleep with men in order to do it."

All of a sudden it felt like I was in the car with my father.

"Do you have any kids, Anastasia?" Tomalis asked.

"No, I don't have any baggage. It can just be me and you."

He shook his head. "That's not why I asked and it could never just be anything because I'm married with children and I'm faithful."

I got smart with him. "Is your wife faithful?"

"No," he said without blinking an eye. "But that doesn't mean I'm going to become a dog just because she's a cat. That also has nothing to do with this conversation. I inquired about children because I'm trying to figure out what reasoning you could have behind your actions. If it's just you and you only have yourself to take care of, there are plenty of things you could do other than have sex for money. You could get a second job. You could start your own business on the side. The same energy you are putting into letting Bradford make a whore out of you, you could put into something productive and really do something with your life."

"You're all I want to do with my life." I tried to touch him again but he swatted me away.

"If that's true, then that's one of the saddest things I've ever heard." He looked at his watch. "I hate to be rude but I'm late for an appointment."

"So that's it? You're just going to reject me like that?" I asked angrily.

"Absolutely. I get the impression that you've never been rejected, so hopefully you have learned something here today. Not every man is guided by his dick. Some of us use the head on top of our shoulders to make decisions."

He reached over me and tapped on the window. Lavar quickly opened it. Tomalis said, "Please get out before I do have Lavar summon security."

I got out, ran down the street into the closest alley, fell down on my knees, and cried. That bastard was going to pay!

Tomalis

Anastasia was truly a sicko. Times had really changed because I had never been attacked by such an aggressive woman. The term "gold digger" didn't do her justice. I didn't know what the hell to call her. I quickly put that little episode out of my mind and went on to handle my business.

I had an appointment with an old friend: Paul Lipford. He was one of the best private detectives in the business and I had hired him on many occasions to check out prospective business associates. I learned early on that, in business dealings, you can often be found guilty by association. Before I signed on to any large contracts, I checked everyone out first.

This time I was going to see him about something more personal. I was passing the Home Depot when I spotted that Chico fellow from the mail room—Zetta's latest man-whore—coming out the front door carrying several bags. I had heard someplace that he was good at building things and was curious about what he was working on. It was ironic. I had started Wolfe because I loved to build things and yet, it was the one thing I rarely had time to do. I only visited my plants once a month on average and I missed the hands-on activity. I missed it a whole lot.

I met with Paul and told him what I needed and then had Lavar drop me off at home where Barron was waiting for me. He would drink most of the night and then sleep all day. It wasn't healthy—it never was—but I wasn't his daddy and he had to make his own mistakes and learn from them.

I went up to the guest bedroom and nudged him awake. "Hey, sleepyhead, get up. We're going out this evening."

"Out where?" Barron asked, propping his elbows on the pillows. "I want to go back to Uranus."

"No, we're not going there." I shook my head. "How many naked women do you need to see on a weekly basis?"

"As many as I can see. There's nothing wrong with naked women. We were all born naked and it's a beautiful thing."

"I guess that's why you're always going to that nude beach, huh?" I chided him.

"Yeah, hell yeah! If I could, I'd live on a nude beach."

"Then it shall be yours, man."

His eyes grew wider than saucers. "Really? Don't play with me, Tomalis."

"Hey, if you want to live on a nude beach, then you shall. I'll have someone start checking out available properties and if they can't find one, then we'll just have to build a custom home. Any preference of location? I know there are numerous nude beaches across the globe."

"Damn, man. Look at how far you've come; from fixing appliances for Pop to being able to snap your fingers and make anything happen."

"Not true. I can't make anything happen. I can't make my son open up to me. I can't make Zetta stop whoring around. I can't make Heather stop using those damn pills."

"She's still on them?" Barron asked. I nodded. "So what are you going to do about it?"

"After Christmas, I plan to fly out to Chicago and offer her some help. She'll probably deny everything and refuse to go to a doctor but I have to try."

"Heather's not coming home for Christmas?"

"No, she's going home with her boyfriend."

"Oh, who's she dating now?"

"Someone named Homer."

Barron guffawed. "Sounds like a big old country buck."

"Hey, takes one to know one." I slapped him on the arm. "Now get your ass dressed and get up."

"Where's Zetta?"

"Hell if I know. Probably burying her head in shame after last night." I knew exactly where Zetta was, where she had been, and what she had been doing but didn't want to get into it. Even though he hadn't asked about Zora, I said, "Zora went shopping. Big surprise. She needs to enjoy this shopping trip like it's her last supper, too."

Barron finally got up off the bed. "Give me fifteen-twenty minutes and I'll be ready to go."

"Just make sure you wash your ass. You're smelling kind of tart."

He gave me the finger. "Fuck you, Tomalis." Barron went into the bathroom and I decided to go see if I could locate Jonah. He was nowhere around.

After begging me relentlessly to take him back to Uranus, I finally convinced Barron to cruise to the Baltimore Harbor with me in the Corvette. We ended up at a cozy little spot right on the water and enjoyed a nice seafood dinner.

Uranus was way too loud and busy for me to have the

type of conversation that I wanted to hold with Barron. I was still concerned about what he had alluded to the other night. After three glasses of Johnny Walker Blue at thirty dollars a pop, I was hoping he'd be relaxed enough to open up to me.

"Barron, what did you mean the other night?"

He tried to play dumb. "I'm not following you."

"When you said that you hope you are around long enough to see me find true love."

"Oh, that. I was just being sentimental. I didn't mean anything by it."

"Barron, I've known you my entire life and I know when you're lying. The corner of your bottom lip starts jerking and you grab your left ear."

"No, I don't," he said defensively.

"Yes, you do. I've just never mentioned it before because I didn't want to give away my upper hand." I reached across the table and touched his wrist. "Come on, man, this is Tomalis you're talking to. If something is wrong with you, I want to know. Hell, after all we've been through, I *deserve* to know."

Barron seemed like he was struggling with making a decision. "Okay, fine, order me another drink and I'll tell you everything."

He got his drink and I got another one also, having a feeling I might need it.

"Okay, what's going on?" I asked, realizing he was still trying to avoid the subject.

"Tomalis, you know, all of us have to leave this world one way or another. Let's just say I'm one of the lucky ones because I already know which way I'm leaving."

"Barron, you're not making any sense."

"Oh, come on," he said. "You know exactly what I'm saying. Some people never have the opportunity to say good-bye to the people they love. They leave their home one morning, thinking they're just going to work and will be back that evening, but they never come back. Car accident, heart attack, whatever. They never see it coming. I see mine coming."

I refused to let Barron witness my tears so I held them back. I needed to be strong for him.

"Don't look so sad, Tomalis," Barron said. "We'll be together again some day. All of us will. Like they say in church, the physical life is just a temporary one. Our souls live on forever."

"I've never known you to be a religious man, Barron," I commented. "You've always seemed to be against it somehow."

"Well, you'd be amazed what a person discovers or starts believing in when he realizes his time is almost up."

"Something can be done, Barron. I don't even know what's wrong with you yet, but the fight's not over until it's over."

"Man, I was TKO'd a long time ago. I did it to myself, though. At least part of it." Barron picked up his glass and finished off his drink. "Liquor. An escape from reality. A way to relax. A bunch of bullshit."

I sighed and pushed my own drink away. "So it's your liver?"

"That's how it all started. Turns out I also have hepatitis C—a viral infection. Let's just say the two don't mix well together."

"How did you get hepatitis?" I asked, finding the entire thing difficult to swallow. Sure, Barron had lived a wild life—he enjoyed his life, unlike me—but he didn't deserve to die because of it.

He shrugged. "They think it was from a blood transfusion. Apparently, I've had the shit for years and it dates back to when I had that surgery on my back about twenty years ago."

"They didn't test the blood first?" I lashed out in anger. "How careless."

"Blood wasn't tested on a regular basis before 1992," Barron answered, shaking his head. "I feel like a medical expert now that I'm about to die. Maybe I missed my calling. I should've become a doctor."

"I've always liked your 'Jack-of-All-Trades' job title myself."

We both laughed. Barron had never really held down a steady job. He skipped around from town to town and from occupation to occupation, never determining what it was he wanted to do. As long as he could make his monthly bills, he was good to go. I had often pleaded with him to work with me. Not for me, but with me. That was how strongly I loved him.

"The women always fell for it," Barron said. "They thought the title sounded mysterious. I had this one chick believing I was an undercover operative for the CIA when I was in London that summer."

"Barron, you are one sick cookie." I chuckled. "Always have been."

He turned serious again all of a sudden. "You've always called me a sick cookie. Now I really am one."

"There has to be something they can do. What about a transplant?"

"I can't get on the list."

"Oh, I will get you on the damn list," I stated defiantly. "Money does a lot of talking."

"Tomalis, give it up. There's something else."

"What?" I asked in shock.

"I also have brain cancer. It's too far gone. I have six months, maybe a year, and then I expect you to give me the ultimate home-going celebration. It better be the shit or I'm going to climb up out of my grave like those people in horror flicks and kick your ass."

Neither one of us laughed. Barron hailed the bartender over to order another round of drinks.

Wednesday, December 20th

The next day Barron slept in late again and I decided not to
bother him. I was at a loss for words anyway. Brain cancer.
Liver disease. Hepatitis C. It was just not fair.

I had breakfast in the kitchen for a change. I didn't always
like the dining room and I wasn't trying to deal with Zetta
and Zora until I had to. I envisioned the two of them sitting
in there wearing silk robes and thinking they were the most
special women on earth. They were both in for a rude awak-
ening. Zetta and I had managed to avoid each other since the
argument about Jonah and Anastasia. Barron and I had stayed
out late, taking our time coming back from Baltimore, and I
opted for one of the guest rooms instead of our bedroom.

Marguerite came in from the dining room with some

empty plates and saucers. She said, "Good morning, Mr. Wolfe. I didn't realize you were in here."

"Good morning, Marguerite. I'm just going to eat in here this morning."

"Would you like for me to prepare something special for you?"

"What did you already prepare?" I asked as I poured myself another cup of coffee and sat back down at the breakfast bar.

"Waffles and bacon."

"That sounds good. I'm easy to please."

Marguerite smiled at me. "You've always been easy to please."

"Thanks for the compliment. How's your kid?"

"Oh, Fernando is great. He's doing very well in school."

"Good." I paused for a second, just staring at her. She always had such a pleasant disposition; even though I knew life had not been easy on her. "Marguerite, I meant what I said before. Fernando is welcome here anytime. Feel free to have him visit as often and for as long as you like."

She sighed as she placed the dishes in the sink. "I appreciate that, Mr. Wolfe, but Mrs. Wolfe has made it clear that she doesn't think that would be professional."

I smirked. "Let's get something straight. Zetta is not your employer; I am. Zetta pays no bills around here; I do. You bring Fernando around and leave Zetta to me. Trust me, when it comes down to it, she doesn't have a leg to stand on." *Just a back to lie on and legs to spread,* I wanted to add but didn't.

Marguerite laughed and she had a beautiful smile. "I'll get your plate for you right away, Mr. Wolfe."

"Please call me Tomalis, Marguerite. If I'm going to call you by your first name, after all these years don't insult me by calling me by my last. We are on the same level. Don't let anyone make you think otherwise."

"Thank you, Tomalis."

"No thanks necessary. Now how about that waffle?"

After Marguerite had fixed my plate, I asked her to join me. She stepped back in surprise.

"I can't do that, Tomalis. I'm part of your staff."

"Didn't I just say less than three minutes ago that we are on the same level." I pointed to the stool beside me. "Please, fix a plate and join me. I hate to eat alone." I nodded my head toward the butler's pantry that led to the dining room. "I just don't want to eat with them."

Marguerite ran her hands down her apron. "Maybe I should go see if they need anything else."

"No, they don't need a thing and, if they do, they can get it themselves."

Zora and Zetta were going to have to do everything for themselves again in a matter of days so they might as well have gotten used to it.

Marguerite giggled, fixed herself a plate, and sat down. "Thanks for the invitation."

"This is something I should have done a long time ago. It makes no sense that you have been here so many years and we have never shared a single meal."

I thought I saw a blush. She tried to cover it up.

"Marguerite, this may not be appropriate and it definitely isn't any of my business, but do you have any time to date working here?"

She laughed. "No, I haven't dated in a long time. I'm either here or with Fernando on my days off. There's no time for anything else."

"Well, that's too bad," I said. "A man would be lucky to have a woman like you in his life."

Now that time she couldn't hide the blush. "Thanks for saying that."

"I only say things that I mean, Marguerite." I really did think she needed someone special in her life; we all do. I felt bad that her time was so consumed with making our home comfortable. I planned to do something to change that; sooner rather than later.

I made some calls to a friend of mine about Barron's health situation. I knew that Camp Parker—one of our oldest friends—would have been the one Barron would turn to in a time of illness. Camp was already a doctor when Barron and I met him during one of our many excursions to Mexico. We would hightail it down to Tijuana at least three times a year when we were younger, get blasted, and party around the clock.

We met Camp at this cantina that was full of people who spoke very little or no English. He was about the only other person there that night for us to hold a conversation with. Camp grew up as the typically spoiled white boy in Southern California. His father had made millions by founding one of the largest department store chains in the country. Appropriately named Parker's, there were at least ten locations in every state and steadily growing.

Camp had gone to medical school because—in his words—"he didn't have shit else to do."

At that time I was still working on making Wolfe Industries a force to be reckoned with. I was making a living but it wasn't anywhere near what it would ultimately become.

I remember telling Camp, "It must be nice to never have to worry about anything in life."

He was the first one who schooled me on the truth when he said, "Money can buy a lot of things, but it can never buy happiness."

How right he was. I got him on the phone. He was somewhere in Puerto Rico when I tracked him down on his satellite phone. Camp practiced but it was limited. He was a damn good doctor but pretty much just treated his friends and family. That's how I knew that Barron had turned to him. Camp was a good man with a good heart and with Barron being so nonchalant and private when it came to certain things, it was a match made in heaven for the two of them to deal with his illness together.

After getting caught up and exchanging pleasantries, Camp was reluctant to take our conversation any further once I told him that Barron was visiting me in Maryland for the holidays. His silence confirmed what I already knew. I went on to tell Camp that Barron had confided in me about his illness and that I only wanted to help. I asked him if there was anything, *anything,* we could do to save Barron's life. I didn't care if we had to do something on the black market. I had no reservations about breaking the law to keep Barron alive.

Camp finally opened up to me, even though it was against his ethical code, and told me there was nothing that could be done. It was all a matter of time. To put it exactly, he said, "You know I love Barron, too. I would never let him die without giving it all that I have. Maybe if he'd come to see me, or any other doctor sooner, we could've done something. By the time he contacted me, it was way too late."

"But there has to be a way," I pleaded.

"There is nothing," Camp whispered. "It's only a matter of time, Tomalis. Barron needs you—he needs both of us— to be strong for him now. Let's make sure he dies with dignity. That's all he wants. He told me so himself. He wants to die with dignity."

"Then he shall," I said and hung up without saying good-bye.

I had barely hung up the phone when Zetta stormed into the cabana house where I had gone to have some privacy.

"Not going into the office today, Tomalis?" she asked nastily.

"That's the beauty of being the boss. I can take a day off whenever I want. I had something to take care of."

She sat down on the loveseat with tropical-printed cushions. "I have to take care of something, too."

"Okay, I'm curious. What do you have to take care of, Zetta?"

"This outlandish behavior you've been exhibiting lately."

"My behavior is outlandish? I think it's more the other way around."

I was walking past Zetta to leave when she grabbed me by the wrist and pulled me onto the loveseat with her. "Look into my eyes, hubby," she said lovingly. "I don't know where you would get the ludicrous idea that I would ever, *ever* sleep with another man. I've loved you all my life. You know that. We have two beautiful children together, two beautiful grandchildren together, and we have each other."

Zetta was laying it on too thick. She messed up when she said something about two beautiful grandchildren. She never even wanted to acknowledge their existence and said the girls who birthed them for Jonah were only after his money. How ironic.

I decided to play along with her little game. I was more worried about Barron than I had ever been worried about her so I would just toy with her feelings a while longer and then throw her away with the trash where she belonged.

"Zetta, I want to believe you. I really do," I lied, managing to keep a straight face. "It's just that I've heard so many rumors throughout our marriage. How can all of them be lies?"

She grabbed my hand and placed it into her lap; smack dab on top of her pussy. She was warm down there. The bitch was forever in heat.

"Tomalis, you said it. They were all rumors. All lies. I have adored you since the moment I laid eyes on you and you have been everything to me ever since. I would never betray you. I would have to be the biggest fool to even consider it. No man can hold a candle to you, hubby."

She leaned over and kissed me on the lips, trying to slip her tongue into my mouth. I turned my head.

"Oh, come on, Tomalis." She grabbed my chin and turned my face back to hers. "Part of the problem is that we don't make love as often as we used to."

Try never, I thought.

She started running her fingers up and down the buttons of my shirt. "You just need for me to make you feel special; just like in the old days. Why don't we go in the house and head up to our bedroom so we can make love for the next couple of hours?"

"Why go in the house?" I asked, egging her on. "Why not just have a quickie right out here and be adventurous like we were when we first married?"

"Anything you wish, my love."

I suppressed a laugh as she got up and started taking off her clothes, slowly and seductively. Now Zetta had always been fine and I was still a man so my dick did get hard. I was torn between letting her take it all off and then leaving her there looking stupid or giving her a fuck for the road. I decided on the fuck for the road because I needed to relieve some stress anyway.

I stood up and started taking off my clothes. Zetta stopped me. "No, let me do that for you. I've always liked undressing you. You have such an incredible body."

"So do you," I said, telling the truth for a change. Zetta was nude and her tits were as pert as an eighteen-year-old's. Probably because five thousand men had been sucking on them since our wedding day. Zetta probably held the world breastfeeding record. "That's it, go for it," I told her as she started working the buckle of my belt. "Why don't you pull my zipper down with your teeth? That always turned me on."

"Sure, baby. Anything you say. Anything you want." Zetta got down on her knees and used her teeth to lower my zipper. Then she grabbed both sides of my pants and pulled them down around my ankles. I kicked off my shoes and stepped out of my pants. Next came my boxers but I kept my shirt on.

Zetta tried to deep throat me but I said, "No, I want you to ride this big juicy dick for old time's sake."

She stood up and pushed me down on the loveseat. "Ooh, I just love it when you talk to dirty to me."

"Then climb on and I'll really talk dirty to you, bitch!"

"Now, I don't know about that bitch thing, Tomalis. I'm your wife."

Zetta had to be kidding. She was the biggest bitch on the planet. "Okay, Zetta, just climb on and we'll forget about the bitch thing."

She straddled my hips and my dick slid into her easily— no big surprise. I had to admit that her pussy was incredibly wet and it felt good when she started moving it up and down on my dick.

"Oh, yeah," I said. "Give that pussy to Big Daddy."

"I love myself some Big Daddy."

"Um, then whose pussy is it?"

"This is Big Daddy's pussy. Always has been," Zetta lied again.

It had been a long time since I'd had sex so after a few minutes, I lifted her and slammed her back on the floor with my dick still planted deep inside her. I grabbed her ankles and wrapped them around my neck and then worked her pussy like a pile driver.

"Damn, Big Daddy's about to come!" I yelled out after about ten more minutes of punishing her pussy.

"Oh, come on, Big Daddy! Give me that shit!"

I started to get bored so I made myself climax and then climbed off Zetta.

"Ooh, Tomalis, that was great!" Zetta cooed and laid there spent. "I knew things would still be the same."

I turned my back to her and smirked while I picked up my clothes. "Yes, Zetta, everything is exactly the same."

I went into the bathroom to wash up and get dressed. I dropped a towel on top of Zetta as I walked past her. "I have to go. There's something I have to take care of," I told her.

Zetta obviously thought everything was cool. It wasn't. It was just a fuck for the road.

After I got into my office, I had an interesting visitor with even more interesting information. Things were getting more intriguing by the day. Being at the top has its privileges; like knowing that when heads start rolling, one of them won't be yours.

Chico

Going to work the next day was hard but I showed up. Razor had come over my house the night before. Luckily, Momma wasn't home. She was over at the nursing home with my grandmother. I had to give it to her. She took her responsibility of being a daughter seriously. Half the time my grandmother didn't know who Momma was because senility had set in, but Momma still went to see her a minimum of three times a week.

Razor banged and banged while his stupid ass dog ran around my front yard. I made sure all the draperies were shut, turned the television down low, and chilled. I had nothing to say to him and little did he know, he had his own problems. Chasing after Judy like she was a princess or some shit. The whole thing reminded me of a movie: *Hangin' with the Homeboys.* In the movie, John Leguizamo had this major crush on this chick that would come into the grocery store where he worked. She would never go out with him but she was all he talked about; calling her innocent and virginal. It was wild as shit when he and his buddies ended up in a booth in an adult store and—after putting a quarter in the slot— the same girl was on the screen involved in an orgy. Razor was just like that; living in a dream world. Great ass movie, though. I made a mental note to rent that shit to watch.

After Razor finally got tired and left, I was feeling kind of down in the dumps about my manhood. I mean, shit, even if I could deal with Zetta fucking someone else, why the hell did it have to be Donald? To think of him as some sort of competition was scary. There must have been something seriously wrong with me if she did him in a supply room instead of calling me up.

I made a call of my own to that chick Carrie from the toy store in the mall. We talked for awhile about a bunch of bullshit. I pretended like I was interested in her educational experiences at Howard. I was really jealous. More and more, I wanted to do something with my life and education was one way of getting ahead. She talked about her dorm, parties on campus, the sorority she wanted to join, how much she missed her family back home, how she didn't know what she was going to do to make money after that seasonal job ended, and about fifty other things. She was really a talker. For the most part, I just sat there and listened. There was nothing interesting about me to talk about. What could I say? I was fucking my boss's wife who was also fucking my supervisor and she happened to be more than twice my age. She would have hung up on me in a heartbeat.

Still, Carrie was very nice. I liked her. I liked her so much that I asked her out the next weekend. She said we'd have to make it the weekend after that because she was going home for a few days. We agreed to meet at her mall and take in a movie and have dinner. I was hoping that I still had two nickels to rub together when the time came. I knew how sisters could get when you asked them to go Dutch or—worse yet—treat. Whoever came up with that "man should always pay shit" had to be a woman. Brothers have it just as tight as sisters.

Anyway, once I got to work Donald was all over me. His odor almost knocked me out but I was ready for him this time. I had a bottle of cologne in my pocket—something I rarely wore—and was splashing some of it on every time he came near me.

Once, when I glanced over at his desk, he winked at me and pulled a pair of pink satin panties out of his right hand drawer. He held them up to his nose and sniffed them as if to say, "Guess who these belong to?"

That made me even angrier. Add to that Miceal and Razor playing twenty fucking questions with me and it was a long ass day. "Chico, what happened to you yesterday?" "Chico, were you sick?" "Chico, we heard you just walked out?" "Chico, were you out fucking Zetta? If so, you are the man?" "Chico, does Zetta have any rich friends that are looking for a young Mandingo to get their freak on with?" It was fucked up! It was all fucked up!

I had never been so relieved to get home in my entire life. I headed straight for the garage to vent the only way I knew how: building things. I had briefly started on the dollhouse the night before but didn't get very far. Trying to hold the cordless while talking to Carrie with one hand and put wood together with the other was damn near impossible.

Building things allowed me to get lost in my own little world. I didn't have to worry about interacting with others, dealing with their bullshit and drama, nothing. I was sitting there on my workbench thinking that very thing when I heard a car pull up in the driveway. I turned and was shocked to see a Wolfe SUV—some hard-core shit that wasn't even out yet—black on black, shining its lights on my back. All sorts of shit ran through my head, including the fact that it could have been Tomalis Wolfe coming to kick my ass. I started looking for a weapon and decided on the drill I was using for the dollhouse. I picked it up and stood to brace myself for whatever was coming. The door slowly opened and the interior lighting was off so I still couldn't see. I wanted to kick myself. In my hood, it was a commonly known fact that you never sat in your garage at night with the door open. Anyone could just roll up on you, catch your ass out, and jack you up.

Finally, I said, "Fuck it," and started walking toward the SUV. "Hello! Who's there?" I asked loudly.

I heard giggling—female giggling—and that's when I realized it was Zetta. She had a lot of fucking nerve.

She climbed out the driver's side, looking like money on

top of money in a cream wool pantsuit and matching FMPs—fuck me pumps. Her hair was pinned up and she had these big ass diamonds hanging from her earlobes.

"Hey, Chico," she said, smiling at me like the shit hadn't even gone down between Donald and her the day before. "I hope I didn't catch you at a bad time."

"Anytime is a bad time." I walked back over to my bench and put the drill down. "What are you doing here? I didn't know you believed in slumming." She didn't say anything so I added, "Then again, I guess you do believe in slumming because Donald lives near here. Let me guess. You just left his crib, right?"

Zetta came up behind me and started rubbing my shoulders. "Chico, baby, don't be so angry. Donald was a mistake. He doesn't mean a thing to me. I broke it off with him after you left yesterday."

I shoved her hands off me one at a time. "Yeah, right. A year-long mistake. You must think I'm a fool. I may be young but I'm not stupid. If I hadn't walked in on the two of you yesterday, you would still be playing us both."

"I'm not playing you, Chico. I drove all the way over here just to tell you how much you mean to me."

"Humph, well, you could've called me with your phoney lies and saved the trip."

"I figured this would mean more. Besides, I wanted to see you." She started fingering my neck. That shit was turning me on big time. "I'm taking a big risk, you know. I could even run into your mother or something."

I jumped back up. *Oh, shit! Momma!*

"Zetta, you've gotta roll. Momma could be here any second and I could never explain this shit."

Zetta laughed. "We'll think of something if she catches

us." She grabbed my dick and started caressing it through my jeans. "After all, we're so damn creative together."

Zetta kissed me on the lips but I didn't respond. Then she started sucking on my neck.

Sit down, dick! Sit down, dick! I thought to myself. It was no use. I was hard within seconds.

"Chico, you know you still want me," she whispered in my ear before flicking her tongue in and out of the canal. "We belong together."

I grabbed her shoulders and moved her away. "We don't belong together. You belong at home with your husband and kids and I'm trying to do right by my own kid."

"You have a kid?" Zetta asked.

"See, that's what I'm saying. We don't have anything in common but fucking. All we've ever discussed is fucking and that's all it ever was."

"Chico, we've only been seeing each other a few days; not even a week. Things like this take time, but I do want this." She started pushing all up on me again and fondling my dick. "So tell me about your child. Boy or girl?"

I recalled my conversation with Carrie the night before. We had discussed just about everything. She knew all about Gina and her bitch of a mother McKenna. She knew that I loved to build things. She knew what I really wanted out of life. All from one phone conversation and not from fucking, like Zetta and I had been doing.

"Zetta, it doesn't matter if I have a boy or girl. We started this out the wrong way. In fact, it shouldn't have ever started. I just got all hyped because you . . ." I held my hands open wide and moved them from her head down to her hips in the air space beside her. "Zetta Wolfe, an older woman with more money than my entire family, everyone I know and their entire families, have ever seen put together, came on to me and told me to hop into your car. I admit that I had no expectations at first—other than hoping for some hot sex. But I started to care for you—too damn fast at that—and that changed everything."

"Let me say something, Chico. I never——"

I put my index finger to her lips. "No, let me finish, dammit! I'm not your child, Zetta! I'm not anybody's child! I'm a man!" She looked shocked but shut the hell up. "You sat there and let me express all these feelings for you, knowing good and damn well that you were fucking someone else all along! For a damn year! A fucking troll at that!"

All of a sudden I was angry. *Real angry.* I started thinking about something I'd seen in a movie once. It was about this female movie star that was fucking all these other men to use them to get ahead in her profession. One of her girlfriends warned her that she better quit before she fucked the wrong man and her career would be destroyed. She laughed in her friend's face and said, "I only fuck men that have as much or more to lose than I do." I remembered that line clearly, word for word. Then it dawned on me. Zetta had fucked up. I had thought about going to Tomalis the day before when I was mad, but didn't want to die. I was barking up the wrong tree. Tomalis didn't have shit to lose in the first place. Zetta had everything to lose.

Zetta was standing there looking like I'd punched her in the face.

"Chico, I don't know how many ways I can apologize for the same thing. Donald and I are history."

"Yeah, and so are we," I said. I calmly sat back down, placed my right ankle over my left thigh and clasped my hands. "Zetta, I've been thinking. It's right here at Christmastime and my kid, who shall remain nameless, wants a lot of things for Christmas. I take that back. My kid doesn't want a lot but my kid deserves a lot."

Zetta seemed lost, like she was wondering how we went from one topic to the other. "Well, I hope your child's Christmas is everything you want it to be, Chico."

I smirked. "I'm glad to hear you say that, because you're gonna help me make it happen."

"Come again?"

"Zetta, you might think running around fucking me one day and fucking Donald the next and fucking your husband whenever is cute—exciting even—but I had real feelings involved and . . ."

"And?"

"And I think you should pay for hurting my feelings."

It didn't take her long to get it. She threw her hands on her hips and started rolling her head from side to side. Zetta seemed to have a little ghetto in her after all. I started wondering where she grew up. "Are you about to try to blackmail my ass, Chico?" she asked.

"Blackmail is such an ugly word," I responded. "Let's just say that you care about my feelings and want to make amends for the pain you've caused me. Making my kid happy in turn makes me happy and that should make you happy so we'll all be happy at the same time."

Zetta stood there for a minute and glared at me with disdain. Then she threw her head back in laughter and shook it like she was acting in one of those shampoo commercials where the shampoo is supposed to be an aphrodisiac or some shit.

"What's so damn funny?" I asked.

She looked down at me and grinned. "You men will never learn. Do you have any idea how many fools have tried to blackmail me over the years?"

"Aw, I get it," I said, understanding her statement the second it left her sucking dick after dick mouth. "So you're ten times a bigger whore than I thought, huh? It's not just me and Donald, is it?"

She held her right hand up and rubbed her thumb over her other fingers, like she was buffing the nails and about to brag. Then she blew on her hand. *Yeah, she was about to brag!* "Chico, I knew from the first time I had sex that it was going to be an essential part of my life. Some women barely enjoy sex, some of them never even cum, but not me. I live for it."

"You sick bitch!" I wanted to pick the drill back up and run the bit right through her eyeball, but she wasn't worth it. "That still doesn't change the fact that your husband doesn't know."

"Oh, Tomalis suspects, but he'll never prove it. I'm just that damn good. If you or Donald or any other *piece of dick* goes to him, it will be your worthless word against mine. I never lose anything and I'm not about to lose my life of luxury."

"Get the fuck out of my garage!" I yelled out at her and pointed to her SUV.

"No, Chico, I'm not leaving," she stated with much confidence. "I came here for some hot sex—some serious fucking—and I'm not leaving here without it."

"In that case, I hope you packed your toothbrush because you're going to be here a long ass time." I thought about Momma—trying to remember if she'd mentioned going somewhere after work or not—and retracted. "No, you're leaving right now. Get in your ride and roll out."

Zetta threw on her seductive face and then pulled the cord to turn off the ceiling light in the garage. "You ever fucked a woman in your mother's garage, Chico?"

"No and I never will." I pulled the light back on.

"Never say never." She pulled the light back off and started unbuttoning her blazer.

I pulled it back on. "This is not turning me on at all," I lied. My dick was heavier than a brick. Something about demanding women always did it for me; whether I wanted it to or not.

"You can keep turning the light on but . . ." she said, pulling it back off. "If you turn it on again, your neighbors are going to get an eyeful."

I turned it back on, despite her threat, and she had managed to free her tits. *Damn, she knew how to get undressed fast!*

Zetta laughed and turned around to face the street. "Fine, you want the world to see, so be it." She spread her arms and started strutting like a model on a runway. "Do you like what you see, Chico's neighbors?"

Now here I was with another dilemma. There was me, Chico, a nineteen-year-old with a hard-on that could be used as a battering ram at the moment, son of an overreligious mother who could creep up any second and find a half-naked woman damn near her own age in her garage, mad at the world including his baby's momma, a supervisor at work who looked and smelled like a troll, and the half-naked woman in front of him. Then there was Zetta, obviously the queen of all whores, ready to fuck me in the open air of my garage for all the wrong reasons because it surely wasn't a love thing, determined to have her way because she probably always got her way, and looking good enough to eat out on top of my work bench.

Damn, what was a brother to do? I could fuck her and risk falling even more in love than I already was. Or I could fuck her and laugh at her ass afterward and try to pretend it was a meaningless fuck. Or I could fuck her and worry about where the cards fell later on.

"Fuck it! Let's fuck!" I told her and cut the light back off.

Diana

"So what made you change your mind?"

My mouth fell open as I tried to think of a response. Stephen waited patiently as he nibbled on a breadstick across the table from me. We were at the DuClaw Brewery—my favorite restaurant—and I was still trying to figure out how I ended up there.

"Well?" Stephen asked, growing impatient.

"Let's just say I had a great day at work." That much was true. "I had a great day at work, things are turning out the way I planned them, and so I decided to give you a break. But, if you want me to go back to treating you like I was before, just say the word and it shall . . ."

Stephen took my hand with his free hand. "Diana, enough. I'm definitely grateful that you called. You can't blame a brother for wondering about the drastic change, though. I'm glad we're having dinner and I hope you'll let me see my sons afterwards."

"Thirteen years is a long time, Stephen," I said to him. "How could you ignore them—ignore me—for thirteen damn years?"

"Diana, I know I was wrong. It was foolish. It was immature. It was selfish."

"Keep going," I said sarcastically.

"It was all of the above and then some. Bottom line: I was stupid. Once I had made the first mistake, it was just easier to keep making them instead of trying to correct them. Life went on. I started meeting other women and—"

"Marrying them and having babies," I added for him.

"I know how much that must hurt you."

I raised my voice and pulled my hand away from his. "You have no idea how much it hurt me! While you were out lollygagging and sowing your wild oats, I was alone *raising your children* and trying to make sense out of your actions. It took a long time for me to realize that it wasn't me with the problem. It was you. It was all you."

"Yes, it was, and I openly admit that."

"Do both of your ex-wives know about me and the twins?"

Stephen shook his head. "Only one of them."

"And she thought it was okay for you to just abandon them?"

"No, she didn't. In fact, when I finally told her everything, that was like the final straw in a borderline marriage and she filed for divorce less than a week later."

I smirked with satisfaction. "Good for her."

"No, it's not good for her, it's not good for me, it's not good for our kids, it's not good for anybody."

"Well, the blame only lies with one person," I reminded him.

"I'm well aware of that and that's why I'm finally trying to make things right." He stared me in the eyes. "Tomorrow isn't promised to any of us and I need to fix this mess so that all my kids will know each other and have each other when I'm gone. It's not fair to them to grow up and not know about each other."

"I agree, Stephen. Too much could happen. One of them could get sick and need a transplant or bone marrow or blood or whatever. They could end up dating or getting married to each other. Anything could happen and that's what pisses me off about shitty ass men like you."

"Contrary to what you may believe, Diana, I'm not that. I'm not a shitty ass man. I believe in providing for my family. I work hard every damn day and I'm doing it honestly; unlike a lot of men out here trying to make a fast buck and not giving a damn how they make it."

"So what do you want? An award? A pat on the back." I took a sip of my wine and then set the glass back down. "Black women have been carrying the world on their shoulders for generations and no one has ever praised us about a damn thing. What's really so aggravating is how the parent that makes all the sacrifices gets no appreciation while the kids cherish and put the one that's missing in action on some sort of pedestal."

"Diana, is that what you think will happen with Dean and Darren if you let them see me?"

"No, I sure as hell hope not. But I have seen it happen. I have a friend whose ex is serving time and her son cries for his daddy every day while she busts her ass trying to take care of him and be a good mother."

"Well, I'm not doing time. I'm a good man and my sons need a role model. Are you even involved with someone, Diana?"

I lowered my eyes in shame.

"If you're not, then who do they have to emulate? You? As much as you want to be, you can't be both a mother and a father. They need me."

"You're damn right, they need you," I said, getting louder again. "That's the whole point, Stephen. They've needed you for the past thirteen years and so have I. I didn't make them by myself but you just rolled out on me like everything was everything and never looked back. That makes you a fucked-up individual, any way you slice it. No matter what happens from this moment on, you can't change the past."

"I'm not trying to change the past, Diana. I'm trying to change the future. Meet me halfway." He held out his hand. "Friends?"

I hesitated and then shook it. "Friends." I frowned and said, "But if you do anything to hurt my sons, I will kill you. I mean it, Stephen. They'll have me locked up someplace because I won't let you hurt them. Don't come into their lives for a hot minute and then break camp again. You do that and there will be no place on this earth you can hide."

"I'm prepared to scour the earth for that motherfucker," Stephen said, deepening his voice and jokingly quoting a line from Ving Rhames in *Pulp Fiction*.

We both laughed.

"You're still silly," I said to him.

"And you're still fine," he said back to me.

It was so strange; the feeling that suddenly came over me. It was fleeting and only lasted a few seconds but it was scary as hell.

Stephen followed me home and I asked him to give me about twenty minutes to go inside and speak with Dean and Darren first. When I went inside the house and announced that their father—who neither one had ever laid their eyes on in thirteen years—was out front, there were conflicting reactions. Darren seemed excited about the fact that he was about to meet Stephen while Dean threw a serious tantrum and said he hated him and didn't have anything to say to him.

I spent a few more minutes trying to calm the waters and then I decided to let live and let go. I opened the door and waved for Stephen to come on in. He got out of his car and took baby steps to the door. Apparently, he was getting nervous about what he might walk into. That's what he deserved.

He came in and, at first, all he did was stand there and smile at the boys. Both of them looked like he had spit them out. He couldn't have denied them in a court of law in a million years. I had often regretted not taking Stephen to court for child support but I didn't want to force the issue. If he didn't want to be a presence in their lives, I didn't want his money; no matter how difficult the struggle.

After five minutes, I went upstairs and left the three of them downstairs to get acquainted. I didn't want to risk saying something negative and influencing the boys either way. They had to determine whether they wanted to spend time with their father or not. I had heard too many stories about children who grew up to hate one parent because they felt like that parent kept them from the other one or discouraged a relationship. That was not about to happen to me.

I don't know how it happened but I dozed off. It was after 2 A.M. when Stephen gently shook me awake. I couldn't believe he was in my bedroom.

"Well, I can see you're making yourself right at home," I told him sarcastically.

"I just didn't want to leave without saying something to you first."

I propped myself up on my bed. "So how did it go?"

He shrugged and sat down on the edge. "I'm not sure if it was a good or bad experience, but it was definitely an enlightening one." He buried his face in his hands. "I feel like shit. The boys needed me with them all along and I was just a dumb ass."

"You won't get any argument from me," I said. "Where are the boys now?"

"They both went to bed. Darren had passed out downstairs but I woke him and told him to go to bed. Dean went right behind him."

"They just fell asleep?" I asked, wondering why one of them didn't come wake me.

"No, they've been out for about an hour."

That made me wonder what Stephen was still doing in my house. "What have you been doing for the last hour?"

"Thinking. Thinking about how I can right so many wrongs."

"That's not possible. All we can do is move on from here."

Stephen reached out and started caressing my cheekbone. "I'm most sorry about what I did to you, Diana. You might not believe this now but I really had feelings for you. I always did."

I snickered. "You had a funny way of showing it."

"I was young, confused, and thought that having kids would mess up my life."

"So instead you just decided that you would let them mess up mine?" I sighed. "That's so reassuring."

"I meant what I said earlier," Stephen told me, gazing into my eyes.

"You said a lot of things earlier," I reminded him.

"You're still an extremely beautiful and desirable woman."

He lowered his hand to my left breast and I swatted his hand away.

"Don't even go there, Stephen."

"I'm not seeing anyone right now, Diana, and I know you're not. I already asked the boys."

"You asked the twins if I was dating?"

"Yes."

"That's none of your business. Oh my goodness, what on earth will they think?"

"They'll think that their father is still very much attracted to their mother. We were obviously attracted to each other at some point or they wouldn't be here."

He had a point but I didn't see the relevance. "Well, that was then and this is now."

"Why aren't you seeing anybody?" he asked.

"It's complicated. The man I want to see is seeing someone else so I just have to wait."

"Wait for what?"

"To see if he becomes available again."

"And what if he never becomes available again?"

"Then I'll just have to hope that someone else becomes appealing to me."

Stephen started trying to fondle my breasts again and I didn't stop him. My mind said no but my body craved for some affection. Being near him was such a familiar feeling; a comfortable one even though I despised what he had done to me.

Unfortunately, I was beginning to understand how some women—especially those who tell all their dirt on talk shows—could have a man run over them and still want to fuck them. After all that time, I wanted to fuck Stephen again; if only for that night.

"We can't do this here," I told him.

"Do what?" He grinned. "Make love?"

"You and I both know that isn't what it would be between us. If nothing else, let's keep it real, Stephen."

"Okay, fine. Then you don't want to fuck here?"

"No, not with the boys at home."

"They're knocked out. Are they usually sound sleepers?"

I had to admit that they slept like logs. I had trained them that way, but I didn't respond.

Stephen got up off the bed, went over to my bedroom door, closed and locked it. Then he turned to me and started taking off his clothes. *Damn, he still had it; big, juicy dick and all!*

Anastasia

Bradford had a lot of nerve; coming up to Shakia and me when we were on our way out the door and demanding we be at the penthouse within an hour for an *important* get-together. I didn't feel like fucking; not at all. I was still trying to get over what had happened with Tomalis the day before in his limo. He'd treated me like shit and I didn't appreciate it. That's the only reason I showed up at the penthouse with Shakia in tow. There was no way I was going alone and I never wanted to see that whore from last time again.

Tanaka was there, along with one of the Japanese men I had known in the Biblical sense before, and two black men I didn't recognize.

"What's Tanaka still doing here?" I asked Bradford after he'd buzzed Shakia and me in.

"Minding his damn business."

Bradford was such a wiseass. I couldn't stand him.

"Okay, fine," Shakia said. "Then what are we doing here?"

Bradford slapped Shakia on the ass. "What do you think?"

She giggled and held out her hand. "No cash, no ass."

Bradford slapped some cash into Shakia's hand and then into mine. "I don't know which one of you is worse. Both of you are completely useless."

Shakia put her hands on her hips. "If we're so useless, then why did you just give us money?"

"Because I'm about to be a very wealthy man, filthy rich. Giving you some chump change to help me get what I want is nothing but a part of the game."

I eased up behind Bradford, wrapped my arms around his waist and whispered in his ear, "Filthy rich, huh? I might just have to stop being your fuck partner and become your full-time lady."

He took my hands off him, turned around and grabbed both of my wrists forcefully. "You're not a lady, Anastasia, and I have certain standards for the women I show off on my arm. You don't meet the requirements. Sorry, baby." He let go of one of my wrists but pulled the other one up so he could kiss the back of my hand. "That's about as close as you're going to get to being treated like a lady. Cherish the moment."

He swung me around and slapped me on the ass. "Get in there and treat those men like royalty. If things work out for me over the next couple of days, I might just give you two a bonus."

"Now you're speaking my language," Shakia said. "I love the hell out of some bonuses."

Bradford rolled his eyes at her. "I just bet you do."

She brushed by him and said, "Let's get this party started right! Where's the champagne?"

I had always been the wilder one but something had come the fuck over Shakia that night. I didn't know if she had started popping pills or some shit but she was all the way live. For the most part, I just sat back and watched her act a fool.

I was surprised because Bradford didn't partake of the goodies. Usually he was the first one in line trying to get some pussy; whether he was playing host or not. *Greedy motherfucker!* It was a nice evening for December and he ended up out on the balcony on the telephone the entire time Shakia and I were mixing it up and playing international lovers. It turned out the other two men weren't black—at least not black Americans—they were from Africa. Let's just say that African men being hung like the elephants some of them ride around on isn't always a myth. When I did one dude, I felt like my pussy was on fire because his dick was so huge. Wide and long, it was almost like fucking three men at once.

Before we even set it off with the sex, Shakia put on one hell of a show. She pulled a CD out of her purse—some shit I had never heard of—and put it into the shelf system. Music started pumping out the built-in speakers in the walls. Weird music. It was some sort of crazy house music. Shakia always was kind of strange but now she was straight-up buck wild. It took homegirl at least twenty minutes to get her fucking clothes off. Now if she was performing at a regular strip joint—like Uranus—men would have been booing her ass off the stage. They want to be seduced but they aren't trying to spend that damn long trying to see some skin. They want a sister to be shaking loose tits and ass in their faces within five minutes or less. The clothes are just a formality.

But Tanaka and his crew were taking it all in with different pairs of eyes glued on every inch of her body. Actually, I was kind of jealous off all the attention she was getting because I knew I looked better than her. I had other things to attend to that night so I was just ready to get the fuck session over with.

While Shakia was still doing her "I am the woman" routine, I grabbed one of the Africans and led him into the "blue bedroom." We called it that because the lights were blue and

Bradford said it reminded him of house parties he used to go to as a teenager. Blues lights in the basement or some shit. That just told me how old he really was but it was his world and I was just a sister trying to help the squirrel get a nut or two or three.

After I had put out as much as I planned to for what Bradford was paying, I left Shakia to hold down the fort and joined Bradford on the balcony. He was still yakking on the telephone so I cleared my throat. He swung his neck around and then said into the phone, "Let me just talk to you tomorrow." He paused and eyed me uncomfortably as I sat in one of the lounge chairs beside him. "Yes, everything is still a go. I have everything in place. You just handle your part and I'll damn sure handle mine."

He hit the off button on the cordless like he was trying to smash it all the way through the phone and sat it down on the table.

"What was that all about?" I asked.

"Didn't I tell you to stay the fuck out of my business?" he came back at me with much nastiness.

"Bradford, listen," I said, leaning in closer to him and taking his hand. He was about to pull it away but then I started sucking his fingertips one by one and the muscles in his face began to relax. Before I knew it, he was grinning.

"Okay, I'm listening," he said. He nodded his head toward the penthouse living room. "But first, did you have a good time in there?"

I snickered. "They had a good time. I got paid." I took his damp fingers and placed his hand in between my thighs and right onto my clit. I had on a dress but no panties. "Only men like you make me wet. See how hot and bothered you've got me."

His grin spread even wider. Men eat up compliments like good steaks. "Anastasia, you know it's not me that gets you hot and bothered. It's what you think I can do for you."

"No, it's what I think we can do for each other." I got up and leaned back on the table, lifted my bare foot, and started giving him a foot job. "Bradford, you've been missing out on a lot and you don't even know it."

"Oh, I know you're good in bed," he said. "That's why this long-standing arrangement has been so beneficial to both of us."

"True, but I can be useful in other areas also."

Bradford laughed like I'd told a joke. "Like? What areas?"

"I'll be honest, Bradford. Until yesterday, I was determined to land Tomalis Wolfe. I wanted to be his second wife."

He shook his head. "Let me guess. Something happened, like you making a fool of yourself with Tomalis, and now you decided to go for second best."

"No, close but no cigar. I'm not trying to marry you, Bradford. I'm trying to partner with you."

"Partner with me?"

I unzipped his pants and took his dick out. It was already hard. *Greedy motherfucker!* I lifted my dress around my hips and straddled him, sliding my pussy down over his dick.

"Yes, partner with you on whatever it is you have going," I whispered as I started riding him. "Tomalis Wolfe deserves whatever it is you have in store for him." I paused and stared Bradford in the eyes. "You do have something naughty in store for him, don't you?"

He smiled. "Maybe I do. Maybe I don't. Why don't you just wait and see?"

"Because that's no fun. I want to be a part of it. I want to know it's coming and take pleasure in seeing the expression on his face when it happens. He's a mean, mean brother and I want to see him go down."

"Awwwww . . ." Bradford started getting into the sex and lowered his head so he could pop one of my tits out my dress and start sucking on it. He was moaning and humping me on the chair. "You think you know so much, Anastasia. Did a little birdie whisper something in your ear while you were inside? A little birdie named Tanaka, perhaps?"

"No, he didn't. Why don't you?"

I started really laying the pussy action on him then and it wasn't long before Bradford was singing sweet music in my ear.

Thursday, December 21st

Chico

I showed up at work the next morning like I was the king of the world. Zetta had laid it on me so hard the night before that I had actually seen stars. Thankfully, Momma didn't get home until late. She had been back over to the nursing home for yet another Christmas program that my grandmother had invited her to.

Zetta sucked my dick while I stood up in the middle of the dark garage. Every now and then a car drove down the street and half of me wanted to piss on myself while the other half thought it was one of the most exciting things that had ever happened to me. After she sucked me off *real good,* I propped that fine old ass of hers up on my work table and ate her like she was a piece of sweet potato cheesecake. Only she tasted sweeter.

Now I know all this sounds crazy, being that she all but wrote a testimonial on the fact that she'd been fucking brother after brother for years. Not to mention that she'd been slapping skins with Donald's ugly ass for more than a minute. Still, the pussy was just that good and I wasn't about to give it up.

I did make it clear to Zetta that she better give up all the other dick though, with the exception of Tomalis. Who was I to tell any woman that she couldn't fuck her own husband? The trip part was that Zetta *claimed* they weren't fucking. She said that he didn't pay her any mind, even when she tried to give him some. Now I didn't really believe that at all. Not for one damn second but she made it sound believable so what the fuck?

I was willing to share her with him; especially after she said that she would hook me up with some extra cash to make sure Gina had a good Christmas. She made it clear that it wasn't blackmail money. In fact, she laughed so much when she said it that I thought she was about to start having convulsions. Zetta was going to give me some extra ends out of the goodness of her heart and because she loved the way I laid down the pipe.

My feelings were still all mixed up, but I did realize that what I felt for Zetta couldn't possibly be love. After all, we hadn't even known each other a week yet. I told myself that I could never let it become that either. Zetta and I agreed that I should probably date someone else from time to time. She just wanted to make sure that she could ride my stallion whenever she felt like it. That was cool with me. Ride, my golden sister, ride.

Razor and Miceal were both in the mail room arguing when I came in.

"What the hell?" I asked as I approached them.

They were being all loud and shit and started swinging at each other like a couple of whores in a street fight.

I stepped in between them. "Hey, what the fuck are you two doing?"

Miceal pushed me away from him and said, "Razor's tripping, man. Over that slut Judy."

"Damn, he found out?" I asked.

Razor pushed me on the shoulder. "You knew, Chico? What the hell kind of friend are you? I thought you were my dog."

"I am your dog, Razor. But I'm Miceal's dog, too. I've only known about this shit a couple days and quite frankly, it's none of my fucking business. You two need to sort this shit out but not like this. Hollering and shit up in the workplace over some chick that's not gonna pay either one of your damn bills when you get fired."

Miceal seemed to be calming down a bit. "Chico does have a point, man," he said, looking at Razor. "I told you that I broke it off with that slut anyway. The only reason she came through your crib and spilled the beans was so she could start some kind of rift between us. You and me are always gonna be down. Always, forever, and the day after that. Fuck Judy."

"See, that's the problem, Miceal," Razor said. "You did fuck her. You fucked her behind my back knowing how much I was feeling her."

"Look, Razor," I jumped in. "You can't make a sister feel you back. Judy wanted to screw Miceal so she did. Move on to the next sister and forget this shit. You look good enough to bed damn near any whore you want. Don't let this be the reason for you and Miceal to end a friendship. Shit's just not worth it."

Razor stood there like he was analyzing the logic I'd just laid down. "You're right, Chico. She's not all that."

"Damn right, she's not," I agreed. "Now, shake hands and make up."

Instead of shaking hands, they gave each other a pound.

"It's all good, dog," Razor said to Miceal.

"Everything's cool?" Miceal asked.

"Yeah, this shit will never be mentioned again. My word on that."

I sighed, shook my head, and went on over to my station. No sooner had I sat down on my stool when Funky Skunk slithered up behind me. "Chico, you're late again."

"Donald, I don't have time for your nonsense today," I told him without even giving him the courtesy of a glance in his direction. "I'm here now and I'm about to try to get some work done."

"Well, you need to hurry up and get to your rounds. To-morrow's the Christmas party so things will be pretty slow around here."

"Does that mean I don't have to come in?" I asked jok-ingly.

"Don't come in and find yourself out of a job."

"I'm surprised I'm not already out of one," I said sarcasti-cally. "I'm sure you're working on it though, huh?"

He gave me an evil grin. "You'll find out soon enough."

I got up closer to him—even though his stank breath was threatening to put me into a coma—and whispered, "It's aight, Donald. If I do get fired, Zetta will take care of me."

Donald shook his head. "Humph, still believing in pipe dreams. That's sad, Chico. Zetta Wolfe is way out of your league."

"But she's in your league?" I picked up a stack of letters and smacked him on the arm with them. "Donald, your little fling with Zetta is over. There's a new sheriff in town and he goes by the name of Chico. You better recognize, old man."

I was a cool motherfucker when I walked away from Donald to get my cart and start my rounds. When I was leaving out of the mail room, I saw Miceal and Razor chilling in a corner staring me down and whispering to each other. I know they were wondering why Donald and I were going at it. Hell, I was not about to admit that I was fucking someone that had fucked Donald; even once. I was their god at the moment; they were in awe of me. Finding out some shit like that about Zetta would've made them revoke my playa card.

Now rounds were interesting that day. There seemed to be mad tension in the air; especially at the secretarial pool. Anastasia and some new chick were making snide remarks to each other as I placed mail on the various workstations. I didn't hear it all but the new chick—a Latina with the only set of tits that could rival Anastasia's and Shakia's up in the joint—said the word *"perra"* over and over. Now I knew enough Spanish to know that meant "bitch." Then she said, *"Usted mejora estancia fuera de mi cara."* Now I could be wrong but I think she meant that Anastasia better stay out of her face. I had dated a Spanish-speaking honie here and there so I knew a little bit.

I was stunned when Anastasia started speaking it, though. She said, *"Si usted piensa que usted es tan lindo, después que hace mi día e intento para saltarme así que puedo batir el infierno fuera de su asno."* Other than *"asno"* meaning "ass" I was completely lost. She started speaking fast as shit then. *"Funciono esto aquí coloco y no quitaré mierda cualquiera."*

The new chick came back with, *"Usted no está funcionando una cosa maldita. Satisfágame en el callejón después del trabajo, usted perra del gatito."*

Now there went the bitch word again. I wanted to ask them to please speak in English so we could all understand more clearly, but they didn't look like they would appreciate the suggestion.

Instead, I went up to Anastasia and said, "Hey, girl."

She smacked her lips. "What's up, Chico?"

"I'm cool. I'm cool. What's up with you?"

"Nothing, just making it clear that I have seniority up in this bitch."

I pointed at the new chick. "So what did she do to you?"

"She came in here like she was a diva and started trying to boss people around. No one around here is anyone's boss. Our supervisor works down the hall and even she can't tell me what to do."

"I heard that," I said. "Well, Anastasia, I'm going to catch you later. You coming into work tomorrow?"

"No, I'm taking the day off to get ready for the party. You coming to the party, Chico?"

"Sure, why not? I've heard so much about it. I feel like I'd miss out on something major if I didn't show."

Anastasia's attitude changed with a quickness. "Trust me when I say this, Chico. You don't want to miss one minute of tomorrow night."

"Really?" Anastasia came off like she knew something I didn't so I asked, "Is something special going to happen?"

She laughed. "Oh, you could definitely say that. Something *real special.*"

"Well, I'll be sure to be there."

"Cool."

"Cool."

When I got to Diana's office, it was empty; or so I thought. I had just placed a stack of mail on Diana's desk when she came out of Bradford's inner office holding a small tape recorder.

"Hey, Diana."

She jumped back like she'd seen a monster. "Oh, hello, Chico. What are you doing here?"

I pointed at the mail on her desk. "Same thing I'm always doing here." She was acting mighty strange; like she'd been caught in the middle of something she had no business doing. "What are you doing?" I asked.

"Oh, nothing. I was just putting some papers on Bradford's desk that he'd asked for."

"I see. Nice tape recorder," I said, pointing at it.

The hand that was holding it started trembling and she almost dropped it. "Yes, they can come in handy. It's how I take dictation instead of the old-fashioned way."

"Sounds good to me." I headed for the door. "I'll see you later, Diana."

"See you later, Chico."

I went back out into the hall and started digging through my cart for the stuff for my next stop. "Some strange shit around here today," I said to myself.

After work, I met Zetta around the corner in her SUV. I had told her the night before that there would be no more of that picking me up in front of the building in her big ass limo shit. I was making all the rules from now on and I wanted to make it known. She seemed acceptable of that and did as I said. If we were going to be able to fool around indefinitely, we didn't need to be flaunting our shit out in public.

Now I did let her have her way about one thing. She offered to take me shopping to hook me up with a suit for the party. I didn't have shit to wear to something like that so I agreed. We drove back out to Pentagon City Mall—The

Fashion Centre at Pentagon City to be exact—where she had stood my ass up earlier in the week. We went into Bernini where she bought a brother a Signature seven-button classic wool suit for a cool six hundred smackeroos.

I hid my face and pulled Zetta on to the other side of the mall corridor right before we passed the toy store where Carrie worked. I glanced over and saw her helping an elderly man to pick out a remote-controlled car. She was as cute as a button and I was looking forward to our date, which I planned on keeping despite the fucking thing I had going with Zetta.

We went to Zetta's crib on Wisconsin Avenue and I blew her spine out her damn back.

Diana

I made sure that Stephen was long gone before the boys got up for school. It would have been a shame for them to know that I had been so weak that I would bed their father so easily after a thirteen-year disappearing act. As I was showering that morning, I tried to rationalize my actions. I came to the conclusion that it wasn't even really about Stephen and me. It was about the fact that I was yearning to be with Edmund. He was inaccessible so I settled for something familiar and convenient.

Bradford was acting mighty sure of himself when I arrived at work. He was being bossy—as usual—but it seemed like he was just trying to pass the time. He kept asking me if he'd missed any calls whenever he stepped out for a moment; even to use the bathroom. That led me to believe that the call he was waiting on had to be of extreme importance. It was time to put another tape in place.

When he stepped out for about five minutes—reluctantly—to have a conversation with another executive about an upcoming conference they were both scheduled to attend together in Dallas that upcoming January—I made my move.

I was coming out of his office with the tape recorder I had retrieved from his laptop case when Chico startled me. He was standing by my desk and I know that I looked suspicious because I was shaking so bad. Oh, well, it would all be over soon enough.

During my lunch hour, I decided to see if I could catch up to Edmund again. When I got down to the garage, I was disappointed to discover that he'd called in sick that day. I wondered if I should call him and check to see if he needed anything. No, that would have made me seem so desperate. Anyway, he had a woman and surely if he needed chicken soup, orange juice, or something that was a combination of the two—hot and juicy—he would call her up.

Before he would leave my house, Stephen had made me promise that I would call him that afternoon so we could all hook up that evening. He said that the twins were looking forward to picking out a tree together and taking it back to the house to decorate it with him. I had good and bad feelings about that. I couldn't get over the "too little too late" scenario that kept popping into my head.

I had to heal, though, and healing started with acceptance and moving on.

In all actuality, I had a great time picking out a tree with Stephen and the twins. The sexual tension in the air was thick but I don't think the boys picked up on it. We found a lovely seven-foot Scotch pine at North Star, the oldest and most well-known vendor of Christmas trees in the D.C.

area. Then we went down to the Ellipse—south of the White House—to see the National Christmas Tree and the fifty-six smaller trees surrounding it. They had one for each state, territory, and the District of Columbia. With more than seventy-five thousand lights illuminating them collectively along the Pathway of Peace, they were truly a breathtaking sight to behold.

Stephen suggested that we have dinner before we returned home. The tree was tied to the roof of his rental car so it wasn't easy finding an underground parking garage downtown were we could fit it. Instead, we opted to head out to Maryland and have dinner at Jasper's in Largo. The place was packed—as always—but luckily the wait for four was a lot shorter than the wait for two or five.

Stephen was staring at me so hard over dinner that I almost couldn't even eat my favorite—mixed grill with shrimp. The boys were more talkative than ever and I was grateful because it meant I didn't have to say much. We topped off dinner with slices of the peanut butter pie and then headed back to the house.

For the next two hours, we had a ball decorating the tree. I had saved every ornament the boys had made since preschool and Stephen seemed disappointed that he had missed out on so many precious memories. Again, he had no one to blame but himself.

Darren and Dean went to bed about eleven; excited about their last day of school before the winter break the following day. Stephen helped me build a fire in the living room and I made us a pot of hot chocolate.

"The boys tell me that you're going to a party tomorrow night," he said after I sat down beside him on the oval rug by the fireplace.

"Yes, I am." I licked some of the whipped cream off the top of my mug and then blew on the steamy liquid. "Just my office party. We have it every year."

"Sounds nice."

"It's okay. A bunch of rich people socializing with people who wish they were rich. There are a ton of phonies that show up and try to pretend like they're more than they really are."

"You make it seem horrible."

"No. Like I said, it's okay. I only go to try to meet people who can help me further my career. In a normal business setting, they don't have time for a peon like me. But when they get a little liquor in them, they become friendlier and open to more ideas."

"I can dig that," Stephen said, drinking his hot chocolate without having to blow on it at all. I guess that's what happens when you're so full of hot air. "Want a date?"

His question almost made me drop my mug out of my hands. "A date?"

"Yes, a date. You know when two people make plans to go to the same place at the same time, leave from home together and return home together. A date."

I rapidly shook my head. "Stephen, I think last night may have given you the wrong impression. I'm not interested in resuming any sort of relationship with you."

"Why not?" he asked in a serious tone.

"That should be quite obvious," I responded. "While I'm more than capable of forgiving—even though I didn't think I was even a week ago—forgetting is something totally different altogether. What's to stop you from allowing me to open my heart to you again and having you rip it apart a second time for good measure?"

"Diana, you know me. I would never do that to you."

"I thought I knew you, Stephen, and I never thought you would have done what you already have." I got up off the rug. "This conversation is going nowhere. It's getting late and you should be heading back to your cousin's."

"I brought my suitcase with me."

"What?" I yelled out. "Why?"

"Because I assumed that I'd be staying here."

"I don't know why on earth you would assume that."

He chuckled. "Because we got busy last night, Diana."

"And one night of getting busy means you can stay here?" I asked.

"That's what I took it to mean."

I folded my arms in front of me. "Well, you took it the wrong way. You can't stay here. Not tonight or any other night."

"This is crazy. I don't even think my cousin's home. He left to go over his girlfriend's house."

"No, you're crazy if you thought one fuck would make me lose my mind over you again."

Stephen and I went back and forth for more than thirty minutes about why he couldn't stay at the house with me and the boys. He finally gave in and left to go find a hotel. I felt halfway bad, jumped on the Internet to use a search vehicle to locate a vacancy, and then called him on his cell phone to let him know which hotel had one.

It was after midnight when I climbed into the tub surrounded by my dollar-store candles. My mind wandered to sex and before I knew it, I was masturbating beneath the bubbles. I could envision him licking all over my body, entering me from behind and taking me nice and slow. "Um, yes, baby," I whispered and then moaned. "Take this pussy, Edmund!" My eyes flew open. *Damn him!*

Anastasia

"*Esa perra!*" I yelled out as I got into my car after work. "That bitch!" I repeated in English. My day had started out great. After all, Bradford and I had officially teamed up the night before to bring Tomalis to his knees. I just knew that I was going to have a fantastic day; what some of us call a "hoochie's holiday." A hoochie's holiday is a day when nothing goes wrong. Nothing can go wrong because you feel so good about yourself and have so much confidence that nothing and no one can get to you. That was how I was feeling when I switched into the office that Thursday.

Then it happened. Shakia introduced me to this new heifer, Benservita, Benvenuta, Benrecevuta, or some shit like that. I gave up on trying to get her name straight. She thought she was Jenny from the block. Not!

Shakia was acting like the *chica* was her new best friend and they'd just met. I didn't like her right off the bat. She kept bragging about how much "*juego*"—game—she had and how she was the "*el más fino*"—finest—woman at Wolfe. Now I knew my shit was tight but I wasn't even prone to stating all that out in the open. While I really didn't give a shit what the other sisters in the pool thought about me, I wasn't trying to have to scrap with someone every day at work over the fact that I looked better than them.

By the time Chico came by with the mail, the Ben whatever woman and I were going for it. I made it clear that she wasn't running shit and told her to stay out of my face or get an ass-whupping she'd never forget. Chico managed to calm me down a little bit—he could be a cutie when he wanted to be—and I ignored the wench for the rest of the day. I also ignored Shakia who tried to apologize for befriending her in the ladies room. I told Shakia to step off and leave me alone.

She and I made a lot of money fucking men together but she was about to be placed on my "talk to the hand" list.

I drove off from the office on my way to get my hair and nails done. I wasn't about to go back to Now Hair This and my shit was still not done because of the interruption—or eruption—from Zora, Zetta Wolfe's mother.

I decided to do a walk-in at Salon Plaza in Largo and hope that I ended up with a sister that could understand how fine I really needed to be when I left the place. I was losing it because when I got out of my car, I started searching for my cell phone. I told my mother—who I was talking to on the cell phone at the time—that I couldn't find it and she asked me if I needed to come home and lie down.

With fifty-two operators, there was no wait to get in a chair and I was digging the sister who was about to hook up my do. As we were chatting, we discovered that we knew a lot of the same people including a lot of the same sorry ass brothers. Her name was Caprice and she was actually boning Dawson who used to bone this sister Panda who used to bone this dude Willie who used to bone my cousin LuLu. Caprice had a brother named Rollie who was currently boning this sister Mink who used to bone this brother Vince who used to bone this sister Yvonne who was the daughter of Tremaine who my mother rushed me off the phone to bone when I had talked to her on my way into the salon.

"Damn, small world," I said after we'd finally run down the entire family tree of fucking.

"Shit, you ain't never lied," she remarked as she plugged up her blow dryer. "We've probably boned the same dude before."

"Somewhere down the line, we probably have." That shit made me feel uncomfortable and got me to thinking that it was time to slow my roll. I decided to change the topic. "Got any hair style books I can look through?"

When I left the salon—looking good as shit—I grabbed a pepperoni and sausage calzone from Cafe Villa and headed to the Bowie Town Center to find an outfit for the Christmas party. I stopped in Karibu Books to kick the breeze for a few with Rico and Oliver—two cool ass brothers—and to see what new books were out. I didn't have a lot of time to read but I had to scoop up *Pandora's Box* by Allison Hobbs while I was there. The back cover said it was about a sister who decided to work in a brothel to make ends meet. I knew all about that and figured I could relate big time.

After I left Karibu, I got some sexy lingerie from Victoria's Secret, got all the shit to make me smell good from Bath and Body Works, and picked up the scented candle-of-the-month from the Yankee Candle Company. Then I went to Hecht's to get my shopping on.

I found a hot red number that showcased my banging ass body. The price was right so I jumped on it. I used to go into stores and buy the highest-priced shit they had on the rack. Then they caught onto sisters like me who would purchase something, wear it, and then bring it back halfway "funktified." First, stores started putting the labels in places where you just couldn't tuck them in or tape them on to the inside fabric so no one would see them. Then they really ruined our shit by not giving full refunds. They even went so far as to only issue a store credit. Some of them got really deep and gave you a credit minus a twenty-percent restocking fee. Now that's some foul ass shit!

I planned to go home early for a change. I needed to get my beauty rest for my big day. Friday night—the Christmas party—was going to be a night to remember and one Tomalis Wolfe surely would never forget. I made one last stop at a drugstore to pick up a vial of new lipstick. You would never believe who I ran into!

Tomalis

I took Thursday off from the office to spend some time with Barron. I tried to get Jonah to take the day off from school to go with us but he swore up and down that he had five exams that day. I got the impression that my son just didn't want to spend any quality time with me. I didn't know where I had gone wrong with Jonah. I had tried to give him everything but—in a sense—I guess all he ever probably wanted was me.

The guilt had begun to set in lately about both of my kids. Running Wolfe had made me miss out on so many milestones in their life. Jonah had played little league baseball as a child and when I thought back, I don't think that I ever made it to more than a handful of games. Zetta was not much better. She was too busy out getting sexed. We would have one of our servants drop him off at practices and games. That was no life for a child.

Same thing with Heather. She had participated in everything from dance to soccer to taking piano lessons. I did attend one of her recitals and she was very good. I had failed as a father and it was time for me to admit it. My daughter had to turn to pill-popping because of me and my son had followed his mother's footsteps and turned to sex. For a brief moment, I considered blaming Zetta's promiscuity on myself but no, she was grown and was responsible for her own actions.

Barron's attempt to ignore his health issues was driving me crazy. For the past couple of days, he had literally refused to even discuss his imminent demise. He woke up Thursday morning and was excited when I told him that we'd be spending the entire day together.

Barron did have one complaint, though. "You always take me to the same damn places every time I come. Let's do something different."

I asked him what he really wanted to see in the D.C. area and there was quite a bit.

He wanted to have breakfast at Ben's Chili Bowl——a legendary restaurant on U Street that had been open since 1958. Everyone from Redd Foxx to Duke Ellington to Martin Luther King, Jr. had once dined there. Now it was time for Barron and Tomalis.

They didn't open until eleven, so technically it ended up being lunch. We were there when the doors opened and quickly grabbed two seats at the counter. I knew that I was risking heartburn when I ordered two chili burgers and a piña colada milkshake. Barron got three chili half-smokes and a chocolate shake. We sat there and laughed and joked just like old times.

When we left Ben's about noon, we headed downtown to the National Museum of American History. The first floor was like heaven to me. It was all about the history of science and technology—invention and building—which was right up my alley.

As Barron and I stood there checking out the history of the automobile, he said, "I know you're feeling this, man."

I grinned. "Isn't this incredible?"

"Yeah, if you say so. I still want to check out the Air and Space Museum."

"We'll go there next. I want to see the planes, too."

Barron chuckled. "I suppose you plan to start building planes next."

"Hey, don't laugh. Remember you did that when I first said that I was going to be the first African American automobile manufacturer?"

"Yeah, and look at your smooth ass now." He shook his head. "You amaze me, Tomalis. You're so full of life. I admire you so much."

"Now that is funny, Barron. It's you who should be admired."

He looked confused. "How so? I have nothing and you have everything. Hell, I'm about to check out and you're in perfect health."

"In most people's eyes I have everything, but in mine I have nothing. I've lost so much along the way by letting my priorities get mixed up. I've had the ability to travel—go anywhere in the world I want to go—but instead I'm always around here trying to make more money. The only traveling I ever did was when we were younger."

"Our infamous trips to Mexico."

We both laughed.

"Yeah, those were something," I said. "You, on the other hand, have seen so much. Like the nude beaches and—"

"Umph, umph, umph," Barron said, interrupting me. "Don't mention the nude beaches. My dick might get hard and this whole museum will look like the power went out."

"Modesty was never one of your stronger traits, Barron." I slapped him on the shoulder. "I'm going to miss you, man."

"Hey, don't get sentimental on me or I'll go find the nearest bus stop and haul ass."

"I'm serious, Barron. I can't imagine my life without you," I told him, fighting back tears. "You're all I have left."

"No, I'm not," Barron said forcefully. "You have your kids."

"They both either hate me or don't even care that I exist."

"No, they don't think you care that they exist. You need to work on that."

"I'm trying, Barron. I really am. I asked Jonah to come with us today."

"And?"

"He said he needed to go to school. Now most kids would jump on the chance to miss school but he'd rather be there than with me."

Barron tried his best to console me. "Things will get better, Tomalis. I believe that and you have to believe it, too."

"Well, I'm definitely making sure that certain things are handled right away," I said, beginning to feel better as I thought about my plans for the immediate future.

"Now I can't wait to see what goes down before New Year's. You did say something major was going to happen before then, right?"

"Oh, yes, it is."

"Good. At least I'll be here to witness it."

"Barron, there has to be something that can be done," I said, my mood darkening again from his last comment.

"There's nothing you can do. Face the facts. I already have. Just let me enjoy the rest of my life and make me a promise."

"What's that?"

"That you will at least attempt to love again."

"What woman in her right mind would want me?" I asked.

"Surely, that was a joke. You're Tomalis Wolfe, dammit. I've met some women who said they would suck out your asshole if you let them. Do you have any idea how much pussy I've gotten over the years just because I'm your best friend? Man, you could get laid ten—hell, twenty times a day if you wanted."

"Getting laid and being in love are two different things."

"True, but getting laid is a good start."

Barron laughed and I began to get this rumbling in my stomach.

"Barron, I need to go find the closest restroom," I told him.

"You and me, both," he said with a chuckle.

After we left the next museum, Barron and I went to check out a movie. Then I told him that I needed to drop him off for a while because I had to run an errand. He asked me why he couldn't come with me and then commented, "I didn't know rich ass brothers like you had to run their own errands. You're up to something, Tomalis."

He was correct but I wasn't going to tell him where I was headed. I dropped him off at the house and then went to keep an appointment. A very important one that would change my life and the lives of everyone around me.

Friday, December 22nd

Chico

When I got to work on Friday, you would have thought that I was Tomalis fucking Wolfe. Every one was riding my jock before I could even get into the front door good. Every one from the guards at the front desk to the housekeeping crew to the executive assistants who always just snarled at me when I looked in their direction. One sister even handed me a small bag of gingersnap cookies she'd baked herself and told me to have a Merry Christmas.

I didn't know what the hell was going on. Then I walked into the mail room and Miceal said, "How does it feel to be the man today?"

"It feels good, I think," I replied. "It will feel a whole lot better when I figure out why everybody's kissing my ass like my crack is full of gold."

Razor came up on the other side of me. "Figure it out, Chico. You make mail rounds. Today is bonus check day. They all want to get theirs before everyone else."

"Get it now, fool?" Miceal asked.

"Damn! No wonder!" I said. "Well, I can tell you who's getting their check first."

"Who?" Razor asked.

"Me, motherfucker." I ran over to my cart and started looking for my check, which should have been right on top since that's where they always put my paychecks.

I heard a throat clearing behind me. "Donald, you missed your calling. You need to be in a profession where they pay you to sneak up on people. You're damn good at it."

"Chico, enough of your mouth for one day."

"I just got here. What are you talking about?" I asked him.

"I came over to inform you that your bonus check has been mailed to you at home. There was some mix-up in Human Resources."

"Mailed to me?" I was pissed. "Why would they mail it to me? That makes no damn sense."

He threw his hands in the air and sighed. "Hey, don't shoot the messenger. I'm your supervisor so they just left me a voice mail telling me what I just told you. Any other questions, go talk to them."

"You are so rude," I told him.

"Then you can always quit and never have to lay eyes on me again, Chico. I promise you that I won't miss you. Not one little bit."

"Donald, just leave me the hell alone, aight?"

"There you go with those Ebonics again. You young fools have a lot to learn about corporate America."

"Yeah, well, you won't be the one teaching us. That's for sure."

I wasn't up to going back and forth with Donald. He and
I both knew what all the drama was really about. I had fucked
Zetta half the night and he wasn't in the apartment with us so
I was the motherfucking king and he couldn't deal with it.

I yanked my cart past him and headed for the door. "I'm
going on rounds!"

Diana

I was so excited about the Christmas party that night. I
stopped by the ballroom on the encased rooftop level of the
Wolfe building to check out the decorations on my way in. It
was out of this world. There were hundreds of red and white
balloons in arches across the ceiling and four vertical
columns of balloons outlining the dance floor.

The tables had red cloth tablecloths and napkins, hurri-
cane lamps with mistletoe rings, and silver placecard stands
so that everyone would know where they were supposed to
sit. I glanced at the huge seating chart they had near the entrance. It was in alphabetical order and it had my name at
Table 18 along with a guest. *Had I responded for two people?* I
definitely had no date. I could always ask a girlfriend. Pinky
was out of the question because she would show up looking
like a streetwalker but maybe Red would be available.

Stephen had called me at 6 A.M., still trying to get me to
rekindle flames that had burnt out a long time ago. After
making it clear that nothing sexual would happen between us
again, he announced that he was going to head on back to Atlanta that afternoon. I asked him if my having sex with
him—or not having it—had anything to do with the twins.
He didn't need to leave town because I wouldn't give it up.

He *claimed* that he needed to get back a few days earlier

than planned and that he would be back to see the boys sometime in the spring. I hung up on his ass. Something told me that he was playing games all along and now I felt bad that I had even let Dean and Darren meet the bastard. Time would determine things—not me pitching a fit—so I decided to let live and let go.

When I got to my desk, Chico was on the roll early and had already dropped off the mail. I was delighted to see my *extra* bonus check—the one I'd just earned the day before— at the top of the stack of letters on my desk. It would really help with additional gifts I wanted to get for Christmas. I wanted to buy one special gift as well. I planned to get something for Edmund; even though I could not have him romantically in my life.

I was also happy about something else but I was never one to count my chickens before they hatched so I opted to just wait and see what happened later that night.

At lunchtime, I went to the bank—which was extremely crowded being it was the last business day before Christmas—and took my place in the long line so I could cash my check directly from the Wolfe account. I recognized numerous other Wolfe employees in line who didn't want to put the checks into their own accounts and have to wait for them to clear before they could get the funds.

I was on my way out of the bank when I bumped into Edmund. "Hey, Edmund. Are you going to cash your check?"

"No." He shook his head and pointed at the ATM machine. "I am just going to do an electronic deposit. My regular account is at this bank but they're too slow for me to stand in line."

I sighed. "I know that's right. It's seems like I've been in there forever." I glanced at my watch and realized I had less than ten minutes to get back. "I'd better run."

Edmund touched my arm. "Do you really have to?"

Something about his touch was so sincere. It made me wonder what it was all about. Bradford would undoubtedly be ready to bitch at me if he found out I'd taken a long lunch. But he hadn't even shown his face that day, which didn't come as a big surprise since I knew what he was up to.

"I can spare a few more minutes, I suppose," I finally replied.

"Just give me a second to make this deposit."

I waited on the corner while he waited behind the two people at the ATM machine and prayed that one of my wishes was about to come true. He finished up and joined me. "Have you eaten, Diana?"

"No, I spent my entire lunch hour in the bank."

"Well, are you hungry?"

"Sure, I could eat something." *Like you,* I thought. *I could eat your ass whole.*

"How about Ortanique over on Eleventh Street?" Edmund suggested.

"Isn't that the place with Caribbean food?"

"Yeah, it's good, too."

"Then let's check it out."

Edmund took my hand like it was the most natural thing in the world and started walking. I wasn't about to complain.

We were able to snag a table with ease and sat by a window while we waited for our food. I ordered the jerked game hen and he ordered the jerked pork chops. I had noticed that they had bread pudding draped with toffee sauce on their dessert menu and I had no intention of leaving without trying it. Hopefully, Edmund would split it with me so I wouldn't seem so greedy.

"Edmund, can I ask you something?" I didn't want to rush him but I knew I couldn't sit there all day.

"Sure, Diana. What's up?"

"Am I wrong or is there something different about you today?"

"Different? No, I'm the same person."

"That's not what I mean. It seems like there's something different between us. A different chemistry."

He smiled at me. "Well, you did say that if things didn't work out with my other friend that you'd like to see where things could go."

I almost toppled my glass of cranberry juice. "The two of you broke it off already?"

"Diana, I'm going to be honest and upfront. There was no other woman. I just said that because I didn't appreciate the way you came on to me after you saw me stripping when I had been trying to get next to you for the longest time."

I redirected my eyes out the window. I hate it when men are right. "I realize how that looked. I was always attracted to you, Edmund. My defense mechanisms just had me making up excuse after excuse not to date. It wasn't just you, either. A lot of brothers have approached me but I always found something wrong with them so I wouldn't have to face the fact that I was the one with the problem."

"So what are you saying?" he asked me.

"What are you saying, Edmund? Are you willing to date me?"

He lifted my hand, turned it over and ran his tongue over the lifeline on my palm. "If you'll date me, I would like nothing more."

I wanted to jump for joy but just giggled and blushed like a schoolgirl instead. I wondered if I should come clean and tell him about jumping into bed with Stephen. Then I decided that should be on a need to know basis and he didn't need to know all that.

"Diana, would you do me the honor of accompanying me to the Wolfe Christmas Party tonight? They have me listed as bringing a guest and I don't have one."

I laughed. "They have me down for one guest, too."

"Well, it looks like they'll just have two extra seats because you and I are going together."

"I can hardly wait."

The waitress came back with our food just as Edmund was getting up from the table. He told her, "Excuse me." Then he came around to my side of the table, pulled me from the chair, hugged me, and then laid the most luscious and sensual kiss on me that I'd ever had.

Anastasia

I couldn't wait to get to the *party!* It was going to be all the way live! Shakia asked if she could catch a ride with me. I told her hell no because she was too damn slow. If I told her to be ready at seven to go someplace, I'd have to sit around waiting on her ass until eight. That shit wasn't about to happen that night and make me late for the event of the century.

When I got there, the band was off the chain. The High Voltage Band was one of my favorites. I would go check their asses out just about every Saturday night over at Chuck and Billy's across the street from Howard University. Talk about getting your sweat on. People up in that joint were drenched when they left but it was all good because there's nothing like a jamming party.

They were doing the damn thing in the Wolfe ballroom. I found the table where Shakia and I were supposed to sit and—of course—her ass was nowhere in sight. Probably just getting out the fucking shower at home.

I was looking good as shit and all the men were wanting to eat my panties off—it was obvious. I spotted Tomalis and Zetta Wolfe as they walked in. She was clinging on to his arm like he would run for the hills if she let go for even a second. Her bitch mother was with them. She would've been in for a serious beatdown if I'd run into her anyplace other than there.

After locating the closest bar in the room, I was ready to get my drink on. The champagne was top-of-the-line and I planned to drink at least three bottles of that shit. Barron was sitting at the bar and had beaten me to the punch.

"Hey there, young lady," he said, grinning at me.

"Hey there, yourself," I said back to him.

"Care to join me in a drink?"

"Certainly."

We sat there and chatted for a while and then he asked me to dance. Now there's booty-shaking and then there's what we were doing. Barron could really get down for a brother his age. It made me wonder what he might be working with in the bedroom.

After an hour of freaking all over each other on the dance floor, I finally spotted Shakia coming in the entrance. Bradford was standing there talking to Zetta Wolfe. I couldn't believe she'd actually turned Tomalis loose.

They slowed the music down while the band took a break and put on "This Woman's Work" by Maxwell. Normally, I didn't slow dance but I was curious about what Barron was holding so I let him grind up on me. I could work with what he was holding.

Once that song ended, instead of the band coming back, they decided to start the little program they usually held. It was more of a formality, with the various supervisors getting up to congratulate their direct employees on having a fabulous and productive year. A bunch of bullshit that I had heard one time too many. Barron and I went to stand against the wall. Neither one of us really felt like sitting down. We were ready to get our groove on and hoping the talking would take fifteen minutes or less.

Everyone seemed stunned when Tomalis Wolfe took the stage first. He always went last and kept it very brief. Even I was shocked that it was about to go down like this. *Damn, I knew I should've bought a camcorder with my bonus check instead of a home theater system!*

Chico

I couldn't believe it when I heard my name called out. *What the hell is this?* was the only question that ran through my head.

Mr. Wolfe stood there at the podium grinning like a real wolf and eyeing me. "Chico Grayson, would you please come to the stage?"

Miceal pushed me on the shoulder. "Man, you hear him calling you. Get your ass up there."

I was frozen. Why would Tomalis Wolfe want me on the stage? I was a mail-room clerk. I searched the crowd for Zetta and spotted her over in a corner with Bradford Haynes. They both had fear written all over their faces.

Donald came rushing up behind me—I smelled him first—and grabbed my elbow. "Chico, don't you dare embarrass me," he said, pulling me toward the front of the ballroom—toward Mr. Wolfe. "Here he is, Mr. Wolfe!" Donald yelled out. "You did say Chico Grayson? Fine boy—one of my best workers."

I looked at Donald like he was crazy. He knew good and

damn well we couldn't stand each other. I definitely couldn't stand his ass after I found out Zetta had fucked him. How skank!

Reluctantly, I walked to the stage. I felt like I was a dead man walking. Nothing good could possibly come from me going up there.

After I was standing beside Tomalis, he placed his left arm around my shoulder. "Now, I would like you all to take a good look at this young man. He's been with Wolfe Industries a little over six months and he is the embodiment of a perfect employee. He's always at work, he's always on time, he dresses neatly, he's well-groomed, he's always respectful, he's always . . ."

All the words started blending together and I could barely make them out. Probably because I was five seconds or less away from passing the fuck out. Tomalis had never said two words to me and now he was giving a speech about my proficiency as an employee? Hell, half the shit he was saying wasn't even true. I wasn't always there and I damn sure wasn't always on time. The dressing neat and well-groomed parts were cool and I could be respectful to some people— like Diana—but definitely not to Donald.

I snapped back into reality when I heard the word "fucking."

I looked over and up at him. "Yes, that's right, ladies and gentlemen, he's even fucking my wife for me." His grip tightened around my shoulder. "Now what more can a corporate head ask for?"

Zetta fell down on the floor—probably from losing her balance when her tongue dropped out of her mouth. Bradford helped her get back up and the bitch just stood there frozen in space.

There was a hush that fell over the crowd at first and then it switched to a bunch of whispers.

One older lady up front asked the man beside her, "Did he just say what I thought he said?"

The man—more than likely her husband—replied, "How the hell should I know, Dorene? I'm the one with the hearing aid."

Everyone searched for Zetta and located her. Good, all eyes were in the right place. At least for a second, until . . .

Tomalis said, "Some of you might be wondering what this is all about. Asking yourselves why a man like myself would get up in the middle of his corporate Christmas party and expose my cradle-robbing wife and her boy lover." He paused and then grinned. "Well, it's like this. For years— decades now—I have known that Zetta was nothing but a whore. She takes after her mother." He waved at some woman on the other side of the room near the back. "Hey there, Zora. Smile for the cameras."

It was then that it dawned on me that there were reporters there from local papers and numerous camcorders running held by various employees. *Oh shit!*

Part of me wanted to steal Tomalis in the face but that would have meant spending at least one night in jail—or the hospital if he beat my ass for doing it.

"Speaking of cameras," he went on. *Will this shit ever end?* I asked myself. "Speaking of cameras, I have something I'd like to show everyone. I'm sure that you'll find it entertaining."

A huge screen emerged from the ceiling behind us and I was afraid to turn around when I saw a projector light come on in the back. People started oohing and aahing. Some people started laughing.

Then I heard the sound and turned around with a quickness. It was from Wednesday; the night Zetta had shown up in my garage and seduced me.

"But the lights were out!" I exclaimed, remembering that I had clearly made sure of that once she started getting buck naked.

Tomalis let go of me and said, "Night vision. Isn't technology amazing?"

The picture was in weird shades and I was so ashamed that I wanted to crawl up in a hole and hide. There I was. Chico, the nineteen-year-old son of an overprotective religious mother who would lose her religion and whip my fucking ass when she found out about this, lover of a woman that had promised to help a brother out but was about to find herself ass out just like me and—on top of all that—my player card was damn sure about to be revoked.

It was fucked up! It was all fucked up!

Tomalis

I was loving it! I looked over at Barron—who was holding hands with Anastasia—and he gave me a thumbs up with his spare hand. I grabbed Chico's wrist and pulled him to the side of the stage. "Let's move out the way," I told him, "so people can get a better view."

Chico was like a lost puppy and obeyed without uttering a word. I felt kind of bad for him but he needed to learn his lesson. Boys want to become men—eventually they have to—but he needed to learn what being a real man was all about.

Zetta tried to get to the projector to turn it off but Phil wouldn't let her anywhere near it. I heard her say to him,

"You ungrateful little fuck! I've let you drive me around all this time and this is what I get for it?"

Phil looked at her and laughed in her face. "Mr. Wolfe has paid me to drive you. You haven't done a damn thing for me except treat me like I was beneath you. It's payback time, my sister."

The tape had been edited to shorten it but people got the gist of it. The dick sucking, the pussy eating, the penetration. Zetta's goose was cooked. But it wasn't well done enough for me.

"Phil, let's move on to exhibit B," I said.

Phil grinned. "Yes, sir, Mr. Wolfe."

He clicked ahead to the next scene, which was also filmed in night vision. Now I knew this one would disgust everyone. It was of Zetta and Donald fucking in the cleaning supply closet and everything that happened between the two of them and Chico in the hallway afterwards. I had seen it numerous times over the last twenty hours but it still made me sick to my stomach. That was low—even for her.

Zetta couldn't take it. I knew that she had never been so humiliated or ridiculed in her entire life. She fled out of the room and the little runt Donald went after her. Zora flung her mink stole around her shoulder and trailed them like she had an ounce of dignity left.

I told Phil, "Cut it off. It's just not the same without her here to witness it."

He cut if off and I pushed Chico away from me. "You can go home now, son. You probably have a curfew and I wouldn't want you to be late."

Everyone fell out laughing as they watched him go down the steps and disappear into the audience. I saw him flop down on a chair in the back with his eyes glazed over like he was in a trance.

The room suddenly grew silent and nobody moved an inch. Most of them didn't want to miss out on whatever might happen next. They probably assumed I wasn't finished. They were right.

"Bradford, could you come up here for a minute, please."

Bradford looked like he was about to shit in his pants. "Tomalis, what do you need me up there for?"

"Bradford, don't be ridiculous. You're my right-hand man. You belong up here beside me." I held my hand up and waved him up there. People stared at him as he made his way. Once he was on stage, I turned to him, "Bradford, I want to thank you also. First, I just have to thank you for fucking my wife." There were oohs and aahs all over the room. "Yes, you've been fucking her, too. I've known about you the longest, which is why I shouldn't be too surprised that you would try to fuck me in the ass also. Without grease, at that."

Bradford's knees started wobbling. "Tomalis, I have no idea what you're talking about."

"Bradford, it's useless to deny it," I told him. "You've always thought that you were so slick, that you could manipulate people—especially women—into doing whatever you want. The head on top of your shoulders might be big but the brain inside of it is just as small as your little head." I pointed to his crotch. "At least, I heard that it's *very small*. Both of them just landed you in serious trouble."

"I won't stand here and listen to this!" Bradford lashed out.

"Fine, you can leave while I tell all the reporters and everyone else how you were trying to take over my corporation, along with Tanaka from Prism Motors."

Bradford's mouth fell open. "How did you . . ."

Diana stepped forward from the crowd. "I did you in,

Bradford," she said with much delight. "I went to Mr. Wolfe with the evidence I've been collecting behind your back and put the nails in your coffin."

Anastasia let go of Barron's hand and walked forward. "And I pounded those motherfuckers into the coffin."

The two women who—from what I understood—previously couldn't tolerate each other, gave each other a high five, struck poses, and grinned at us.

"You fucking traitors, both of you!" Bradford screamed. "I'll fix you!" He glared at me. "I'll fix you all!"

"You do that, Bradford," I said. "But you're going to have to do it outside of this building." I nodded toward the door, where two security guards were waiting. "Security, please escort Mr. Haynes from the premises."

"But what about all my stuff?" he demanded to know.

"You're not stepping foot back into that office," I replied. "I'll have someone gather your personal items and have them dropped off. Other than that, you're not getting a damn thing."

"Severance pay?"

"Consider my not having you arrested as your severance pay."

Bradford balled his left hand into a fist.

I said, "By the way, the locks have been changed on the penthouse so don't even think about going there to retrieve anything you might have stashed away over there."

"You think you're so smart, Tomalis," he stated nastily. "If I really want to do you in, I have plenty of information at home."

I shook my head. "No, I thought of that."

"You broke into my house?"

I reached into my pocket and pulled out a silver key ring with the letter T on it. "Remember when you gave me this a few years ago? You said that I was your brother and your casa was my casa. Well, I took you up on that invitation and made myself right at home."

"I can have you arrested for theft, Tomalis."

"For taking things that belong to me? Even the computers in your home had Wolfe ID tags on them. Same thing with your laptop, which I have also."

Bradford said nothing further. He knew it was pointless. He was on his way out when I said, "Please, don't let all of this ruin the event. Let's get the band started again so everyone can enjoy the remainder of the evening."

No sooner had I said that when Zetta and Zora came storming back into the room with Donald between them.

Zora yelled out, "I will not let you do this to my daughter!"

"What are you going to do, Zora? Send me to my room? Take away my allowance?" I laughed. "Oh, that's right. I give you an allowance. At least, I did. The bank is officially closed."

Zora clamped her mouth and eyes shut, like she was contemplating her next move.

I could tell that Zetta was trying to pull herself together. *Too late, sweetheart.* While I realized there were other ways to just get rid of Zetta—without the public flogging—I wanted to do it in public to prove a point. I did feel bad that Jonah was in the room. He was sitting at a table near the front with a date—one of his sex goddesses that I had never laid eyes on—and drinking champagne like water; even though he was underage.

All those years everyone thought that they were pulling the wool over my eyes. Tomalis Wolfe was never and will never be anybody's fool. I wanted the world to know that.

Zetta came up on the stage and everyone got quiet all

over again so they could hang on every word. "Tomalis," she whispered, touching my wrist. "Can we please go somewhere quiet and talk?"

"There's nothing to talk about, Zetta," I said sternly. "Just to make myself perfectly clear and to make it official, I want a divorce, I'm going to get a divorce, and there's not a damn thing you can do about it. Our prenuptial agreement states that if you cheat on me, you get nothing."

"I signed that when I was drunk," she lashed out at me.

"Well, more than twenty years after the act is a little too late to try to blame it on liquor. Any judge will laugh you out the courtroom with that nonsense."

"But I love you, Tomalis. I realize that I've made mistakes but our love will pull us through."

"The only thing you'll be pulling is luggage, out of the house and into a cab because you're not taking anything else with you but your clothes."

"What about the kids?"

"Humph, now you take our kids into consideration? Zetta, just leave before you make an even bigger fool out of yourself."

That's when it happened. Donald actually grew some balls. "Don't you speak to my woman like that!"

I laughed. Everyone did.

I stopped laughing when he rushed the stage and tried to punch me in the stomach. I had hoped to avoid a physical altercation and—quite honestly—I thought that Chico fellow would have been the person to initiate it being that he was so young. But when Donald came at me like that, there was only one thing left to do. I knocked him the hell out.

I don't know how it happened but that one fist to the head must have set off a chain reaction because the next thing I knew Zora and Anastasia were going at it; obviously an aftereffect of what had gone down between them at the hair salon. Zora could fight pretty good for a woman her age but Diana teamed up with Anastasia and then Zetta jumped into it to protect her mother.

Men started fighting other men—over what I have no idea—and before I knew it, we had a brawl. Barron came up on stage beside me and hugged me tight, "Man, you sure know how to throw a party. This is just like old times."

I grinned. "Thanks, man. I wanted to give you a night you'd never forget."

"Well, you've damn sure done that. I'm so fucking proud of you." Barron pointed down into the mass confusion. "You think we should at least break the women up?"

"No, let them have their fun. They probably have years of pent-up frustration to get rid of."

We both laughed, descended the steps of the stage, and walked out.

I saw that Chico fellow sitting on a bench at the bus stop across the street when we were getting into my limousine. He had his head buried in his lap and he was weeping. "Become a man, son," I whispered.

"You say something, Tomalis?" Barron asked.

"No, nothing important." I shrugged. "We won't leave but let's just sit in the limo and relax."

"Got any porno DVDs?"

"No, just bullshit love stories."

"Hey, all love stories are not bullshit. I still say you'll love again."

"In your dreams, Barron. In your dreams."

Saturday, December 23rd

Chico

It was fucked up! It was all fucked up! I was still telling myself that the next morning when I dragged myself out of bed.

How could things have gone so wrong? Zetta, that bitch! At least she was going to get what she deserved; absolutely nothing. I have to admit that Tomalis Wolfe was cool as shit with his game. The way he went about exposing her ass and sending her to pack her shit was amazing. Classical, even. Too bad all the drama had to happen at my expense. I considered myself an innocent victim. Yes, I'm a man but even men have to watch out for spiders. Zetta lured me into her web and I fell for it hook, line, and sinker.

Razor had warned me that Momma had heard all about it, which made me even more depressed. I would never be able to live down my actions. I had bedded a woman old enough to be my mother. A woman with a son two years younger than me. What the hell was I thinking?

I sulked into the kitchen. Momma was sitting at the table mixing a bowl of stuffing. "Good morning, Chico."

"Good morning, Momma." I poured myself a cup of coffee and sat down across from her. "I already know you heard about last night."

"D.C. is a big city, but it's not that big. Miceal came back around here telling everyone who would listen. Those people told other people and by two in the morning, the phone was ringing off the hook so bad that I finally unplugged it from the wall."

"That damn Miceal. And he calls himself a friend."

"He probably is your friend, baby. He's just got a big mouth and people with big mouths never consider the repercussions of their actions." She kept stirring the stuffing when she added, "Just like you didn't consider the repercussions of yours."

I lowered my eyes to the table in shame. "I could lie and say that Zetta Wolfe used me, Momma. Without question, I hate the bitch."

I waited for Momma to tell me how inappropriate it is to call women bitches but it never came. In fact, I could've sworn I saw her nod in agreement. "I was so caught up in the fact that an older, *rich* woman wanted to get with me that I didn't think about what could go wrong. She made me feel like I was special, like I was the only one for her."

"Let me guess. You weren't the only one?" Momma asked.

"Humph! Not hardly. Zetta's been with just about every man at Wolfe. Even Donald."

Momma looked like she was about to choke on her own

saliva. She'd heard too much about Donald. "Tell me you're kidding," she said in disgust.

I shook my head. "Nope, she even did him. Talk about having sexual issues, huh? I guess Miceal and Razor would've been next."

Momma smirked. "I better get this stuffing in the stove. I have to get it to the nursing home for Grandma's party by noon."

"Momma, I really do apologize for hurting your feelings. All the neighbors are going to be talking."

"They're already talking but let them talk. They didn't run me away from here when your Daddy left me for that slut and they won't run me away from here now. You made a mistake, Chico. All that proves is that you're human."

"And I'm also immature."

Momma pressed her palm over her chest. "I never thought I'd hear you say that."

I laughed. "I know—at least I know now—that I still have a lot of growing up to do. What happened last night, I don't ever plan to put myself in a situation like that again. Not ever."

"You just need to find you a nice girl and settle down. I still don't understand what happened between you and McKenna."

I was about to fix me something to eat but the mention of McKenna made me lose my appetite. "McKenna's evil. I hate to say that about the mother of my child, but it's true. She changed up on me completely and when it's all over and said and done, she'll have to pay for her actions. I plan to get myself a better job and fight for custody of Gina. McKenna tried to make me out to be unfit but she's the one unfit to be anyone's parent."

"What kind of job are you planning on getting?" Momma asked. "I still say education is everything. I wish that I'd gone further than high school."

"You need me to help you pay the bills."

"True, but you can work and go to school. All you've been doing when you get off work at Wolfe is hanging out with those fast boys and sleeping. I take that back, you've also been having sex with a woman my age."

I frowned. "Only for the last week, Momma." I wanted to add that at least it had been mind-blowing sex but decided against it. Bottom line: fucking around with Zetta wasn't worth the aggravation.

As if she'd read my thoughts, Momma asked, "Was it worth it?"

"No, it sure wasn't," I replied. I got up from the table. "I'm going to hit the pavement and see if I can find another job."

"On a Saturday? The Saturday before Christmas at that."

"Hey, it could happen. Besides, anyone can find a job. It's just a matter of not being picky and in my situation, I can't afford to be. I have a child to take care of." I walked around the table, leaned over and gave her a kiss on the cheek. "And I have you to take care of."

"What about school?" she asked me over her shoulder.

I shrugged. "I'll think about it."

"Chico . . ."

"Seriously, Momma. I'll really, really think about it. Until then, I'm going to make some money doing *something* so I can finish buying the things for Gina that I want her to have for Christmas."

"Don't do anything crazy or illegal."

I rubbed her shoulders. "I may be a lot of things but I'm not crazy. Like you said last week, I probably wouldn't last in jail and I have no intention of finding out. All I know is if people with one arm, no legs, and other handicaps can find a job in this economy, I'm not about to sit on my ass. Gina already has one parent setting a bad example. I won't allow her to have two."

Momma got up and wrapped her arms around me. "I really am proud of you, Chico. One day you will come into your own. You just have to figure out what you want to do with your life."

"I will, Momma. I will." I turned to leave the kitchen but paused. "What about the neighbors gossiping."

Momma laughed. "Hey, there could be worse things than having a stud muffin for a son."

I grinned and went to get dressed. I was going to make it; one way or another.

Diana

Well, he definitely didn't make it easy for me but I got my man. Waking up the next morning in Edmund's arms was nothing short of heavenly. We'd left the party—after I had helped Anastasia beat the hell out of Zetta Wolfe and her lunatic mother—and hightailed it to the nearest hotel that we could afford. We definitely couldn't afford a room at the one next door to Wolfe Industries. They started at three hundred and went up to two thousand. Neither one of us is rolling like that.

I wasn't sure if I would stay at Wolfe or not. Too much had happened. I was just glad that Bradford finally got what he deserved; thanks greatly to yours truly.

Dean and Darren had asked if they could stay over at their friend's house again that night so I had a full twenty-four hours more to get my groove on before I had to pick them up. I planned to make the best use of it.

Edmund was snoring lightly; even that made me horny. It had been so long since I could watch a man sleeping. He seemed so peaceful; probably because I had laid all my built-up sexual desires on him. With Stephen, it had been different. Just simple sex but it didn't fulfill my desires that way being with Edmund did. I did things with him that I never thought I'd have the nerve to do. As far as I was concerned, it was only the beginning.

I had just finished brushing my teeth—luckily I always carry a toothbrush and a small tube of paste with me along with my tampon in case Aunt Flo shows up—when I heard my cell phone ringing. I rushed back into the part where Edmund lay sleeping to grab my purse up off the floor. I didn't want him to wake up just yet.

I rambled through my purse to retrieve it, glanced at it, and recognized the number. For a brief moment, I debated about answering it. Then I decided that it might just be an interesting conversation.

"Bradford. What can I do for you?" I asked after pressing the talk button.

"I hate fucking caller ID," he hissed back at me. "I hate your ass, too. You fuckin' bitch!"

"Thanks for the compliment," I stated jokingly. "Have a good time last night?"

"I just called to officially fire you."

"You must be confused, Bradford. You can't fire me because Tomalis Wolfe fired you last night."

He was silent on the other end but I could hear him breathing heavily. "Tomalis will change his mind. I'm much too valuable to his organization. He'll see the light."

"Humph, I don't see why he would consider you valuable. After all, you were trying to rob him blind."

"I'll make sure you never work in this town again."

I couldn't help but laugh. "I'm still working. I wasn't fired. Not hardly. For the record, I was given a raise for exposing your scandalous business dealings."

"A raise!" Bradford screamed into the phone. "No way! No fucking way!"

"Yes, way." I heard Edmund stirring in the bed so I slid the glass door open and stepped out onto the balcony, closing the door behind me. "Maybe you and Mrs. Wolfe can both get jobs someplace else together. Someplace where they don't mind hiring sexually deviant women and men with sticky fingers."

"I should come over there and whip your ass."

"Feel free to go over to my place. I'm not home."

"Well, you have to come home sometime."

"And I will." I waited for him to say something else but he didn't. "Bradford, I wish I had the time to sit here and listen to your idle threats but my man is waiting for me in bed. I'm going to hang up now so I can make love. You have a nice day."

"Diana, I'm gonna——"

I cut him off by cutting off the phone.

When I went back into the room, Edmund was propped up on the pillows in bed. "Cheating on me already?" he asked sarcastically.

I sat the phone on the nightstand and slid into bed next to him. "What woman in her right mind would cheat on you?" I ran my fingers over his smooth chest. "She would have to be a fool to even think about being with another man."

Edmund blushed uncontrollably. "Stop flattering me so much."

"Or what?" I climbed on top of him. "Will you spank me if I don't stop?"

"Hmm, the way you say that so seductively, it makes me think you want to be spanked."

I licked a trail across his chest from nipple to nipple. "It could be interesting; if you spank me the right way."

"What way is the right way?"

"Um, I could bend over on the bed and . . ."

"Naked?"

"Of course, baby." I kissed him on his lips and darted my tongue in and out of his mouth. "I could bend over on the bed *naked* and you can get down on your knees behind me so I can swirl my pussy in your face and then you could take your palm and whack my ass to your heart's content."

Edmund licked his lips and whispered, "Damn! I knew there was a reason I wanted you so bad."

"Now that you have me, I hope you treat me right. After all, you're just a baby."

He chuckled. "Was I a baby last night when I made love to you all night long?"

"No, you were a king among men."

We both grinned.

"Then let me lead you back into my kingdom for another round," he said.

He flipped me over onto my back and starting suckling on my breasts. I pushed him away.

"Why?" he asked.

"What happened to me swirling my pussy in your face?"

He got off me. "Don't let me disrupt your plans."

I got on my knees and pushed my ass up as he got behind me. I started gyrating my hips while I reached between my legs and fingered myself. Edmund pulled my hand out and yanked it further toward him so he could suck my fingers. Then he started fingering me and slurping on my pussy at the same time.

He started tapping my G-spot and I came within a matter of seconds.

"Shit! I'm such a bad girl!" I screamed out as I came.

He kept tickling my clit with his tongue as he said, "Yeah, you are a bad girl and you have to be punished."

Edmund started spanking me. My, oh my. I was in for a long twenty-four hours. Thank goodness because I planned to make up for lost time.

Anastasia

Okay, stranger things have happened. I just don't really know how my particular situation happened. All I know is that I woke up on Saturday morning with Barron's dick in my mouth. Yes, all up in my mouth. I must have slept like a baby and his dick was my pacifier.

I wasn't even sure where we were. It was a fly ass suite so I assumed we were in the Belvedere; next door from where the infamous party had taken place. I got so drunk that I didn't remember a thing after Tomalis going off on any and everybody. Barron said I was in a fight. *Moi?* I found that hard to believe but I'll be damned if I didn't have scratches all over my arms. I asked him to give me the details and he said he would after we fucked the life out of one another.

I had run smack dab into Barron at the drugstore on Thursday night when I was buying lipstick. He was getting a prescription filled and recognized me. He asked if I wanted to join him for a drink. The word "opportunity" started flashing in my head. It was a chance for me to get the inside scoop on Tomalis so I'd have even more information to help Bradford bring his ass down.

The exact opposite happened. Barron went on and on about Tomalis and how much he meant to him. He told me how they had met, how many traumatic experiences Tomalis had been through, how kindhearted Tomalis was, and how Tomalis was the most loyal man he'd ever known.

While I still had the hots for Tomalis, Barron made me realize that it was my problem and not Tomalis's. He didn't have to be with me if he didn't want to. Barron, on the other hand, was feeling me. He didn't seem like a bad catch either. I still wasn't clear about what he did for a living. He just said he was a "Jack-of-All-Trades"—whatever the fuck that meant.

By the time Barron had taken me back to my car, everything had changed. I actually got to ride in Tomalis Wolfe's prize Corvette with Barron. He was rocking that shit, too. It was there in the parking lot that I revealed everything I knew about Bradford and Tanaka planning to steal Wolfe Industries right from under Tomalis's nose.

I could never and would never return to Wolfe Industries; even though I wasn't fired. I just wouldn't have felt comfortable being there after so much had gone down.

I could have always gotten a job at Uranus again, but that was not really my thing. Maybe I'd catch the train to New York City and barge into Jay–Z or P. Diddy's office and convince them that I was the best chick to star in their next videos. After all, I had all the elements. I was fine, I could shake my ass, and I could suck a mean dick if I had to in order to make ends meet.

I was still lying there with Barron's dick in my mouth

while I considered my option. Actually, his dick was kind of good. Tart but good.

I wasn't sure about Shakia's plans. I was confident she wouldn't show her face around Wolfe again either. Maybe she and I could hook up and do some things together. Meanwhile, I decided to suck Barron off again. Being the best friend of Tomalis Wolfe meant he had access to the cheddar. *Things might be looking up after all,* I thought as I deep-throated him as a wake-up call.

Tomalis

Even though it was near freezing outside, I decided to sit out on the portico and have breakfast. Marguerite had prepared my favorite: Belgian waffles with Canadian bacon. The Saturday before Christmas was the only one Marguerite worked. She insisted on it because there was always so much to be done in preparation for the holidays. I was hoping to be left alone to enjoy in peace but I realized quickly that there would be no such luck.

Jonah was the first to locate me where I didn't want to be located.

"Dad, can I talk to you?" he asked from behind me, after I'd heard footsteps approaching.

I sighed and then pointed to an empty chair. "Sure, Jonah, have a seat."

He and I just stared at each other for a couple minutes.

"Jonah, I want to apologize for my behavior last night. I'm not sorry that I did what I did. I'm just sorry you had to witness it."

The sides of Jonah's mouth curled up into a smile.

"Dad, no need to apologize. I thought what you did was awesome."

"Awesome?"

"Yeah, man, I mean Dad." He laughed. "Mom deserved everything she got. She had it coming and so did Bradford."

I was stunned. "Jonah, I thought you'd be upset about me talking to your mother like that."

He really laughed then. "Dad, you don't have to pretend around me. We both know what Mother is. Hell, I'm a whore because I'm following in her footsteps."

"That's not a nice thing to say, Jonah."

"Yeah, but is it a lie?" he asked. I didn't respond. "That dude she was doing from the mail room could've gone to high school with me. I've seen him around; I just can't place him."

"So he travels in your circles?"

"I wouldn't say all that, but I've seen him someplace. We've definitely been at the same party or same event at least once. We pretty men tend to familiarize ourselves with other pretty men so we know our competition."

I shook my head. "Jonah, life isn't about being pretty or seeing how many women you can bed down. Look at you, seventeen with three kids."

"I only have two kids," he corrected me.

"Two and one possible," I corrected him back. "Either way, one child is one too many. I've worked hard to give you every advantage in life and I don't want to see you screw it up. One day, you'll be running Wolfe Industries and—"

"What if I don't want to run it?" Jonah asked with disdain.

"What do you mean?"

"Like I said, what if I don't want to run it? What if I want to do something else with my life?"

"I can't imagine it. How often does a young man have the world placed in his lap?"

"Not too often, I'm sure," Jonah responded. "But that's not the point. Heather's older than me. Why isn't she the one who's supposed to run Wolfe?"

"Because Heather's almost a doctor and you're my son."

"And?"

"And sons take over the businesses of their fathers."

"In what rule book?"

It was at that point when I realized that I didn't know my son—at all. He was a complete stranger.

"Okay, Jonah, what do you want to do with your life?"

"I want to become a translator for the United Nations," he said with a straight face.

"Really?"

"Yes, Dad. I want to go to college, major in international trade or political science, and then become a translator for the United Nations. That way, if the translator thing doesn't work out, I can go into the trade industry."

This was the first intellectual conversation Jonah and I had engaged in; possibly ever. "Sounds interesting, I must admit. Where did all this come from?" I asked.

"I already speak fluent Spanish and German." He eyed me suspiciously. "You knew that, right?"

I was ashamed. "I knew about the Spanish."

Jonah sighed in disgust. "Dad, I've been taking German for four years."

"I'm sorry, Jonah. I'm really sorry." I felt like crying but I held the tears back. "I've been so caught up in running this business that I've neglected the truly important things in life. All of that's going to change. I promise. From now on, you and I are going to spend a lot of quality time together. I want to spend more time with my grandkids, too." I paused. "How are Justin and Jana?"

"They're fine, Dad." *Whew,* I thought to myself. *At least I got their names right.*

Jonah glanced at his watch. "Dad, I have to run. I promised a friend that I'd take him Christmas shopping today."

I cleared my throat. "Are you going to go say something to your mother? She's going to be moving out today."

Jonah grinned. "Just tell her good luck and good riddance."

Less than five minutes after Jonah had left me alone, here comes Zora. She looked like she'd been crying all night. I wasn't surprised at all. Her meal ticket was gone and there wasn't a damn thing she could do about it.

"Tomalis, I want to have a word with you," she stated angrily.

"Okay, you can have a word with me. One word. How about good-bye? That's the only word I'm trying to hear from you."

At that point, I had given up on the cold waffle and moved on to trying to enjoy *The Washington Post.* It seemed like having privacy was a lost cause.

Zora sat down and yanked the paper out my hands, crumbling it up and throwing it on the ground. "You will show me some respect. I'm your mother-in-law."

"Yes, you are my mother-in-law and that's exactly why I don't respect you." I gestured toward the house, where Zetta was supposed to be packing her things. "Look at what you raised."

"Zetta has given you the best years of her life and now you just want to toss her out. What kind of man are you?" she asked.

"A man with a backbone," I responded. "Zetta preys

upon the weak and she made the mistake of assuming I was weak all these years. I was never weak. I just left her to do her dirty deeds so she'd leave me alone. Now, I've grown tired of it and she has to go; along with your ass in tow."

"But what about the children? How can you just disrupt their happy home?"

It took all the strength I could muster not to get up and walk away. I was determined not to let anyone run me off from my spot so I held my ground. "There has never been a happy home and there are no children here. Heather's grown and living in another state and Jonah has two kids. He's a man."

Zora looked like she was trying to come up with something else to say; something convincing. "What will become of us? Zetta and I are used to a certain lifestyle."

I laughed in her face. "Aw, you poor, poor things. How about becoming self-sufficient for once instead of relying on me? If that doesn't work out, I'm sure you can both find some other unsuspecting fool to play for his money. You can do a tag team. Both of you can sex him down."

Zora stood up. "That's disgusting!"

"Disgusting enough for you to leave now?" I asked, hoping she would leave me the hell alone and go help Zetta pack her shit.

"My daughter has made you the man you are. You owe her. She has stood beside you, supported your efforts, birthed your kids, and—"

"One of those is debatable," I said. "Neither Jonah or I am convinced he's truly my son. Either way, biological or not, I'll always be his father."

"You're sick!"

"No, you're sick!" I got up to face her on eye level. "As far as Zetta making me the man that I am, that's a crock of bullshit. I became successful not because of her and not for her, but in spite of her."

"How dare you!" Zora pawed at her chest like she was having a heart attack.

"How dare you pretend like you didn't know what Zetta's been up to all this time. I'm taking my life back, piece by piece, and it all starts with clearing all the trash out my house."

"Trash?"

"Ghetto trash, to be more exact." I sat back down at the table. "Go help your bitch of a daughter pack. I want you both out of here within the next two hours or I'll have you physically removed."

Zora stormed off. I picked my paper back up to smooth it out and read the business section.

Chico

Okay, what's a brother got to do to get a job these days? Fuck somebody. I already did that and it got me absolutely nowhere. I got back home after beating the pavement half the damn day and collapsed on the sofa in the living room. I glanced over at Momma's Nativity scene. Boy, oh boy, would I be glad when Christmas was over. I wasn't in the mood for any sort of celebration.

The Wolfe annual Christmas party had been the shit all right. People would be talking about it for months to come; possibly even years. I was surprised that shit didn't make the news but there was still time for that. I just hoped they didn't name names; even though no one would recognize mine. Shit, I was a nobody.

I heard barking in the front yard and said, "Fuck!" I knew it had to be Razor because Brutus's noisy ass bark was unmistakable. I just hoped Miceal wasn't with him.

There was banging at the door and I got up to pull it open. "What the hell, Razor? Where's the fire?"

Miceal was standing behind him while Brutus was running around the yard with that damn tire around his neck.

"That dog is going to choke one of these days," I said. "Mark my words."

"We came over to check on you," Razor stated, ignoring my comment about Brutus. "Are you okay?"

"No, I'm not okay, fool. Did you see that shit that happened to me last night?"

Miceal snickered. "Who didn't see it?"

"The better question is who didn't hear about it." I snarled in his direction. "I heard you came back here running your fucking mouth and telling everyone my business."

Miceal pushed Razor out his way. "Don't front, Chico. If the tables were turned, you would've done the same shit to me. The shit was off the hook, man."

"And it was funny as hell," Razor added. They gave each other a high five and I wanted to knock both their asses off the front porch.

"It might've been funny to you but I wasn't amused. First Zetta played me for a fool and then her hubby embarrassed my ass in front of the world." I went out on the porch and closed the door behind me. "Where were you fools anyway? You're my boys. You're supposed to have a brother's back."

They eyed each other. Then Miceal said, "Hey, Chico, we are your boys and we do have your back. I was in the men's room draining all that free liquor they had at the party out of me when the shit went down."

"Miceal, you're a lying ass!" I yelled out. "You were standing right beside me when that man called me up front. What the fuck? You think I have amnesia?"

Miceal didn't reply. He just sat down in one of the wicker chairs and folded his arms across his chest.

I looked at Razor. "Razor, you're supposed to be so damn tough. What the hell was up with you?"

"Hey, I didn't get the benefit of the pussy," he replied. "Why should I risk everything for some ass you tapped?"

"See, at least you're keeping it real." I pointed at Miceal. "Unlike this fool over here; claiming he was taking a leak."

Razor sat down and I joined them. "So what you been up to all day?" he asked. "We rolled through earlier but you weren't here."

"I was out looking for a new job. Christmas is in two days and I didn't even get my check yesterday; rather less my Christmas bonus. I knew some shit was strange when Donald told me they'd put my check in the mail instead of leaving it with him to distribute it."

"I wouldn't hold your breath waiting on it," Miceal said.

"Thanks for the advice, genius." I wanted to slap him so damn bad. "I still can't get over the way Zetta played me. I thought she and I had something special."

"Hey, I told you from jump old girl was using that apartment for a fuck palace."

I leered at Razor. "Now you're wanting an ass-kicking for real, huh? You two keep it up and I'm either going to jack you up or end this friendship right fucking now."

Miceal slapped his knee. "Hey, Chico, it ain't that serious. We're going to always be your friends. No matter what, man. Fuck a Zetta Wolfe and fuck a job. If you aren't welcome there, I'm quitting first thing Monday morning.

I'm sick of smelling Donald's stench day in and day out anyway."

"Shit! Donald's ass won't be there on Monday, either," Razor said. He opened up his flip-top cell phone and started dialing.

"Who you calling?" I asked.

"That Mexican restaurant over on Third Street. I have a taste for some enchiladas."

I thought about the restaurants in the immediate area and couldn't recall a Mexican one. "Where's there a Mexican joint on Third Street?"

Miceal started laughing. "Man, he's talking about that white panel truck that's always parked over there by the school. They sell food out that bitch."

I had to chuckle myself. "Let me get this straight. You're ordering from a truck over the damn phone?"

"Hell yeah. That's some good shit."

"You better be careful what you eat, Razor. It'll fuck your stomach up."

"Look who's talking," he responded. "The man who lives off beer and bad wings."

"Hey, all wings aren't bad."

"No, but they're all bad for you."

"Damn, answer the phone!" Razor screamed into it. A few seconds later someone picked up and he placed an order. After he hung up, he said, "Want to go with us to pick it up? I ordered enough for all of us. We can eat on the playground at the school."

I waved him off. "Fool, I ain't going nowhere. I'm planting my ass right here."

"Whatever, man," Razor said. "Come on, Miceal."

I watched them walk down the sidewalk. "Don't forget your runt!"

• • •

Life is pitiful without cable. *Pitiful!* I sat there for two hours watching Christmas programs. The same damn ones that had been coming on since I was five. I could understand people wanting to relieve the past but what about the here and now?

I had just dozed off from complete boredom when I heard a horn blowing out front. I couldn't imagine who it could be. I pulled one of the drapes to the side and fell backwards, tripping over an end table when I recognized the car out front. It was Tomalis's Corvette. The one everyone knew about, had heard all the stories about, and knew better than to ever touch.

He was sitting in the driver's seat, staring at my front porch.

"Oh shit!" I exclaimed out loud and started pacing the floor. "He's come to kill me!"

Damn, why did I let Razor and Miceal leave? I needed them—and Brutus—to protect me. Momma wouldn't dream of having a gun in the house—even though I had encouraged her to get one in our neighborhood—so I was basically ass out.

I could have just pretended not to be there, but I wasn't a coward and wasn't planning on being one. I decided to break bad with him and hopefully scare his ass off.

I yanked the door open, stomped out on the porch and yelled, "What the hell do you want?"

He cut the engine off and opened the car door. *Shit, he wasn't going to leave!*

Once he'd gotten out, he leaned against the car. "Chico, I'd like to talk to you."

"About what?" I lashed out in the meanest voice I could come up with. "You had your little fun last night at my expense. What more do you want?"

He came walking toward me. I balled my hands into fists so I'd be ready if he tried to steal me one.

"Chico, this is going to sound really strange but . . ." He hesitated. "I came here to help you."

I relaxed my hands. "Say what?"

"I came here to help you." He came up on the porch and pointed at one of the wicker chairs. "May I?"

I exhaled, realizing he might not be there to do me bodily harm after all. "Sure, why not? Take a load off, Mr. Wolfe."

"You can just call me Tomalis. After all, we've both been intimate with the same woman."

I shook my head. "Mr. Wolfe, I—"

"Tomalis."

"Tomalis, I really do owe you an apology. Even though we've never formally met, until last night that is, I've always had the utmost respect for you. After all, you're a brother who came from nowhere and you're living every man's dream."

"Or every man's nightmare," he came back at me.

"I can't tell you how sorry I am. I know you must be in a mountain of pain, finding out so many people betrayed you."

He laughed. "I knew about their dirt all along. I knew Zetta fucked you right after she did it. Actually, before, because my driver Phil called me from the car while she was sucking your dick in the back seat."

My mouth fell open. I was stunned.

"Don't look so shocked. As you apparently realize now, Zetta's nothing but a sex machine. She has no morals. You were simply a pawn in her game. A boy toy and I don't blame you. At first, I did, but not any more."

"Seriously?" I asked.

"Seriously. Zetta's a sexy woman and she's learned to use

that attribute over the years to get whatever she wants. You're just now becoming a man and she took complete advantage of you. Ninety-nine percent of the men your age would've fucked my wife."

"So that's what you came here for? To tell me that you understand why I fucked your wife?"

"No, not really. I came here to make you a proposition. Hopefully one you can't refuse."

"A proposition?"

"Yes. Being that what happened wasn't your fault and being that I confronted you in front of everyone last night, I feel sorry for you. I'd like to help you out, if I could."

I shifted in my seat and then pinched my own arm to make sure I was awake. I felt the pain so it wasn't a dream.

"Mr. Wolfe, I mean Tomalis, I'm not quite sure I'm following you."

"Chico, I'd like to make you my apprentice."

"Come again?"

"I heard through the grapevine that you like building things."

"Yeah, yeah, I do." I suddenly grew excited. "I just finished making this dollhouse for my daughter."

"Oh really?" Tomalis said, moving up on the edge of his seat. "Where is it?"

"In the garage. I also made something else. Actually, it's a toy that I invented for my two-year-old daughter Gina. It will keep her entertained when her sorry ass mother is sitting on her behind watching soap operas all day."

Tomalis shook his head. "And they say men are lazy."

"They must not know McKenna."

"Or Zetta either."

We both laughed.

Tomalis started rubbing his chin. "Toys, huh? There

aren't any major African American players in the toy industry. Maybe we can make it happen."

"Get real, my man. Are you trying to fake me out?"

"Not at all. Granted, I haven't seen your device yet but if
the concept makes sense, design engineers can be hired to
flesh out the rest."

"Hold up!" I rose and started pacing the porch. "This shit
can't be real."

"Well, it is. That all takes time so how about you coming
on as my personal assistant at Wolfe Industries for the time
being?"

"You would hire me as *your personal assistant?*"

"Yes. I could start you at eighty a year plus incentives and
bonuses."

"Eighty as in eighty thousand?"

"That would be the one."

I felt weak in the knees. "Why would you do this?"

"I see part of you in myself. I found out today that my son
has no interest in the company. I plan to retire soon so I can
enjoy some downtime and travel for fun instead of for business. There are different types of freedoms, Chico. There's
financial freedom and then there's time freedom. I have the
first but time is more valuable and I can never get it back." He
paused for a moment and said, "This is my day for playing
Santa Claus."

"What do you mean?"

"I have this housekeeper, Marguerite, who's had a really
troubled life. I wanted to do something extra special for her
so I fired her earlier today."

I was confused. "Firing her was nice of you."

"In a sense. I fired her from my home but I hired her for
my office. She's my new administrative assistant. Human Resources is going to have a fit because she doesn't have the de-

gree they require but I own the corporation so there's not a damn thing they can do about me hiring her. Nor can they do anything about me hiring you."

"But why me?" I asked, still not buying it. There had to be a catch.

"Why not you?"

"This entire thing is insane but if you're even halfway serious, then I'm down."

"So you can start on Monday."

"Monday's Christmas."

"Humph, you're right. Let's make it Wednesday then."

"Cool."

This shit was just too easy. Come hell or high water though I was going to see it through. If he turned out to be bullshittin' me, I'd just head over to that truck on Third Street and ask them if I could make tacos for them or hand out fliers. Anything to make a buck.

"See you bright and early Wednesday," Tomalis said as he walked back toward his Corvette.

"Um, Tomalis, can I ask a favor?" I was about to be bold but I didn't have jack shit to lose.

"Yes, what is it?"

"Can I get a little advance? I'd really like to make this Christmas special for my daughter."

Tomalis pulled a money clip out his pocket and pulled off five crisp hundred-dollar bills. He handed them to me. "Merry Christmas, Chico."

"Merry Christmas, Tomalis."

He got into his car. "Hey!" I yelled after him. "You want to go grab a bite to eat or something?" I held the money up. "My treat!"

He grinned at me. "Thanks but no thanks. I have to go find my best friend Barron."

"Is he all right?" I asked, remembering the dude from the night before and how he was cutting up something terrible before the drama even started.

"Barron's always all right. If he's going to check out, he's going to do it between a pair of creamy thighs."

"What do you mean, check out?"

Tomalis didn't answer me. He got into his Corvette and rolled out.

I decided to go peep the food from the truck on Third Street. As I was passing a group of prostitutes, three of them were dressed up in Mrs. Santa Claus lingerie.

"Want a date?" one of them asked me.

I pointed to them one at a time. "Hoe! Hoe! Hoe! Merry Christmas and hell no!"

They copped major attitudes but they couldn't faze me. Nothing would ever faze me again.

Christmas Eve the Following Year

Chico

Chico kept his date with Carrie from the mall. They ended up dating heavily but Chico refused to have sex with her until they knew each other well enough. Carrie was stunned because it was usually the woman who wanted to wait and the man that wanted to slap skins after the first date. During a dinner of pepperoni pizza, buffalo wings, and beer at a local pub, Chico asked Carrie to marry him. That was in June and they still hadn't had sex. They were married in August. Tomalis was the best man and Razor and Miceal were groomsmen. Tomalis also paid for the entire wedding, which had more than a thousand guests. Chico and Carrie invited everyone they knew and those people invited everyone they knew after they found out "the Tomalis Wolfe" was the best man and paying for the wedding. Carrie wore a Vera Wang gown, Chico's tuxedo cost more than three grand, and the wedding cost close to two hundred grand. Everyone had a grand time.

Chico and Carrie finally had sex during their honeymoon in the south of France. Chico gave in and got on a plane, despite the fact that he said he never would put his life in the hands of one man; alcoholic or not. Carrie was everything in bed that Chico had hoped for and once they started making love, they started having sex, and then they got down to the real fucking about two months into their marriage.

On Christmas Eve, Chico presented Carrie with a brand new Wolfe XJK 420, the first one off the factory floor and the first one he helped Tomalis design. It had everything imaginable in it including separate televisions for each passenger, a Playvision—a system not even on the market yet and the toy Chico had originally invented for Gina—and a wet bar with a working sink.

Carrie and Gina trimmed the tree in excitement. Chico had obtained custody from McKenna after Tomalis hired the best attorney in the world for him, and McKenna was so distraught that she decided to try to get back at Chico by messing around with Razor. Razor fucked McKenna but dumped her after two months because he said she didn't give good head. Razor finally landed Judy—who had been previously fucking Miceal—who was now fucking Shakia and about to start shacking up with her.

Carrie gave Chico her present at 11:59 P.M. on Christmas Eve. She handed him a silver baby spoon and told him that he was going to be a daddy. Chico cried and then they fucked.

Chico's mother spent Christmas Eve at the cemetery, visiting the grave of Chico's grandmother. Then she went to church and thanked the Lord for the complete turnaround in her son's life. She went back to the same home she had lived in for decades and refused to leave, even when Chico offered to purchase her a new one. She did enjoy watching the new sixty-one-inch television Chico had given her, though.

Anastasia

Anastasia spent Christmas Eve by herself. She had learned so much about herself and had extremely matured over the past year. Having spent Barron's final months on this earth with him, she finally realized the significance of living and the insignificance of having a lot of money to live off. In fact, after making sure Barron died with a smile on his face in May—on a nude beach as the sun set—she used the money he'd left her from being a Jack-of-All-Trades throughout his life to found a nonprofit organization called Barron's Gift. Barron's Gift guided youth who had been brainwashed into believing that they could never be somebody into believing they could be whatever they want to be.

Anastasia really concentrated on helping young girls who allowed men to define them and made them understand that they alone defined themselves. She wanted them to realize that spending time on bettering themselves and getting set in careers was more important than trying to land a man who would take care of them. Anastasia went on to win many awards, and much recognition was given to her from magazines and newspapers who jumped on the inspiring story of a young African American woman who went from being a part-time call girl to a full-time motivational speaker and organization head.

Anastasia felt her appearance was contradictory to the image she was trying to give the world so she had a breast reduction, switched to a short haircut reminiscent of Joan of Arc, and started dressing conservatively. Her mother didn't approve of the drastic change but Anastasia reminded her that she was grown and had to live her own life.

On Christmas Eve, she poured two glasses of sparkling cider—she had given up alcohol because of the effect it had on Barron's health—and toasted him. "Barron, I miss you, but I know one day we will see each other again. Until then, I plan to make you proud of me. No, I take that back. If you were here, you wouldn't want me to say that. Until then, I plan to make myself proud of me."

Anastasia drank both glasses of cider and climbed into bed alone.

Diana

Diana spent Christmas Eve with Edmund and the twins. She had agreed to allow Darren and Dean to fly to Atlanta the day after Christmas to spend their winter vacation with their father. Stephen still wanted to get into Diana's pants again but she made it clear that they would never sleep together again.

Stephen was distraught but moved on to a woman he met at a golf tournament for charity and decided to make her his third wife.

Edmund and Diana decided to continue to take it kind of slow; even though they were madly in love. Edmund realized that Diana needed time to heal and he needed time to learn to handle the damage that the pain she had been through had caused her.

They became engaged in early September but decided to have a long engagement—two years or more.

Bradford Haynes—Diana's former boss—had continually called Diana's office and home making threats or hanging up. Tomalis Wolfe had an investigation launched and Bradford was arrested. Tanaka from Prism Motors paid his bail and then promptly told him to go to hell. When last seen, Bradford was panhandling in front of the coffee shop across the street from Wolfe Industries. Donald Coleman—the former mail-room supervisor—was often standing right beside Bradford with a mug in his hand also. Bradford—still attractive even though downtrodden—got most of the handouts from the women and even a few quickies in a nearby alley. Passersby often just sneered at Donald and held their noses. One old lady—a regular customer at the coffee shop—showed up one afternoon with a bag full of toiletries for Donald and told him to go wash his ass and brush his teeth.

Tomalis

After sending both Zetta and Zora back to the ghetto where they came from, Tomalis spent most of his time at the office inventing things like he did in the beginning. He grew to adore Chico and they often came up with ideas together, including the design for the Wolfe XJK 420. In his spare time, he hung out with Barron until he fell too ill to be able to and then sat by his side night after night telling old stories in laughter.

When Barron died, Tomalis was devastated, but Chico, his children—including Heather who moved back to the D.C. area and transferred to a local medical school after she found out she would not have to deal with her mother—and Marguerite—Tomalis's new administrative assistant and his new love—helped to comfort him.

Zetta showed up at the wake but Tomalis had her tossed out, realizing that is was just a ploy to try to get back into his good graces.

Jonah decided to get his life together—even though he didn't know if Tomalis was his biological father for sure—went to college, majored in political science, and became a translator for the United Nations. It had been many years since someone had blamed a pregnancy on him and he planned to keep it that way by always carrying a twelve-pack of condoms with him.

Zetta and her mother Zora became the first mother-daughter act at Uranus. Zetta's tips were decent—since she had decades of experience making dicks hard—but Zora's were horrid.

Both of them eventually turned to prostitution on the side and they spent Christmas Eve at an orgy thrown by a hundred-ninety-year-old white man in Potomac and his friends.

Tomalis spent Christmas Eve with Marguerite. While Marguerite didn't think she was good enough for Tomalis, he felt differently and tried to convince her of that on a daily basis. His divorce had recently gone through—after a long, nasty battle that netted Zetta zero—and he didn't want to rush into another marriage. However, he felt strongly for both Marguerite and her son Fernando. Wolfe Industries went on to become the largest automobile manufacturer in the world and Tomalis became a multibillionaire.

Merry Christmas from Zane

Bonus Section

CHRISTMAS PRESENTS FROM ZANE

I hope that you enjoyed *Skyscraper*. I truly enjoyed penning a Christmas book—even though it is not the traditional kind about people engaged in a joyous celebration. That is just not my cup of tea. I am a little on the wilder side. With that in mind, I wanted to do something special for my readers so I have four presents for you. Use them sparingly because I do not want any one ending up in traction or having a baby they were not planning to have. With that in mind, I must also say that while I write about wild sexual experiences, I do not promote promiscuity—which you will understand once you read my last story. This is all in fun and I cannot stress enough the importance of practicing safe sex and getting to know your sexual partners first. If you do find that special person—and you have both been tested—then I hope you have a whole lot of fun together. Sex should never be about pressure, about pleasing someone else without gaining pleasure yourself, or about keeping up with what your friends are doing. This is not meant as a lecture, but if nothing else, I always keep it real.

Merry Christmas everyone and look for *Chocolate Flava: The Eroticanoir.com Anthology* in January 2004. It is the perfect companion to put sparks in your Valentine's Day.

Peace and Much Love,
Zane

Present #1

Wanna spice up your sex life? Wanna turn your mate the hell out? Then stop doing the same things in the bed all the time and get creative. I often get requests—from both men and women—wanting to know how they can enhance their sex lives. So, here is my rendition of the ABC's.

ASSUME THE POSITION. This is fairly simple and has different variations. You handcuff or tie your partner's hands to the headboard, or if you prefer, you can tie them behind their back. They are at your mercy and you can have your way with them all night long. If you live in a basement apartment with pipes on the ceiling or have something else you can use, you can tie them up to the ceiling while they are standing. This is great with the woman tied up because you can fuck her while she is standing or you can lift her up on your shoulders and eat her pussy.

BELLY BUTTON SHOTS. Pour tequila into your mate's belly button and lick the right side of his/her chest and shake some salt on it. Squeeze some lemon or lime juice on the left side of his/her chest and then lick the salt and make your way down to the belly button with your tongue so you can lap up the tequila. Then, trace a trail back up to the lemon or lime juice with your tongue and lick it off. Repeat on each other until you can no longer refrain from jumping each other's bones.

CUM FOR ME, BOO. Resort to drastic measures and whip out the sex toys to see how many times you can make each other cum in the span of one evening. Whoever makes the other person cum the most wins the bet and gets pampered and waited on for an entire weekend or whatever else you may want to wager. This can be very delightful, especially if both partners have an oral fixation.

DO NOT DISTURB. Spend an entire weekend in a hotel room with the DO NOT DISTURB sign on the door. Take snacks and plenty of water for hydration purposes and fuck the hell out each other until neither one of you can barely walk. It may sound harsh but you can't knock it until you try it.

EROTIC ENDEAVORS. Both you and your partner make a list of your sexual fantasies you want to play out. Trade lists and then set a deadline to make all of each other's fantasies come true.

THE FEAST. Zane's variation of cleaning out the fridge. Instead of throwing away all the half-empty bottles of this or that lurking in your fridge, take a blanket and place it on the floor (so your asses won't get cold) by the open fridge door and get down on the blanket butt naked. One at a time, take turns selecting items from the fridge to eat off each other. If you are one of those people who eats out every night because of a busy schedule and has an empty fridge, pick up a couple of items such as whipped cream, chocolate syrup, and cake frosting (yes, I said cake frosting) on your way home and satisfy your sweet tooth.

THE GAME. Break out all the old favorites like Monopoly, Scrabble, checkers, Chutes and Ladders if you are a bit slow, or chess if you got it like that and play. You can even play charades. Whatever game you choose, whoever loses has to become the "sex slave" of the winner and do "everything" they demand.

HAPPY BIRTHDAY. Throw your mate a private birthday party when it is not anywhere near their birthday. Take them totally off guard, order a birthday cake, buy them presents that are all sexual in nature such as lingerie, sex toys, and edible underwear, and watch their face light up when you take them by surprise.

INDECENT PROPOSAL. This is a variation of truth and dare but truth's ass is out of town. Dare your mate to do something outrageous sexually. Something you know their ass thinks they are too prim and proper to do. This game only works if both partners are willing to let go of all sexual inhibitions.

JUST DO IT. Meet your mate at the door one day and cut the bullshit. Like Nike says, "Just do it!" Oftentimes, people dream about fucking all day and then tense up when the time comes to put up or shut up. They wait for their partner to make the first move. Fuck all that! Go for yours and break the world record for getting naked in the least amount of seconds. Better yet, answer the door butt naked.

THE KINKY GAME. Sit down together and compile a list of kinky things you both want to try such as S & M, using Ben Wa balls, butt plugs, anal beads, dildos, whatever and make out a schedule for the week. If you are not quite there yet, make out a list of unusual positions you want to try. No matter what, stick to the schedule and do a different thing every single night for an entire week.

LIFE IMITATES ART. Very simple! Watch some movies, preferably pornos but some R-rated movies have vivid sex scenes as well. Pick out some of your favorite scenes from movies and act them out with your partner. If you really want to get jiggy with it, break out the camera and make your own carbon copy of the original film.

MOTHER MAY I. Enough said. Play Mother May I in the bedroom and you can't do a damn thing without getting permission first. Okay, so I still have a little girl lurking in me.

NAKED TWISTER. It doesn't get any easier to explain than this. Hit up a toy store and buy the old-time favorite kids game, Twister. Take it home, get butt naked with your mate, pop in Cooley High or Shaft, make a pitcher of Kool-Aid and play the game. Of course, being naked gives it an interesting "twist" (no pun intended).

OPEN HOUSE. This can be done one of two ways. If you live in an area where kids go to bed at a decent hour, open up all your curtains, shades, and blinds late one night, turn on all the lights and freak the hell out of each other. I know it sounds silly but the mere thought that someone "might" be watching can be a fantastic turn-on. The other way it can be done is to fuck each other in a house full of people while taking the risk that someone might walk in on you. This can be very exhilarating at holiday dinners where some old-fashioned relatives might catch you getting busy.

PUBLIC DISPLAY. Now, you have to be very sexually open to do this shit but, hey, I am so I can recommend this shit. Fuck your mate in a public place such as on a subway train, city bus, or even airplane. Go to the movies and buy some nachos. Take the warm cheese spread and pour it on your mate's dick or pussy and perform oral sex in the theater and then fuck them. Go to a fancy restaurant and disappear under the linen tablecloth and have oral sex. Fuck in elevators, in public restrooms, on a picnic table, in the laundry room, in the stacks at the library. Let me quit cause my ass is getting excited just thinking about it.

Q & A. One of my favorites, 'cause no one likes a dumb-ass person in their bed. It is a trivia game. In fact, you can play an actual game if you like such as Trivial Pursuit. Tell your mate that they have to get a certain amount of answers right or they can't get none that night. You can even watch *Jeopardy* or *Wheel of Fortune* and play this, or if you have been with your mate a considerable amount of time, ask them questions about you that they should know the answer to. This game can be fun, especially when your mate is feenin for some sex and you make them earn it.

THE RECYCLED VIRGIN. Both you and your partner take turns pretending you are virgins. You take one night of the week and they can take the next one. Have your partner walk you through it and calm your "imaginary" fears by giving you step-by-step instructions. You can act shy and timid and keep pushing them away when they get to certain "bases" and it can be interesting to see how long you can pretend not to know a damn thing. I mean how many "experienced" people can just lie there when they are getting fucked royally?

THE SPELLING BEE. Umm, another favorite. For the men, spell out the alphabet on your woman's clit and even spell out her name. For the ladies, do the same with the dick and/or balls. You can blindfold your partner or have them close their eyes while you spell out something and they have to try to guess the word. You have to have some major tongue skills in order to pull this one off though because I don't think they sell *Hooked on Phonics* for oral sex.

TALK DIRTY TO ME. Phone-sex the hell out of each other, pure and simple. If you have a cell phone, call your mate from the car and have phone sex with them on the way home so that by the time you get there, it will be time to set it off and I don't mean robbing banks like in the movie. Unless, of course, you are talking about robbing cum banks.

UNDER NO CIRCUMSTANCES. You have to love this one and it is a game of mind over matter. It also requires a hell of a lot of willpower. Without tying your partners' hands or confining them in any way, tell them that they cannot touch you no matter what you do to them. That means you mean can't touch a woman if she does a lap dance or even if she sucks your dick. Same goes for the women. No touching whatsoever or you will have to pay the penalty. My suggested penalty is that you must perform oral sex on your mate for twelve hours straight if you fuck up.

VISION QUEST. Bet your partner something sexual in nature and then go outside. Pick a certain item such as a red canary or a squirrel or a butterfly. Whoever is the first one to spot the object and, yes, it must be verified by the other party to prevent cheating, wins the game. If you really want to get creative, play that old favorite, "Cars," and pick a certain make or model of vehicle beforehand. Whoever's turn it is when that type of car drives by is declared the winner.

WHAT FLAVOR IS IT? Go to a sex shop and purchase different flavors of body oils. If you happen to live in a small-ass town where the local Wal-Mart is the closest thing to a sex shop, go to the cosmetics section and get some different flavors of lip gloss. This game works better with the woman as the test subject. Place a different flavor on each part of your body. Your lips, your neck, each breast, your belly button, the inside of each thigh, and your clit. Your man has to lick each spot in turn and guess the flavor correctly or no "nookie." Hmm, I wonder what flavor works best on a clit. Cherry maybe; get it?

XTRA NAKED. Cover the bed or floor with an old blanket or something you don't mind messing up and then get naked. Cover each other with baby oil from head to toe so that you are both very slippery and then fuck. It will be hard to even hold on to each other and private parts will be slipping and sliding everywhere but it is mad funny.

YOU DO ME. Mutual masturbation. Get each other off. Or, for those who have a dildo hanging around, men can fuck their women with a dildo until they cum. Whatever's clever!

THE ZANE. The Zane means talking all of my suggestions for sex games and playing each and every one of them in the span of two months. I wonder how many of you can do it 'cause that means fucking *every night*. If you decide to take the "Zane Challenge," email me at zane@eroticanoir.com and let me know the results.

Present #2

A lot of you may be wondering what the perfect gift would be for your lover. Below are a few of my suggestions—from nice to naughty.

1. one dozen chocolate roses
2. body tea
3. bubble bath in wine bottles
4. home spa kit
5. jigsaw puzzle made from a picture of the two of you together
6. talking picture frame that says "I love you"
7. erotic story written by you
8. chocolate tattoo paint kit
9. striptease instructional video
10. French maid costume

11. coupon booklet for free sexual favors
12. flavored nipple drops
13. flavored massage oil
14. scented candles
15. sexy lingerie
16. body glitter
17. bondage kit
18. erotic massage book/tape
19. furry handcuffs
20. edible panties or briefs
21. vibrator
22. sex swing
23. glow-in-the-dark body paint
24. liquid latex
25. bull ring
26. double-headed dildo
27. French tickler
28. anal beads
29. penis pump
30. gift certificate to a spa
31. sexually explicit personalized license plate
32. matching key rings with your initials on them
33. gourmet cookbook
34. blindfold
35. *The Sex Chronicles: Shattering the Myth,* by Zane
36. *Gettin' Buck Wild: Sex Chronicles,* by Zane
37. huge smile
38. hug
39. foot massage
40. your everlasting love

Present #3

AN EROTIC STORY

Tattoo—Zane

I still don't know what drew me to Chinatown that night, other than complete boredom. Marques and I had been broken up for a little over two weeks and he had yet to call. Not only was I offended, my feelings were genuinely hurt. I'd expected him to come groveling back to me just as he had the previous times we'd parted ways out of anger. *How dare he change the rules on me without asking my permission?*

Marques and I had been going strong, on and off, for more than two years, ever since I'd moved to Washington, D.C., from Dover, Delaware. D.C. was fast paced, but you never would have known it from my lifestyle. Other than the occasional dinner and movie, Marques never took me out anywhere. He just came over, did his business, rolled over, and fell asleep before I was even warmed up. Looking back at it now, I wonder why I even cared that he hadn't called to make up. All of my girlfriends had tried to convince me that he wasn't about anything but sex. It took meeting someone else to finally drive the point home.

That evening, I decided I was through with sitting around the house like an idiot. I sat down at my dining room table and made a list of all the sites and attractions I planned to take in by the end of the coming summer. There was the National Gallery of Art, the Museum of Natural History, the Museum of American History, the National Museum of African Art, and tons of other museums I had yet to step foot in. There was the National Zoo, the Lincoln Memorial, the Jefferson Memorial, the Washington Monument—the list went on and on. The more I added to the list, the more ashamed I was about never having experienced those places.

After I finished my list, I caught a glimpse on the six o'clock news of the Chinese New Year parade going on in Chinatown. America at large had gotten through the new millennium without a glitch or act of terrorism, and now at the beginning of February they were bringing in the Chinese New Year in style.

People looked like they were having so much fun that, by the time the reporter said, "Back to you at the studio," I had jumped up off my sofa, run into my bedroom to slip into a pair of jeans and a gray wool sweater, pinned my hair up, grabbed my waist pouch, and headed for the door. Enough was enough. No more sitting around the crib watching women fight over trifling men on *Jerry Springer*.

I drove my car to the Shaw Metro Station and then hopped a train down to Chinatown. The reporter had griped about the parking situation, and I wasn't taking any chances. It was bad enough sitting in work traffic—I didn't need the stress at night to boot.

Surprisingly, the train was pretty empty. There were only two other people in the car with me: a couple who were obviously in love, lust, or both. I watched them making out from the corner of my eye and got the feeling they knew I was into it. They didn't seem to mind my voyeurism, so I just went with the flow. They slowed their roll when an elderly woman climbed on at Union Station. She looked like everybody's grandmother, and the expression on her face clearly objected to their behavior. By the time she had actually taken a seat, they had stopped all the fondling and kissing and were idly chatting about the club they were headed to.

I got off in Chinatown; the music was blaring even before the train doors completely opened. I could hear people laughing and partying as I made my way up the escalator to the exit. A group of teenagers passed me carrying balloons and sparklers, and eating something that smelled damn delicious. My stomach immediately started growling. I had neglected to eat the microwave dinner I'd nuked before the news came on.

The parade was still in full swing as I made my way through the thick crowd on Sixth Street. The Chinese lanterns people toted around on poles, native apparel, and floats were spectacular. Being that I didn't know a lick of Chinese, I couldn't understand the lyrics to the songs people were belting out at the top of their lungs. Still, I found myself swinging back and forth to the sound of the music. It was very soothing.

My stomach was still calling out, "Feed me, you witch!" Okay, so maybe that's a slight exaggeration, but if my stomach could talk, that's probably what it would have said. I walked inside a carry-out on the next block and ordered some shrimp lo mein. The carry-out was pretty deserted since most people were enjoying the parade, so I had my little white carton box and a pair of chopsticks within minutes. I wanted to ask for a fork, but I figured when in Rome, do as.

I bumped into two little boys on my way out, neither one of their heads as high as my shoulder. They had piles of T-shirts around their necks. "Hey lady, you want to buy a T-shirt?" one of them asked, holding up a poorly silk-screened white shirt with "Chinese New Year 2004" smeared across the front. "Only five dollars for you since you're so pretty."

They were adorable and I was flattered, but I was no fool. They had probably used that line on every woman they came across. "Are those shirts a hundred percent cotton?" They glared as if I'd asked the one-million-dollar question on *Who Wants to Be a Millionaire?* "What about preshrunk?"

"Look lady, do you want the shirt or not?" the other one asked sarcastically. "What do you expect for five bucks?"

"Something I can wear more than one time," I replied jokingly, yanking the Baltimore Orioles baseball cap up off his head and putting it back on so it covered his ears. "Keep your ears covered up. You don't want to catch a cold."

"Great!" He took the hat off and stuffed it in his jacket pocket. "Now she thinks she's our mother."

His friend cackled. "Let's get out of here before she tells us it's past our bedtime."

"Now that you mention it," I responded, glancing down at my wristwatch, "what time is bedtime?" They looked at each other, rolled their eyes, and started speaking to each other in Chinese. "Hey, that's not fair," I complained. "I don't know what you're saying."

"Exactly," one of the smart alecks replied. They exchanged high fives, laughed, and walked away.

"Fine then!" I yelled out after them, my childish side

emerging. "Whatever you said about me, goes right back to you!"

I noticed an older man looking at me like I had lost my senses. I grinned at him and he flashed a toothless grin back. I decided to push through the crowd a little so I could get a good look at the parade.

I was used to forcing my way through crowds. My parents had started taking me to Mardi Gras when I was about ten. Sitting on my daddy's shoulders and screaming, "Throw me something, Mister!" had been the highlight of my youth.

I was standing there reminiscing about the good old days when the loud banging of approaching drums broke me out of my trance. A group of young men, maybe thirty or forty of them, were beating the hell out of large drums strapped to their chests. I started shaking my ass to the beat. It was like being at a Howard/Grambling State football game at half time.

I had just struggled to pick up some lo mein noodles with the chopsticks, still gyrating my hips, when I saw him. No, scratch that! I saw *him*.

Now don't get me wrong. I have never had anything against men of other races. I had just never been attracted to them. I have always loved the brothas and bought into that whole "the darker the berry, the sweeter the juice" mentality. That is, until I saw *him*.

He was coming my way, beating a drum, and had the strongest, biggest, prettiest damn body I had ever seen. If Mother Nature made anything better, she'd kept it for her damn self. He was about five-foot-eleven, the color of sand, smooth as satin, and had the most beautiful smile. I could see it a hundred yards away.

I sucked in some air and the noodle that had been dangling from my mouth went down my windpipe. I started coughing, about to choke, when someone slapped me on my back, dislodging the noodle. I turned around and whispered, "Thank you," to the petite Asian woman standing behind me. She threw her hand up and said, "No problem."

I turned back to face the street. He was less than twenty feet away from me. *Damn! Damn! Damn!* He was so fine, he looked like the words "F-U-C-K M-E" spelled out.

I have never been one to throw myself at a man, but I knew right then, at that very second, that I was going to get some of that by the end of the night. No matter what. I forgot all about Marques, and trust me, that is saying something, because he had been weighing heavily on my mind.

When Mr. Fine walked past me, I whiffed the air and it smelled like heaven. Even his cologne was all that, a bag of chips, a Popeye's three-piece, and a pack of Bubblicious. I wasn't sure but I thought he was grinning at me. One thing is for sure; I was grinning at him.

I pushed my way along the side of the street, trying to keep up with him. I tossed my food carton into the first garbage can I ran across. People were getting upset with me because I was obstructing their view. One lady pushed me off the sidewalk. I stopped long enough to give her a tongue-lashing. I was about to get into a full-blown altercation when a police officer told me to move it along and get back onto the sidewalk.

I caught up to the pack of drummers, but I didn't see Mr. Fine anywhere. I threw my hands on my hips and yelled, "Shit!" to no one in particular. I started sulking away, with my shoulders drooped in disappointment, ready to go home, crawl into the bed, and dream about what I'd missed out on when something compelled me to turn around. I saw a group of young men headed down an alley. Mr. Fine was one of them. Even in the dark shadows, I could make out the outline of that finely sculpted body anywhere.

I paused, albeit briefly, to contemplate whether or not I had any business going down a dark alley in pursuit of possible dick action. I didn't need to. I needed to take my ass home and be a good girl, but I inched my way down the alley anyway. I had lost visual contact of them but I could still hear their voices.

Something huge scurried across my black leather boots as I passed a trash Dumpster; I shuddered to think about what it might have been. For those of you who don't know, D.C. is famous for cat-size rats. Once I saw one sitting up in a chair chomping on a wedge of cheese bigger than a cantaloupe at a diner down in Adams Morgan. Needless to say, my date and I didn't eat there. We hauled ass.

I got to a curve in the alley and noticed there was a neon light up ahead, some sort of storefront. When I got closer, I realized it was a tattoo parlor. *Cool,* I thought to myself. I had always wanted to experiment with tattoos. I was nervous as hell about going in there, following a group of men into such a place. What if they were some sort of gang or something? I immediately decided that was a ridiculous assumption. Whenever nonblacks see us grouped together, they tend to think the same thing. I wasn't even going to fall into that mentality. I peeped in the window. There were six of them, sitting around drinking beer and laughing.

I walked in, surveyed the place in a matter of seconds and came to the quick conclusion that I liked the joint. It had character. The men grew silent when I came in. All eyes were on me.

"Ahem." I cleared my throat. "Does anyone here speak English?" I directed this question to Mr. Fine himself. They all guffawed.

He was sitting on a stool but stood up and walked toward me. *Damn!* "This is America," he chuckled. "Of course we speak English."

His accent immediately turned me on. "I-I-I was just wondering," I stuttered. "Just making sure before I started carrying on a conversation with myself and looking like an idiot."

He grinned at me. "You could never look like an idiot. You're beautiful." He glanced around at his friends, who physically expressed their approval of his obvious come-on. *Getting the dick was going to be easier than I thought.* "Can I help you with something?"

"I'm just checking things out," I replied, walking deeper into the store. There were photos all over the walls of various body parts sporting tattoos. "I was considering getting a tattoo. Which one of you is the artist?"

"We all are," a shorter one responded, getting up from a tattered leather armchair just long enough to grab another beer from the small refrigerator against the back wall. "I have a feeling you want Chen to help you out, though."

Mr. Fine had a name. Chen. The name was music to my ears. I walked up closer to him, just enough for my nipples to brush his forearm. "So, Chen," I whispered in his ear. "You think you can get rid of the rest of the crew?"

He blushed, flashing a beautiful set of teeth. I could only imagine the pleasure a mouth like that could bring to a woman's body. "You want to be alone with me, huh?"

I made eye contact, taking his hand and entwining our fingers. "Well, the place I was thinking about getting a tattoo is kind of personal. I wanted to show it to you first and get your opinion. You know, let you decide what type of tattoo you think is best for me."

He didn't hesitate for a second. "Lann, Bruce, and the

rest of you. Why don't you all go on back out to the parade? I'll catch up to you later."

"Good idea," I said, delighted. I stood on my tiptoes and kissed him gently on the cheek. "I wish I had thought of it myself."

They all made their way to the door, grabbing some extra beers, and saying things in Chinese to each other and to Chen. I wondered what they were saying, but I know men are men. They were probably saying things like, "Fuck the shit out of her!" "Damn, your ass is lucky!" and "Wish it was me!"

Chen closed and locked the door after them and pulled the metal blinds down. There we were, alone. Just me and Mr. Fine. Less than twenty minutes from the first spotting out on the street. That was definitely a record.

"So where are you originally from?" I asked. "I noticed your accent."

"Beijing." He licked his lips and my panties got wet. "I've been here for ten years."

"How old are you?"

"Twenty-eight. And you?"

"I'm twenty-six." I slapped my forehead in dismay. "I'm straight up trippin'. I haven't even told you my name." I reached out my hand to shake his. "I'm Jolene."

"Nice to meet you, Jolene." He went over to the leather-covered table in the middle of the room and switched on a bright lamp. "So what did you want to show me?"

Part of me wanted to run for the train like those people at the end of *Rosewood* when he turned that blinding-ass lamp on. I wasn't used to feeling so *exposed*. But it was no time to start frontin'. I came there for some hellified sex and I wasn't leaving without it.

"I want to show you everything." Slowly and seductively I

unbuttoned my sweater, letting it fall gracefully off my shoulders and tumble onto the floor. "But we can start with these right here."

His eyes ballooned as I unfastened the front clasp of my demi-bra and let my breasts, hardened nipples and all, escape from their cotton prison.

"Very nice!" He made his way over to me from the door, reaching out his hands for my breasts before he even got there. He palmed them gently and I moaned. "Very, very nice!"

"Do you think a tattoo would look good on one of them?" I asked, continuing to pretend I was actually there for cosmetic purposes. We both knew the real deal. "I mean, does it hurt when you tattoo breasts? I'm not real big on pain."

"Not if I take my time." He let go of my left breast and rubbed my nipple between his thumb and forefinger. "I think a red rose would look lovely on you."

Our eyes met again. I pulled his head down to mine and slipped him the tongue. His was thick and warm, just like I like them. I ran my fingers through his fine, straight hair. Deeper and deeper, his tongue delved into my mouth until no more could fit in. I sucked on his tongue and drew his bottom lip into my mouth, gently nibbling on it when we came up for air.

He kissed me on the forehead and put his arms around my waist, moving one down to fondle my ass. "Of course, the rose might look better someplace else."

"Oh yeah?" I started my own exploration of his body, pulling his blue sweatshirt up over his chest and off. "Where might that be?"

"Right down here," he answered, patting an ass cheek. "Let me see your ass."

I was more than happy to oblige. I stepped out of my

boots and unzipped my jeans. "You sure no one is coming back in here?"

"This is my shop." Chen helped me get my jeans down over my hips; I guess I wasn't moving fast enough for him. "I let some of my buddies do work out of here from time to time, but I'm the only one with a key."

"Cool!" We got my jeans off and I was about to start on my panties when he ripped the suckers clear off. "Damn, baby! It's like that, huh?"

He chortled. "I know what I want when I want it. Why waste time on bullshit?"

It was obviously time to throw any remaining inhibitions out the window. Mr. Fine meant business. A phrase from *Midnight in the Garden of Good and Evil* came to mind: "Two tears in a bucket. Motherfuck it."

I swung him around, though he outweighed me two to one, and slammed him down on the leather table. I climbed on top of him and ran the tip of my tongue from the crest of his chin down his neck, over his chest, licking a trail down to his belly button. He had a tattoo of a woman over his heart; I was immediately jealous. "Who's that?" I asked with disdain, poking my finger into her eyeball. "Don't tell me you're married? Got a sistah up in here all ass out and everything."

He fell out laughing. "No, that's my mother," he answered, taking my finger off his chest and placing it in his mouth. He sucked my fingers one at a time, and I knew he had me then. Finger sucking is one of my weaknesses.

"Does your mother live here in D.C.?"

A frown overshadowed his face. "No, she died a long time ago. Before I moved here with my father."

"I'm sorry. I didn't mean to spoil the mood."

"That's okay." Chen grabbed both sides of my head and pulled my face to him. "Come here, Jolene."

We kissed for a few more minutes, feeling each other up and getting to know each other intimately. He was very gentle, and I could tell he intended to make whatever the hell was happening between us more than a one-night stand.

He flipped me over on my back, ground his dick in between my legs and then got up from the table. I marveled at his physique as he took off his jeans. He was holding quite a surprise between his legs: He was much larger than I'd expected. *Bonus!*

He went in the back of the store through a hanging, beaded curtain and emerged a few seconds later holding a small satin box. "What's that?" I asked, my curiosity piqued.

He opened the box, revealing two small paisley-printed balls about the size of jawbreakers. "These are Ben Wa balls. Ever heard of them?"

"Aren't those used for exercising your hands and relieving stress?"

He grinned from ear to ear. "Among other things."

"Like?"

"Spread your legs, Jolene." I didn't know why I was letting this complete stranger dominate my every move, but I was spread-eagled in seconds. "Watch this." He seductively licked one of the balls and then pressed it slowly into my pussy. I jerked when I felt the cool metal enter me. "How does it feel?"

"Strange," I replied. "And the purpose of this exercise is?"

He didn't respond. He just spread my legs wider, licked the other one and then pressed it up my anus. Then he leaned over and starting licking the lips of my pussy. He lapped them up and down and then allowed his tongue to invade my sugary walls. It was the most erotic experience. I could actually feel the ball moving around inside me while he bounced it up and down with the tip of his tongue.

Someone started making these growling noises and I thought a rabid dog was outside the door. Then I realized it was me screaming out in delight. *Fugg a Marques!* Chen and I were into some of the *HBO Real Sex* shit now!

He ate me out for a good twenty minutes until I decided it was time to reciprocate. When it comes to making love, reciprocity is everything. "I want to taste you," I told him.

"You want to suck my cock?" he asked, lifting his head up from between my legs so he could look me in the eye.

"I'm a sistah. I don't suck cock," I giggled. "I suck dick."

We both laughed. He stood up and I got off the table just long enough to push him down on it and mount him in the sixty-nine position. The balls inside me were making me feel weird but it was a nice kind of strangeness.

I sat on his face and he commenced eating his meal again while I took the head of his dick into my mouth, suckled some of the pre-cum out of it and started humming on it. He moaned, and I contracted my cheeks on it tighter, withdrawing some more. I took his balls into one hand and rubbed the shaft of his dick with the other.

He grabbed onto my ass cheeks, spread them open and slipped the tip of his tongue in my anus, another one of my weaknesses. I licked his dick like an ice cream cone and slipped a finger into his anus, moving it in and out.

Come was trickling down the inside of my thighs as he moved his mouth back to my pussy and sucked on my clit. I could feel the ball vibrating inside my pussy, and the one in my ass popped out when I came. I heard it hit the floor somewhere under the table.

I couldn't help but laugh. Chen didn't say a word. He just kept handling his business. I took the head of his dick back into my mouth and moved my mouth up and down on it, taking more and more in each time. I deep-throated him for a good ten minutes, being that's my specialty. He was about to come. I stopped abruptly.

I got off him. "No, I don't want you to come yet."

"Damn, baby," he complained. "I was just about to bust a nut."

"No nut busting allowed," I replied, going over to the armchair and climbing on it, my knees in the seat, facing the wall. "Not until you hit this."

"Hit it, huh?" He got up off the table and walked up behind me. He had to bend his knees a little to get inside me from behind but it was the bomb diggity when he did. "I'll hit it all right."

I pushed my backside out to meet his thrusts and he moved his dick in and out of my pussy with a vengeance. "Damn Chen, when's the last time you had sex?" I couldn't help but wonder.

He didn't answer. He just fucked me, pulling me by the hair and yanking the pin out of it until it was free-flowing over my shoulders. I arched my back and ground my pussy hard onto his dick.

"I love the color of your skin," he commented, leaning over to bite my shoulder. "You have to let me tattoo you for real some day."

I was speechless. I couldn't even breathe. I had never been fucked so royally. I could see our shadows on the wall, moving back and forth; it was so erotic. He stuck a finger in my ass and moved it around and I started coming all over again.

That must have motivated him, because he started fucking me even harder. He was moving in and out so fast that his balls were slapping up against the back of my thighs.

I reached my hand over my head and grabbed the back of his neck. "Aw shit yeah!"

We went at it for a few more minutes before he suddenly pulled his dick out and came all over my ass cheeks. I turned around, plopped down in the chair exhausted, and then pulled him toward me by the hips, drawing his dick into my mouth so I could savor the last drops.

We sat and talked for a couple of hours after that, getting to know each other. The parade had long since ended; it was well after midnight. In the morning, we started going at it again. He spread my legs over the armrests of the chair and knocked the bottom out of my pussy. I was whipped when I got back to my apartment around noon the next day.

The phone rang. The caller ID showed Marques's number; I didn't pick it up. As far as I was concerned, he couldn't do a damn thing for me. Chen and I had made plans to see each other again that night. This time, we were going out on a *real* date.

He picked me up promptly at seven and I took him to a soul food restaurant. It was his first experience with ham hocks and collard greens, and he loved it. He couldn't get enough of the homemade apple cobbler either.

We've been together six months now and I've never had more fun. His father is mad cool and I'm taking him home to Delaware to meet my folks next weekend. We have hit just about every place I wrote down on my list the night I met him. I finally found a man that likes to get out of the house.

It's funny how things happen when you least expect it.

I guess you're wondering if I ever got that tattoo. Yes and no. I didn't get the rose but I did get Chen. His face is engraved on my left ass cheek.

Present #4

I wanted to end this book with a story that I wrote a few years ago as my Christmas present to a lot of my family and friends. It is a story that I feel reflects the true meaning of Christmas—something we often forget. I hope you enjoy and—more importantly—I hope you understand it.

I'll Be Home for Christmas—Zane

Everything looked the same. The house looked like it had a fresh coat of paint but other than that, everything was the same. The same huge oak tree in the front yard. The same white picket fence. The same ceramic bird bath with a statue of a frog that squirted water out of its mouth. The same mailbox designed like a Washington Redskins helmet. Everything was the same. Everything but me.

"Miss, is this the right house?" the cab driver asked me. The scent of his aftershave mixed with the must from his leathery skin had invaded my nostrils the entire drive from Union Station and had me teetering on the brink of nausea.

"Yes, this is the right house," I hesitantly replied.

He tapped his right index finger on his meter. "That'll be fourteen-fifty."

I reached into my handbag and removed a twenty, handing it to him over the seat. "Keep the change."

"Thanks."

I didn't budge. I contemplated having him drive me right back to the train station so I could hop on the next train back to New York. I'd come so far though. So very, very far.

"Is something wrong, Miss?"

"No, but can you give me a moment?"

I could hear his lips smack together and our eyes met in the rearview mirror. His gray ones were narrowed with malice.

"I really need to get going," he said with disdain. "Today's Christmas and since I *have* to be out here, I might as well pick up as many fares as I can."

"I understand."

I pulled out a compact, fingered my hair, and messed with the mole on my left cheek. It wasn't there thirteen years ago. It wasn't there when I left.

The driver's pale skin was turning red. It was only a matter of time before the situation turned ugly, even with the five-dollar-plus tip I'd given him. I opened up the door, grabbed my garment bag off the seat beside me, and got out of the cab.

It wasn't a white Christmas, but it was an icy one. A rain storm had come through Washington, D.C., the night before and froze overnight. I stood there on the sidewalk, willing myself not to fall because the soles of my black leather booties were slippery, and stared at the house. My parents' house. My house.

The street was extraordinarily quiet. Most of the people were probably eating dinner or opening up presents. It was way too cold to be outside for any reason. I glanced next door and noticed that Mr. Walker had added at least four more cars to his automobile graveyard behind his house. My daddy used to argue with him endlessly about the cars. Mr. Walker could never seem to let one of his precious commodities be towed away. I shook my head. Some things never change.

"It's now or never, Noelle," I told myself aloud.

I marched up the front walk to the steps and froze in place. I thought I saw some movement behind the curtain in the living room. Maybe my eyes were playing tricks on me. What if they didn't still live there? What if a stranger opened the door? What if one of them had died? What if both of them had died? What if I were too late to make things right?

The thick mahogany door flew open and startled me. A little girl, about eight, stood there glaring at me. She was wearing a red sweatsuit with a snowman embroidered on the front. Her hair was long, black, and wavy. I recognized her. She was me twenty years earlier.

She recognized me, too. "I know who you are." She giggled.

I inched my way up the steps and dropped my bag into the antique rocking chair that Daddy used to sit in at dusk and read scriptures to me. "I know who you are, too," I told her.

"Oh yeah." She blushed and swung her hips from side to side. "Then who am I?"

"I don't exactly know your name, but I know your mommy's name."

"What's my mommy's name?"

"Hmm, is it Janet Jackson?" I said jokingly.

She threw her head back in laughter before replying, "Nope. She's a singer."

"You're right." I pretended to be stunned. "I'm getting everything mixed up. Now I know who your mommy is."

"Who?"

"She's Halle Berry."

She stomped her foot and rolled her eyes at me, grinning from ear to ear. "Halle Berry's an actress. My mommy ain't no actress. She's a school teacher."

"Aw, a school teacher." I cupped my right elbow with my left hand and rubbed my chin like I was deep in thought. "Let me see. If she's a school teacher, then she must be Carolyn Mitchell."

The little girl held her stomach and exposed an array of baby teeth, adult teeth, and teeth that were somewhere in between as she giggled. "Actually, her name is Carolyn Mitchell Smith."

"Carolyn Mitchell Smith," I repeated. So my baby sister was all grown up and married with a beautiful daughter. A school teacher no less. And there I was all alone.

"You're Aunt Noelle," she whispered, taking a step out onto the cold porch in her tight-covered feet. "I've seen your pictures."

I smiled. At least they still had some pictures of me around.

"No fair. You know my name, but I don't know yours."

"My name's Noelle, too," she announced proudly. "Mommy named me after you because she missed you so much."

I bit my bottom lip and fought back a tear. It was a mistake coming there. It was too late to turn back though.

"That's a very pretty name, Noelle," I told her.

"Of course you think it's pretty. It's yours."

I winked at her and she winked back.

She took two steps backward. "Aren't you gonna come in?"

My eyes began to water as I stepped into the house. I could make out the distinct odor of my mother's homemade corn-bread dressing with chicken giblet gravy. No one else was in sight, but the dining room table was decorated with ivory linen, fine china, and expensive silverware with a large red poinsettia as the centerpiece.

I looked down at my clone, who had taken my hand. "Where is everyone?"

"Grandma and Mommy are in the kitchen and Grandpa and Daddy are downstairs watching football."

She said Grandma and Grandpa! I was so elated. I wasn't too late to try to make amends with both of them.

She started dragging me down the hallway toward the rear of the house, but before we got halfway there, the door leading from the dining room to the kitchen swung open and my mother walked in carrying a turkey.

"Noelle, go tell your daddy and Grandpa to wash up for dinner," she said, without even looking up. "Why's it so cold in here? Did you have the door open, honey?"

I tried to respond but couldn't find any words. I just stared at my mother as she carefully placed the roasting pan on the table and removed the plaid oven mitts from her hands. She looked exactly the same except for a touch of gray around the edges of her long hair she had pushed behind her head in a bun. I wondered if time had caused her to turn gray or the stress of my disappearance.

My clone responded instead. "Grandma, I was letting Aunt Noelle in."

My mother must have then sensed my presence because she didn't look in our direction. She took a deep, restorative breath, clamped her eyes shut, and gripped the edge of the table with her fingers.

"Momma," I whispered.

Her lips were moving. I couldn't make out the words, but I could tell that she was praying. Then she opened her eyes and glanced at me. She looked like she was about to faint so I let go of Little Noelle's hand, and rushed to her side, catching her before she collapsed into a side chair.

"Momma, are you okay?"

She stood erect and started feeling all over me, pulling the black wool hat off my head and running her fingers through my hair, squeezing my cheeks, and gripping my shoulders. She smiled at me and I felt so relieved.

"You're real!" she squealed.

I laughed uncomfortably. "Yes, Momma, I'm real!"

She threw her palms into the air. "Thank you, Jesus! Thank you for bringing my baby home!"

"Momma, what are you doing?" I heard Carolyn yell out from the kitchen.

"Carolyn, get in here!" she yelled back.

Carolyn came into the dining room and fell back against the doorframe.

Little Noelle said, "Look who's here, Momma."

"Hello, Carolyn," I said hesitantly.

Carolyn didn't look too glad to see me. I guess that's why it didn't surprise me when Momma let me go, thinking Carolyn would embrace me, and she slapped me hard across the right cheek instead.

"How dare you?" she screamed at me. "How dare you do this to us?"

Momma jumped in between us and rubbed my cheek. She glared at Carolyn. "How dare you, Carolyn? How dare you hit Noelle after she's been gone all this time?"

I was the one that needed to sit down. I expected Momma to be angry. I expected Poppa to turn his back on me and not even speak; especially because of things that happened between us before I ran away. I didn't expect Carolyn, the baby sister that had looked up to me, to haul off and slap me.

"That's exactly why I hit her, Momma," Carolyn replied. "She left us, not giving a damn about anything or anybody but herself. Now she comes back here, after all these years, and expects a warm homecoming."

"I didn't expect my homecoming to be warm," I uttered. "I just needed to do this. I needed to come here and explain."

"Explain what?" Carolyn asked, taking a threatening stance. "Explain why you ran off with that no good Reno that you thought was the reincarnation of Casanova?"

Momma glanced at Little Noelle. "Carolyn, not in front of the child."

Carolyn looked at her daughter. "Noelle, go upstairs and watch television."

"I don't want to go upstairs," Little Noelle protested, typical of most children that want to be in grown folks' business.

"Get upstairs now!" Carolyn blared at her.

"You don't have to be mean to your daughter because of me, Carolyn," I said in my niece's defense as she ran up the stairs on the brink of tears.

"Don't even! Don't even try to come in here and tell me how to raise my child!"

"You're right, Carolyn. I apologize," I said, only halfway meaning the words but putting forth an effort to calm her down. "She is your child and it is none of my business."

She looked sated for a few seconds and then tore into me again. "So where's Casanova now?"

Momma objected. "Carolyn, leave Noelle alone about Reno. The important thing is that she's here and we can all be a family again."

"A family?" Carolyn asked incredulously. "Noelle ripped this family apart when she hauled ass out of here in the middle of the night thirteen years ago." She leered down her aquiline nose at me. "Thirteen years, Noelle! Thirteen damn years!"

"I would like to see Poppa now." I decided that trying to explain everything more than once would be too much for me to handle. I wanted my father there so I'd only have to go through with it once. "Is he downstairs?" I asked, already knowing the answer.

"I'll go get him!" Carolyn hissed at me, stomping out of the room.

Momma sat down next to me and took my hand. "Listen to me, baby. I don't want you to think that you have to make amends for anything. I'm just glad you're back." She leaned over and kissed me on the cheek. "I have missed you so much. We didn't know whether you were alive or dead. All these years have been hard on us, but the moment you walked through that door, everything got better. Everything's okay now."

I wanted to believe her. I really did, but I knew Poppa would feel differently. He came flying around the corner a moment later, with Carolyn and a handsome young man in tow. Obviously, Carolyn's husband.

He picked up the nearest piece of china he could find, a

saucer, and flung it up against the far wall. He didn't say a word, just stared at me. His bottom lip was quivering out of anger and he didn't even bother to catch a stream of saliva that escaped the side of his mouth, trickled down his chin, and onto the floor.

No one said anything. We all just waited for him to explode. He didn't. He just looked at my mother and said, "Teena, I'm sorry about the dish. I'll replace it." Then he walked away and stormed out the back door without even putting on a coat first.

My mother was in shock. Carolyn looked pleased. I picked my hat up off the table, put it on my head, and stood up. "Well, I guess that's it. He'll never forgive me, Momma. I have to go."

She grabbed my wrist. "Let me go talk to him. Please don't leave me again."

"Let her go, Momma," Carolyn said sarcastically. "That's what she's good at anyway. Running away at the first sign of trouble."

Momma tried to push me back down in the chair. "Noelle, just sit down and let me go talk to him."

I refused to sit, but I also refused to back down from my father again after Carolyn pointed out my predilection for running away from my problems. "No, Momma. I'll go talk to him and he *will* listen to me. He's going to listen this time, so help me."

I brushed up against Carolyn on my way to the hallway. She was trembling, she was so angry with me. I looked her in the eyes. "Carolyn, I know that I hurt you and I'm sorry. I know I let my baby sister down, but believe me when I say that I love you and I missed you every second of every day. It's just that once you make a mistake, it's hard to turn back. You just end up stacking one mistake on top of another until your life is in shambles and you're too ashamed to turn back. To let those who loved you see what you've become. I didn't come back here sooner because I was ashamed. I was ashamed that I left. I was ashamed of what happened to me once I did. I was ashamed of everything."

She looked moved, but still hissed at me when she asked, "So why come back now?"

I diverted my eyes to the floor. "Because something happened last week that made me realize how short life is and how important it is to tell people you love them. I had to come back here and tell all of you how much I love you."

I felt my mother at my back. "What happened, baby?" she asked.

I looked from her to Carolyn and then back at the floor. "Reno died."

I walked out of the dining room before they could react. Carolyn's husband was standing there with his mouth hanging open. I would just have to be formally introduced to him later. It was time to face the music. It was time to face my father.

He was out in his woodshed, chopping wood with nothing on but a flannel shirt, jeans, and a pair of worn Timberland boots. My daddy's six-foot-five frame towered over the tree stump as he placed a log over it and started slamming the ax down on it.

I stood in the doorway watching him for a few moments. He knew I was there, but paid me no attention. He was venting. He was just as muscular as I remembered, but his hairline was receding and his hair was made of salt and pepper.

He finished on the fourth log and I couldn't take it anymore. "Poppa, can I please talk to you?"

He didn't look at me when he answered, "I have nothing to say to you."

"Well, I have something to say to you and I won't go away until you listen to me." I walked closer to him and touched him on the shoulder, hoping he wouldn't swing around and slice the ax he was holding into my throat, accidentally or otherwise. He lowered it and tossed it on the ground. "I ran away thirteen years ago because you wouldn't listen to me. I won't run again."

He turned and glared at me, his sepia eyes boring a hole through me just like they used to. "You ran away because you were fast. You thought you knew everything when you didn't know anything at all."

"That was part of it, but—"

"But nothing! You thought that idiot boyfriend of yours was more important than your entire family. In the end, I guess he was since you left with him."

"Poppa, I left because I was ashamed," I readily admitted.

"Ashamed of what?" he asked snidely. "Ashamed of the fact that I wouldn't let you run the streets at all hours of the night? Ashamed that I wanted you to be a lady instead of a whore? Ashamed of what?"

I sat down on the tree stump, immediately feeling chips of wood clinging onto my wool jacket. "Ashamed of the fact that I was pregnant."

Poppa was stunned. He started pacing the ground. "Pregnant? Well, if you were pregnant, where's my grandchild? Is it a boy or a girl?"

He actually seemed pleased. "Poppa, did you hear what I said? I left because I was pregnant. The one thing you told me never to be. The one thing you told me was unforgivable."

"I heard you and I did say that, but you were fifteen and what's done is done. So where's my grandchild?"

Tears starting cascading down my cheeks and I couldn't hold back the sobs. He knelt down and grabbed the back of my head, pressing my face into his shoulder. His strong hands around me gave me instant comfort. I had missed them so much.

"Noelle, tell me what's wrong?"

I threw my arms around his shoulders and whispered, "I lost the baby. Reno and I ran away to New York, thinking we could make a go of it, thinking we could find work and a home and be together. Reno tried to do the right thing by me, Poppa. He wasn't like other boys that claim the baby's not theirs. He tried to do right by me."

"I understand." Poppa said in a comforting manner. "I understand. I just wish you would've told me the truth."

"I lost the baby in an alley, Poppa," I continued. "I was in so much pain and Reno tried to stop the bleeding, but he couldn't. He couldn't. And then it just happened. Our baby, our precious little boy, came out of me already dead before he ever had a chance to live."

"Oh, baby!" Poppa exclaimed. He started weeping. "I'm so sorry!"

"We buried him, Poppa. We named him after you. We named him Anthony."

"I'm so sorry, Noelle," he repeated. "I should've been there for you. I made you afraid to come to me and look at what happened. If you hadn't run away, we could've gotten you medical care. This is all my fault."

"It's not your fault, Poppa. It's mine."

He pushed my head away from him slightly so he could look at me. "Why didn't you come back afterwards?"

"Shame," I replied without a second's hesitation. "I was ashamed. I couldn't bring myself to face you."

"What about Reno? What happened to him?"

"He stayed with me all of these years, Poppa. We both ended up getting our GEDs and finding work. It wasn't easy. People in New York don't like each other very much so we kept pretty much to ourselves."

"Did he come back to D.C. with you? Is he at his parents' house explaining all of this to them?"

"No, Poppa," I uttered. "Reno didn't come back. Reno died last week from colon cancer. Reno's gone. He'll never get a chance to explain his actions to his parents. I guess I'll have to."

Poppa didn't say anything else to me. He just held me and cried with me. We both let all of the pain that had accumulated over the years escape right there in his woodshed.

When we returned to the house an hour later, Momma's dinner was sitting on the table cold and all of them, including Little Noelle, were seated at the table waiting patiently.

Poppa directed me to a chair and then stood at the head of the table. "Listen up," he said, getting everyone's attention. "Noelle is home to stay and I will not have anyone treating her badly. She made a mistake, one she paid dearly for, and she understands that. But, I also understand that I made a mistake, an even bigger mistake. I wasn't there for my daughter. I wasn't there to listen to her when she needed me."

My mother let out a sigh of relief, realizing that we'd made our amends out in the backyard.

"Things are going to be different now," Poppa continued. "Different from this moment on. Today is Christmas and it's time for forgiveness, it's time for sharing, and it's time for expressing the love we have for one another."

Carolyn got up from the table, walked over to the side where I was sitting, and embraced me. "I love you, Noelle," she whispered into my ear.

"I love you, too," I replied, yet again on the brink of tears, my eyes still red and swollen from the last round.

She pointed across the table. "I'd like you to meet my husband, Sam."

I reached over and shook his hand. "It's nice to meet you, Sam."

"Likewise," he replied.

Carolyn retook her seat and Poppa sat down. We all clasped hands. "Shall we pray?"

Merry Christmas from Our Family to Yours